THE NEANDERTHAL'S AUNT

THE NEANDERTHAL'S AUNT

GINA DEMARCO

ScienceThrillers Media

This is a work of fiction. All of the characters, organizations, and events portrayed in this novel are either products of the author's imagination or are used fictitiously.

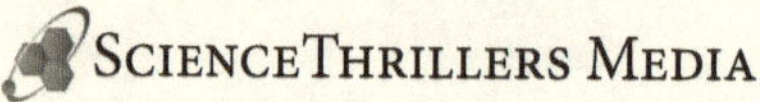

www.ScienceThrillersMedia.com
Publisher@ScienceThrillersMedia.com

First print edition, 2014

Library of Congress Control Number 2014950222

ISBN 978-1-940419-03-9 (trade paperback)
ISBN 978-1-940419-04-6 (ebook)

Cover concept by ZMC
Cover design by Ian Koviak, TheBookDesigners.com
Interior design by Amy Rogers

For Munch, with love

chapter one

On a winter evening, Achilles and I drove down from Boston, where the scientists live, to New York, where the socialites live.

Hank, the doorman at my sister's building, greeted us as we trudged out of the gritty slush and into a brightly lit marble foyer.

"You need to stop feeding that dog of yours, Dr. Nicoletta," he said. He was ex-army so he addressed everyone, even his friends, by rank.

"Achilles isn't fat!" I said, looking down at the muddy ball of white wool at my feet. "He's just fluffy."

"If you say so," Hank said. "Liz left for yoga a couple hours ago."

"How is she?" I asked.

"She seems okay lately. Or more cheerful anyway. Keeps talking about cavemen or something. Do you need me to let you up?"

"No, I still have the key."

Liz lived on the Upper West Side in a pre-war building in an apartment fancy enough to have elevator doors that opened directly into her living room. It had furniture that was thoughtfully placed, and artwork that was made by people you might have heard of. It had carpets that were so old that the child laborers who made them now had grown children of their own. Liz was tidy and fussy about her things so I wiped off the muddy dog and when I raided her kitchen I chose chardonnay and crackers, even though what I really wanted was Chianti and tomato soup.

During the drive down, and while I waited for Liz to come home, my mind was nervously preoccupied with the conversation I was planning to have with her. She was devastated when John died, but I thought she was finally doing a bit better. She was leaving her apartment more and exercising again. But when my mom called me and told me to read Liz's latest blog post, my heart sank. I had come down to talk to her about it, to find out what was really going on. What she had written seemed too outlandish to be true.

The dog and I were cozy on the couch when Liz stepped off the elevator. She was wearing her yoga outfit under a big brown wool coat and a large shawl.

"Sara!" She greeted me with a big smile.

Achilles jumped off the couch and howled with joy. Then he gave Liz his characteristic greeting for her: he humped her leg. I think he must have liked the way she smells because she was the only person he did that to since he became a castrato.

Human males have always had a similar reaction to Liz. You wouldn't have expected it from looking at her. She really was not much prettier than me, except she was a bit taller and put more effort into her makeup. Once, John made the mistake of show-ing her a trashy gossip article that listed the "Ten Plain Wives of Über-Successful Men." Liz was plain wife number seven. I told her it was better than being plain wife number one. There were six wives uglier than her. Liz cried and slammed doors and then fired both her hairdresser and her personal trainer. But it had never occurred to John that anyone would think she was unattractive and he had only shown her the article because he thought it was so absurd it was funny.

Liz shoved the dog off her leg and I held out one of my crackers, which it turned out he was also attracted to.

"Oh, Sara, I thought you were taking that thing to obedience classes," she said.

"I did! He got thrown out. Or, he didn't get thrown out. I refused to pay the guy because he promised Achilles would roll over and then after an hour and a half he started making excuses about him being 'incorrigible', like that kid in *The Sound of Music.*"

"So *you* got thrown out?"

"Yeah, I guess you could say that."

Liz came over to give me a hug. It would have been nicer if she hadn't smelled a little sour from yoga. I think she was doing that kind where they turn the heat up too high so everyone sweats. It sounds like torture to me, but she used to say it helped her stay centered. "I'm so glad you're here," she said.

Her shawl was soft against my face. "Don't you love it?" she said. "It's Peruvian cashmere. I got it at a fair trade store in the Village. Have you had dinner yet? There's some quinoa salad in the fridge."

"We stopped for hot dogs on the way down," I said.

"I'll have to send you my blog post about sulfites again." She put away her coat and gym bag. "Mom said you're coming with me to Barlas Labs tomorrow."

"Yeah, I'm supposed to find out what's going on with this Neanderthal stuff."

"Well, you're going to just love it! Theo is going to give you a tour of the labs, and show you all the sciencey stuff."

"Oh. Great." I'd meant to say it matter-of-factly, but I was tired from the drive and from Liz's expression I could tell it came across as sarcastic. "Sorry, I don't really understand what's going on. It sounds…crazy."

She frowned. "I know this is a lot to take in," she said, tilting her head slightly, "but Theo will explain it all tomorrow. I'm going to bed. I'm just exhausted!"

It was clear that the conversation I had driven down to have was not going to happen that night.

"Just promise to keep an open mind," she said, walking out of the room.

"I always keep an open mind," I said.

"And an open heart!"

chapter two

I was in New York because my mom had called me a few days earlier, in something like a confused panic, and told me to read Liz's blog. It said:

An Important Announcement

My dear readers,

I am writing this to let you know that I am about to embark on a new and exciting journey in my life.

As you all know, the year since I lost John has been a period of recovery and personal growth. Over this time, I have concentrated on learning to trust myself again and not being afraid to follow my heart. Part of this growth has been learning to observe the moments in my life when I can hear the universe speaking to me.

One of these moments happened a few months ago when I was introduced to some entrepreneurs in the biotechnology field.

Theo Barlas told me that his company, Barlas Labs, had developed a technology that could be used to recreate extinct species based on their DNA sequence. Yes, I know what you're thinking – Jurassic Park, right? No, I'm not going to put a dinosaur on the shared roof deck! The co-op board won't even approve a gas grill. LOL! No, the technology is going to be used to allow the rebirth of a very special group of people that lived many thousands of years ago called the Neanderthals.

Well, I have never felt such a calling to be part of something in my entire life. The idea of a little baby being born from a race that was thought to be lost forever just absolutely tugged at my heartstrings. I asked Theo if it would be possible for him to consider allowing me to raise the first child. Well, I did not think that I had any chance of being chosen, since I would be a single mom. But, to my extreme joy, Theo called me today and told me that his company has chosen to go forward with plans for me to adopt the world's very first resurrected Neanderthal baby!!!!

I am going to be a mom! =)

I know that some of you would have been more comfortable with my decision to become a single mother if I had chosen to adopt a phylogeny-typical child. However, as I embark on this journey, I hope you will understand that this is a decision that I have come to after a great deal of meditation. This is perhaps the one time in my life when I have decided to trust myself wholeheartedly, and if you have doubts, I hope that with time they will go away, and you will come to trust me as well.

I wish much love to all of you, and especially my loving family, which will soon grow by one!

Namaste,
Liz

In the comments section, first:

Great news sweetie! Didn't quite understand all of it. Is Neanderthal in Russia? Jeanie's daughter adopted a little Russian boy. He's just adorable! I know you're busy! I will look it up on the google.

Love, Mom

Then there were about a dozen comments from her followers, all saying some version of congratulations. Then a dissenting voice from our brother, Luka:

Liz, this is a terrible idea.

When we were younger he would have just called her an idiot, but he became much more tactful after he went to priest school.

And another from my mother:

Liz, sweetie, call me. I think we need to talk about this.

And they were all dated three days prior so not one of them had bothered to let me know I was about to become the aunt(?) of a resurrected cave baby.

Typical.

My mother had, eventually, and I expect with some difficulty, looked up "Neanderthal" on the Google and became quite alarmed when she discovered that they were not only German but also extinct. To appease her, Liz arranged for me to visit Barlas Labs on the coming Friday, I guess momentarily forgetting that I have a job. Liz's idea was that I would go down and then make a scientific report back to my mother that everything was great.

I agreed to go down but was expecting the opposite findings.

To me, the mission reminded me more of a phase from our childhood, another time when Liz got a funny idea into her head. When she was about eight she became convinced there was at least a *possibility* that there were monsters living under her bed. Even though I was a year younger than Liz, I knew this was a silly thought, that monsters were imaginary and the only things under her bed were her dirty socks (probably mine). But Liz would not be convinced. Every night, before we turned off the lights, she would order me to check under her bed. "Why don't you look?" I would ask. "Because there might be MONSTERS!" she would squeal. I was, apparently, expendable. So I would get on my knees, lift the edge of the bedspread, peer at the nothingness, and say, "Nope, no monsters under there."

And so I went down to New York expecting a repeat of this event. I would go to Barlas Labs, meet this man, and expose his scheme for…well, for whatever it was. Only this time, instead of monsters, I would say, "Look, Liz, no Neanderthals!"

I really thought there would be no Neanderthals. I did not believe that Theo Barlas, or anyone else for that matter, could make a Neanderthal baby. I thought it was just too technically difficult.

This was, after all, the very earliest days of synthetic biology.

One of the basic objectives of synthetic biology was to create new living things from a customized DNA sequence. But we had not made many things yet, and nothing very big. There were so many hurdles.

First of all, you needed to know the DNA sequence that you wanted to make.

You might remember from high school that DNA is a molecule consisting of a sequence of nucleotides (adenine, thymine, guanine, and cytosine) strung together to make a code. When I looked at them on my computer we used letters, A, T, G, and C, to show the string. So a piece of DNA might look like:

ATGATCAAACGTTAGGGACTCTCGAGGAGAAG

We were, at that point, pretty good at reading DNA sequences. We had sequenced the human genome, and we had sequenced a thousand more genomes during the 1,000 Genome Project. It was not routine yet, but we were beginning to sequence the DNA of children with genetic diseases and people with tumors, sometimes saving their lives. The Neanderthal's genome had been sequenced, too. Old Neanderthal bones from a cave in Croatia still contained bits of DNA that was sequenced by Svante Paabo's lab in Germany. In 2010 the draft sequence of the complete genome was released. But the sequence of a Neanderthal was harder to read than the sequence of a living human. The DNA was ancient and falling apart.

A single mistake in the sequence of a vital gene, an A instead of a G for example, could give the Neanderthal a devastating illness, or, more likely, the cells would not even live long enough to develop into a baby. And there are tens of thousands of genes, most thousands of nucleotides long.

Once we knew the sequence we wanted, we would have to generate the DNA molecule in some sort of DNA printer. These printers didn't work all that well then, not for long pieces of DNA. At that point we had taken the DNA sequence of a bacterium and made… bacteria. That was about it. We had not made anything bigger yet: no yeast, no fish, no mice.

I know it seems naïve in hindsight, but I honestly thought that making a Neanderthal person from an ancient DNA sequence was impossible.

At the same time I was not really sure what Barlas's motives were.

Money was the obvious choice. There had been so many con-artists since John died, all trying to get a piece of his wealth from his bereaved widow. But as loony as some of Liz's ideas could be, she was quite conservative about what she did with her money. I think in some ways she still thought of it as John's money and she had sent the police after more than one scoundrel. I could not understand why she would be involved in something like this.

But I didn't have any evidence that Theo Barlas was one of those people. He could just be an idiot. Hanlon's razor tells us to never attribute to malice that which is adequately explained by stupidity. Humans have a long history of underestimating the power of science. But they overestimate it as well, like the alchemists who tried in vain for centuries to make gold from pieces of other metals. It can be done now, but only by using a particle accelerator or a nuclear reactor, neither of which was handy during the Renaissance. Theo Barlas could be some sort of biological alchemist, trying to make a Neanderthal from bits and pieces of genetic material.

I admit that I initially did not give much thought to the consequences of making a Neanderthal baby. The idea that it might actually happen never even entered my head.

chapter three

It was late the next morning when Liz and I pulled into the sprawling Long Island office park that housed Barlas Labs. The architecture was purely utilitarian: the buildings were rectangular cubes of brick, unadorned by anything except doors and windows and some straggly trees standing humiliated in hills of dyed red mulch. The parking lot was vast and bordered by the trees of a suburban conservation area. According to the directory in the lobby, there were several tenants, mostly small biotech startups renting lab space. I recognized a few of the company names from the vendor tables I had visited at conferences. Achilles liked to play with a ball that had one of their names on it.

We had left the city a little late because I had to drag my dog out into the rain so he could pee on the street sign at 77th and Columbus. Like most bichons, he didn't like getting wet, and so he had to be coaxed, and Liz didn't like being late and so she had to complain. She covered the traffic, my driving, and how embarrassing it was to be seen in my car in some depth. When I managed to steer the conversation towards the Neanderthal project she was both joyful and vague. "Oh I'm so looking forward to this! You are going to love Theo. He's so charming. I wish we were going to be on time. I don't want him to think I'm disorganized."

We found the locked door to the lab and rang the bell. It all seemed surprisingly low budget. Barlas Labs didn't even have a sign, just a suite number glued to the wall beside the door. And there was no receptionist. Liz was bestowing air kisses on the man who let us in before I realized that it was Theo Barlas himself.

He was in his late thirties, I guessed, but still had a full head of thick brown hair. He had a rugged, masculine face, olive skin, and green eyes framed by black rectangular glasses. Had those come back in style? I thought they looked a little nineteen-nineties-ish, but his suit and shoes looked as expensive as his office space looked cheap, so I guessed that he would know better than me. I had pictured him being taller.

He introduced himself as Theo and held out his hand with a friendly grin. He wore a cologne that made him smell like a mixture of suede and cucumbers.

I took his hand and introduced myself as "Dr. Nicoletta," not grinning at all and smelling like a mixture of this morning's coffee and a little wet dog.

He took us into a small, windowless conference room where he offered us a hot drink and started up a projector. We didn't pass any other people in the office, just a couple empty cubicles.

"I'm so glad you were finally able to come out to our offices, Liz," he said.

"Well, Grandma insisted that Auntie Sara come out to see the science."

He turned to me. "Unfortunately, Sara, our chief science officer is out of the country this week, so I'll warn you in advance that I may not be able to answer all of your technical questions."

"It looks like everyone is out of the country," I answered. Making a Neanderthal baby, however it was done, would be hard. I was expecting, you know, staff.

"We're not early risers," Theo said

"It's ten thirty," I said.

"That early?" Theo replied. Liz giggled.

"How many people work here?" I asked.

"Not as many as you would think," he said. "We take pride in being a lean startup." He told us that he had prepared a little presentation to give us an overview of the project. He dimmed the lights and started a PowerPoint. The first slide, sepia toned with the company logo on it, was titled, "The Barlas Lab's Place in Earth's History."

"Now the first question you may ask," he said, "is why have we undertaken this project, this project to resurrect the Neanderthal person? Why have we chosen, at this time and in this place, to resurrect humanity's closest living relative? Why have we chosen to resurrect Homo sapiens Neanderthalis?"

Theo looked at us, pausing.

"For Barlas Labs the answer is simply because we can. Simply because we can."

He paused again to let that sink in, and I began to worry that this could end up being quite a long presentation.

"That may seem trite, like climbing a mountain because it's there, but at Barlas Labs our mission, our fundamental mission, is to push the boundaries of biotechnology, to make the impossible possible. At this time in history it is possible to undo the extinction of an ancient human race. And so we have chosen to resurrect the Neanderthal person…simply because we can." He looked around at Liz and me. I guessed that his spiel had been rehearsed for a larger audience. "Now, let me first give you a little background on how closely related the Neanderthals are to modern humans," he said.

"About half a million years," I said.

Liz hushed me.

Theo showed us the standard evolutionary tree, the one that everyone uses when they want to show the relationship between humans and other primates. It starts with the common ancestor that chimpanzees, humans, and Neanderthals all descended from, some sort of ape that lived around six million years ago. The lines in the tree fork to show how the descendants of the common ancestor split into two groups. One group became chimpanzees. The other group became more and more human-like, evolving as a single species. Then, about half a million years ago, that branch also split into two separate groups. One group became the Neanderthals. The other group became us.

"Half a million years," Theo said. Biologists measure the relationships between living things in units of time. "A good long while indeed, but a blink of an eye for evolution. So short of a time, in fact, that scientists have determined that modern humans, us, and the Neanderthals, them, are actually the same species. The same species. We see this in their Latin names. The genus *Homo* means man, and the species *sapiens* means wise. Modern humans are *Homo sapiens sapiens*: the wise, wise men. Neanderthal humans are *Homo sapiens neanderthalensis*: the wise men from the Neander Valley."

The Neander Valley is the place in Germany where the Neanderthal's bones were first found. I couldn't tell if Theo's presentation was well-rehearsed or if he was just naturally relaxed in front of people. He projected total self-confidence. There were no unscripted hesitations in his speech. His eye contact alternated between Liz and me like a metronome, engaging our attention, smiling at the appropriate intervals, managing the inflection in his voice. He was slick, I thought. Smooth. Scientists were never like this – only the sales reps.

"Now the question becomes, how do we at the Barlas Labs bring one of these people back to life?"

Theo showed pictures of fossilized Neanderthal bones. A bit of one of these bones yielded the fragmented DNA that was used to generate the genome sequence of the Neanderthal.

I already knew all of this so my mind and gaze wandered around the room. There wasn't much to look at. Plain walls, no windows. There was a print on one wall of a mountain with a quote, the kind of poster they sell in airplane catalogs: "The best way to predict the future is to invent it." It was attributed to the computer scientist Alan Kay.

Theo was trying to invent the future. Or was it the past? I looked at him a little more closely. He really wasn't bad looking. He seemed pretty fit, athletic and a little bulky. I noticed he had a nice, round ass. I wondered if he rode bikes or something. I should get a bike, I thought. I could get a little basket for the dog, like the witch in the *Wizard of Oz*.

"Do you have any questions on that part?" Theo asked. No, Liz was good and I was thinking about getting a pair of ruby-red shoes.

Theo continued, "The DNA molecules that remained in the Neanderthal's bone were extracted and sequenced with machines like the one we have in the lab."

I was in the lecture hall when Svante Paabo announced that his group had finished sequencing the first version of the Neanderthal genome. The Neanderthal sequencing project was a lot harder than Theo made it sound, a monumental task. Dozens of people had worked on it. All of the samples had to be prepared in ultra clean rooms to avoid introducing contamination. The DNA was old and degraded so it was read in short fragments, a few hundred bases long, riddled with errors. Most of the DNA they found was not even from the Neanderthal but from bacteria and other organisms that had taken up residence in the bone over the millennia since the Neanderthal died. A team of computer scientists had to write special algorithms to sort out all of the data.

But Theo's presentation seemed to be geared more at Liz than at me. She was paying attention, rapt attention, as if this was the first she had heard of some of it. I thought it seemed peculiar that someone who had volunteered to adopt a Neanderthal baby would know so little about Neanderthals.

But then Theo got around to what I considered the meat of the project: the technique they had developed at Barlas Labs for making a Neanderthal.

The first step, he said, was to use the genome sequence as a template for synthesizing the Neanderthal's DNA. While people had made short strands of DNA before, such as when the Venter Institute made a bacterium, Barlas Labs would need very long strands to make a complete Neanderthal chromosome, up to a quarter of a billion bases strung together. The chemical reactions used to make DNA fizzle out after a while so it is more difficult to make a long strand of DNA than a short one. Short strands can be stitched together, but that has its own complications.

"You've already made the Neanderthal chromosomes?" I asked.

"Yes."

"From scratch?" I asked.

"Yes."

I had a lot more questions about this process. How did it work? How many errors were in the sequence? How long did the chromosomes take to generate?

But Theo's talk had picked up speed. It was no longer peppered with dramatic pauses that I could use to interrupt him and I felt silly raising my hand in a room with only three people. He moved on to making the actual Neanderthal embryo. The DNA cannot function on its own. It needs a cell to live in. When the Venter Institute made the artificial bacterium they removed the DNA from an existing bacterial cell and replaced it with the new artificial DNA. This was the approach that Barlas Labs would use. But, because he was making a mammal, he would need to start with an embryo, a cell that could divide and divide again, growing into a complete baby.

"What kind of embryos will you use?" I asked. "Are they human?"

"No, chimpanzee."

"Her name is Linda," Liz added.

"Who?"

"The chimpanzee," Liz said.

"What?"

"Can we go on the tour of Barlas Labs now?" Liz asked. I expect there were more slides, but Liz knew when she had had enough science.

"I still have a few questions," I said, as Liz and Theo stood up and walked out of the room.

I followed them from the conference room, back through the empty cubicle farm, and into the main laboratory. It was standard: harshly lit with the usual gray linoleum floor, black lab benches, and the clutter of glassware, scales, and machines. It was like any of the dozen or so other labs I had been in throughout the years. But it, too, was empty of people.

Then I noticed the big glass wall at the back of the lab, the one with a sturdy door in it that led into another room. On one side of the room, along the width of the glass wall, there was a small corridor, about three feet wide. Then along that there were bars. And on the other side of the bars there was something like a bedroom. It was a large room, bigger than any bedroom I had ever slept in. There were no windows, but there was a single bed with flowery sheets, a red chair, and a television mounted to the wall. There were all sorts of colorful plastic things around that I guessed were toys. And sitting on the red chair, watching the television, was a fully grown chimpanzee.

Theo unlocked the door and the chimp looked up. She saw him and began making a joyful "Ooo, ooo" noise. She got off her chair and lumbered over to him at the bars, not quite walking upright and not quite dragging her knuckles on the ground.

"This," he pronounced as we entered the room, "is Linda."

I was too surprised to say anything. Chimps are usually only kept at enormous research facilities, not at suburban biotech start-ups. Was this even legal?

Linda stretched her hand through the bars, and Theo touched her hand. She responded with excitement, "Oooo ooo ooo ooo," like a teenage girl who had just touched Justin Bieber.

"She likes you!" Liz said. "Oh! I brought her some bananas from the farmer's market. They're organic, of course."

Liz was carrying her favorite handbag. It was colored like an Indian sari and so enormous that she produced a bunch of bananas without it having any obvious loss in volume. She began peeling them and handing them to Linda one at a time through the bars, sometimes touching fingers with the chimp affectionately. "Here you go, honey."

"Linda is going to be ready for her implantation in a few weeks," Theo said, "so we're giving her lots of fresh fruits and vegetables."

"Wait, what?"

"Her implantation," said Liz.

"Of what?"

"Of the baby, silly. Linda's the surrogate mother."

I guess I hadn't really thought this through. Theo claimed he could make an embryo. He would have to put it somewhere warm for nine months if it was going to grow into a baby.

"We would have preferred to use a human surrogate, naturally," he said, "but our lawyers couldn't make that work."

"Oh just look at her!" said Liz. "She's so beautiful! Look at her eyes!"

"You're putting a Neanderthal baby into a chimpanzee?" I asked.

"Next week." Theo smiled with pride.

"And this Neanderthal baby is going to grow inside her belly?"

"If all goes well."

"Of course it will go well!" Liz said optimistically.

Linda looked at Theo, and then at me. She made a small shrieking noise, like she was trying to get his attention.

"Liz, you're adopting this…this baby that will come out of the chimp's vagina?"

"Of course not!" Liz said. "She's going to be delivered by cesarian. Her head will be too big for Linda's vagina, won't it sweety?" Liz pushed another banana through the bars. "You don't want that. That would be a big ouchy, wouldn't it?"

The presentation had been long and tiring, but the details of these biomechanics were making me feel woozy. Theo put his hand on my shoulder. "I know this is a lot to take in," he said.

Linda stepped back from the bananas, and started shifting her weight from foot to foot, making that chimp calling sound that you see them make at the zoo when they're about to get into a fight.

"Ohhh, what's wrong honey?" Liz asked.

"Maybe we should let Linda have some time alone," Theo suggested. And with that he began ushering us out of the room. As he did this, he put his hand across my shoulder, not a push but a suggestive nudge.

The moment that Theo's hand touched me, Linda's calling became louder. She seemed irate.

"Sometimes she gets a little nervous around visitors," Theo said.

I didn't see it coming. I don't know where it came from, or how Linda's aim was so good that she missed Theo completely. But I felt it. A sudden splatter of warm, wet, sloppy goop running from my hair, down my face, and across my shirt, smelly, gross, and brown. Linda had thrown chimp shit at me.

"Uh-huh!" I shouted, stepping back from the impact. I looked at Linda, she looked at me. She cackled. I shouted. "You bitch!"

"Sara!" my sister chastised. "She's an innocent animal."

Linda cackled again.

"She did that on purpose!"

Linda confirmed this with shrill, satisfied mockery. "Ooooo, oooo, oooo."

And then she squatted.

"Oh no! I think she's reloading," Liz said.

"There's a sink through here," Theo said. This time he really was pushing us out of Linda's area, as the foul mess dripped off of me.

In the laboratory we could still see Linda dancing through the glass. We could hear her ooo-ooo-oooing until Theo closed the door to her room. Then we could only see her, waving her arms, a chimpanzee on mute. And then a huge splatter of poop hit the glass wall, right in front of my face.

"I don't think she likes you, Sara," Liz observed.

"Sorry, she's never done that before," Theo said as he turned on the sink and moistened some paper towels. "Here, let me help you get cleaned up."

"Do you think she's jealous?" Liz asked Theo. "Maybe she doesn't like you talking to other women." She walked over to the glass. "Are you jealous, sweetie?"

Linda continued her silent dance.

Her excrement was smeared across my head, my face, my chest. In the lab its rotten, organic smell was mixing with lab odors – chemicals like ethanol and cleaning agents. And now at the sink Theo was standing very close to me, wiping my face. He was so close that I caught the vapors from his cologne, the sweetness of it, the artificial mixture of cucumbers and suede. It was this last smell that threw me over the edge. The mixture of odors became overwhelming. I felt my whole body spasm, the hot acid of vomit welling up in my throat. I stifled the first heave. I remembered that we had passed a bathroom as we entered the labs and so I ran for it.

Just in time, I was sitting on the linoleum floor, in the under-lit room, my head over the toilet, the room spinning as I heaved again and again. The toilets in the Barlas Labs hadn't been cleaned in a while and now all the other smells were mixed with stale urine and vomit. The problem compounded itself.

Liz was outside the door. "Sara, are you okay?"

I answered her by vomiting again. This went on for a while, ten minutes maybe, until the entire contents of my stomach, the coffee and the Upper West Side salt bagel with cream cheese, had spewed into the Barlas Lab toilet.

And then I could hear Theo through the door. "How is she?"

"She does this," Liz said. "Sara Jean the Barfing Queen."

I don't "do this." I have a naturally strong vomiting reflex. I wish I didn't. She and Luka called me that as a kid because whenever one of them would get sick the sound alone would send me running to the bathroom, too. My middle name isn't even Jean. It's Margaret.

"Well, I think anyone would have difficulty…under the circumstances."

Eventually I was able to pull myself together enough to start cleaning myself off. It took a while. Linda's crap was smeared all down my face and in my hair. The smear on my face was dangerously close to my mouth, but I don't think I ate any of it. My good sweater had a big brown smear down it so I took that off and put it in the sink. It took a lot of water to get the soft brown globs out of my hair. The poop didn't quite rinse through the drain hole so I could see Linda's last meal in the sink. Brown goop. Corn. They feed the chimps corn at Barlas Labs?

There was another knock on the door. I was woozy. My head was still spinning as I pulled it open. I was expecting Liz but it was Theo. "Here. I thought you might need a clean shirt." When I was able to focus on his face through my haze he was grinning from ear to ear. No, smirking. He was smirking and holding out a T-shirt.

"Enjoying this? You're enjoying this?"

I took the shirt from his hand and slammed the door. I had answered the door wearing only my most utilitarian beige bra and pants that cut into my waist, leaving me with a small roll of fat sticking out over the top of my pants. I had been standing in front of Theo Barlas wearing an old lady bra and muffin tops with chimp poop soaking into my wet hair.

I didn't care. I just wanted to leave. I rinsed and rinsed some more.

chapter four

Liz drove us back to New York. I was slumped over in the passenger seat of my own car with soaking wet hair and wearing a tight-fitting sky blue T-shirt with a cartoon of a pensive Neanderthal man on it. It said, "Barlas Labs."

I stared out the window as Long Island slowly passed by. Raindrops dulled the colors of the surrounding cars to a palette of gray. The sedan next to us had writing on it saying it was from the New York State Department of Corrections. A prisoner sat in the back, looking out the window. I wondered how long it had been since he had seen traffic like this and how long it would be before he saw it again. He reached his hands up and touched the bars that surrounded the back seat. I couldn't tell if he was wearing handcuffs. He was only a shadow through the reinforced glass and rain. The wipers on my car squeaked back and forth. I didn't say anything. I wanted my dog.

Liz broke the silence by asking me how amazing I thought our visit to the labs was. Not very, I thought, but felt too frail to reply. She went on about how much she enjoyed it, how wonderful Linda was, what an amazing man Theo was.

I asked her, "How do we know he isn't just a man with a chimp?"

"What do you mean?"

The rain was thickening, now, turning to sleet. Our lane was the slowest. The corrections car left us behind. Liz rarely drove and was not aggressive enough to change lanes.

"How do we know there is anything at Barlas Labs besides a man who rented some office space and bought a chimpanzee?"

"Oh Sara, don't be silly."

"We saw him. We saw the chimp. We didn't see anything else."

"What are you talking about? We were there for two hours. I mean, half of it was you puking, but he explained the whole thing to us."

"No. He didn't really. I don't know how a Neanderthal is made. He just said stuff. He just told us that he has a process. I could have made that same PowerPoint presentation five years ago. But I don't know how to make a Neanderthal. Not really."

It was like he was demonstrating he knew how to make a cake by saying it required flour, sugar, and butter. Yes, but how much of each? One pound of each makes a pound cake. An extra pound of butter makes sweet grease. Techniques in biology are fussier than cakes. They succeed or fail by margins of nanograms. How much DNA is in the tube relative to the enzymes? It has to be a certain amount, at a certain temperature, and we sometimes don't even know why. Biology can be a process of trial and error, trying a technique and then seeing how it goes, tweaking the protocol and then doing it again. Doing something new is hard.

"He doesn't even seem to have any staff," I added.

"They're a start up! Those people don't get up before noon. Don't you remember what Corbit Chips was like, in the beginning? John would get in at eleven o'clock and have to turn the lights on."

"Have you seen anyone there before?" I asked.

"I haven't been there before. I met Dr. Zhao, though. On the night I met Theo."

"Alright, so they're two men with a chimp. Like organ grinders or something. A duet."

I could see from Liz's face that she was mad. She had been elated, joyful, for the first time in years, and I was saying, "See, no Neanderthals!" This time, instead of making her feel safe, I was bursting her bubble, trying to break her grasp on the only shred of happiness I had seen in her in such a long time.

"I'm sorry, Liz. It's just that there didn't seem to be anything substantive in anything he said. I'm used to going to conferences and reading papers where people have charts and stuff," I explained.

"And that means they did what they said they did? Because they have a chart?"

Usually, I thought. People get caught making up data sometimes, but it ruins their careers. I didn't know what Theo's objective was, but if your credibility is expendable you don't need to tell the truth.

It was taking us a long time to get back to the city. The traffic had come to a stop.

"How much money did you give him?" I asked.

"None."

"None?"

"None."

I watched the windshield wipers go back and forth. It didn't make sense.

"How does it work then? How will he make his money?"

"I'll pay him when the project is complete."

"He doesn't get anything until you get the Neanderthal baby? Then he gets a lot?"

Liz stared out at the road for a while. Swish, swish. Then she turned and smiled at me.

"He gets a lot when the whole project is done. And nothing at all before."

The traffic crept forward. In a while we passed a black traffic sign flashing an orange warning: Multi-vehicle accident at Exit 43. Escaped prisoner. Remain in car. Keep doors locked.

chapter five

I stayed for the night at Liz's apartment in the city.

The accident and the manhunt that followed stopped traffic on the highway. The traffic delayed the arrival of the police. The weather delayed the arrival of the helicopters. I could barely see the car in front of me, so I didn't know what the cops on the ground could do and the ones circling overhead would not fare much better. They were using thermal imaging cameras, but even those would be blurred by the sleet. The water cools everything, reducing the contrast between objects, turning black and white into shades of gray. Or so we learned from the commentators on the radio, which Liz and I listened to instead of talking to each other.

My mother phoned us after seeing the escape on the news. Both of her daughters were on a highway in terrible weather with a convict on the loose. She imagined our charred bodies, mangled in a car wreck, having our last grasp on life extinguished by the prisoner slitting our throats. We were the stars of the snuff film that ran on a perpetual loop inside her head. She pleaded for me to stay at Liz's for the night. I said that it seemed unlikely that I would run into the prisoner on my way through Connecticut since he was presumably in leg irons. "How many miles can a man hop?" I asked. She countered that the sleet would soon turn to snow and I would be dead in a snowdrift before he got there anyway and I should think of dear little Achilles.

I had lived in Boston for over a decade. This wasn't my first snowstorm, and thanks to the Marathon bombers it wasn't my first siege, either. But we reluctantly acquiesced and assured her that the car doors were locked.

I saw Hank later in the evening when I was taking the dog out. He told me my mom was right. He had driven in from Queens where he had been visiting his mom and the roads had gotten even worse. New York was being snowed in. "At least all you'll have to worry about tonight is Liz wringing your neck."

"Oh, you've talked to her?"

"I'm just saying that I would lock your door tonight if I were you."

Hank actually talked to Liz quite a lot.

He was only in his early forties when he retired from the army and his plan had been to work as a doorman for about a year, make some connections, and then open his own private security firm. After John died, he stayed on as the doorman. It was not a bad job. With Christmas tips he probably made more money than I did. But it was not his dream to be there working for someone else. It would not be anyone's dream to be serving the whims of the over-privileged co-op board, but Hank was not just anyone and he had a drawer full of medals to prove it. He was capable of more than opening doors and hailing taxis, but he stayed on after John died, at least partly, I think, to look after Liz.

In the weeks after John died Hank really was Liz's primary caretaker. And she did need a caretaker. She was a mess. Grief had, of course, taken over her entire life. She had lived in a state of denial for so long about the finality of John's illness that when he passed away, she was totally unprepared for the sadness that came rushing over her.

But she knew, and we reminded her, that John would not have wanted her going on like that so she tried her best to get through it. She signed up for a yoga class. Gentle yoga, it was called. She stretched and meditated slowly in a calm, dark room circled with lit candles on a mat stretched out on the bamboo floor. She went out with her friend Billy to the farmer's market and fair trade stores. Hank made sure she ate three meals on the days when he was working and called her three times a day on the days when he was not. In a few months she had color in her cheeks again and I finally stopped driving down to New York every weekend.

But now there was this, this crazy idea of making a Neanderthal.

Liz did not say much to me when we got back from Barlas Labs. I stayed in my room and watched the television news. The manhunt for the escaped convict continued. His name was Peter Ward. His victim was Janice Bowen.

She was a singer and Ward had been convicted of climbing through her bathroom window one night. His plan, he said in a television interview, was to surprise her in her kitchen. He had read that she liked a man who could hunt his own food. He did not hunt and he lived in the city so he was planning to make her squab. She would smell the food wafting through the house, come down, and fall in love. But the bathroom was as far as he got. The singer just wanted to pee in the privacy of her own home, but instead she walked in on a man standing on her toilet holding a bag of dead pigeons. He had never actually hurt anyone, but his cousin was on the television saying that he was quite unhinged, so my mother may have had a point about the convict too.

Later that night we ate dinner together in Liz's apartment. She called herself a vegan but had ordered us both a portion of Szechuan chicken and some spring rolls. Stress always made her crave poultry, and she was still seething over my lack of support for the Neanderthal project.

"Thanks for ordering the food," I said. "It's really good."

"Theo recommended the place," she said. "He spent some time in China."

"Did he?"

"That was where he met his business partner, Adam."

"So what would happen if they succeeded?" I asked, thinking that I could guide her towards some sort of realization about what a bizarre idea it was. "Would it come live with you?"

"It's not an it. It's a she."

"Sorry. Would she come live with you?"

"That's what adoption means," she said sulkily as she took a bite of her spring roll.

"What do you expect her to be like?" I asked, in my best therapist voice.

"She's going to be lovely."

"Like a human?"

"Like a Neanderthal human. A little Neanderthal girl."

"I don't want us to fight."

"Well don't act like that, then."

"Like what?"

"You promised you would at least keep an open mind."

"I am trying to keep an open mind," I said, pretending I was doing my final exam at calm therapist school. "I just don't understand why you're making a Neanderthal baby. Why don't you just adopt a regular baby?"

"There is no such thing as a regular baby."

"Human. Why don't you adopt a regular human baby?"

"There are *Homo sapiens sapiens* babies. I have chosen to adopt a *Homo sapiens neanderthalensis* baby," she said, a little condescendingly I thought, especially because I was pretty sure she had only learned those words in the morning. "And as my sister I expect you to respect that."

"But why? Why a Neanderthal?"

"Why anyone? Why an orphan? Why a child of color? Why a disabled child? They're all children, even if they're different from you."

"Those are humans, Liz, modern humans who already exist and need a home."

"You adopt the child that you make an emotional connection with. I made a connection with this Neanderthal child."

"How do you make a connection with something that doesn't exist?"

"She's not a something. She's a someone. And she should exist. And when she does she will have no one. Her whole race is extinct because we drove them to extinction. We owe it to them. To undo what we did in the past."

"We don't know that humans made the Neanderthals extinct."

"Well of course we did."

This was an idea she kept bringing up in the beginning, the idea that modern humans caused the Neanderthal's extinction, and we owed it to them to bring them back, to undo our actions. The case against us was mostly circumstantial. Neanderthals lived in Europe for about half a million years. By dating the Neanderthal bones that have been found, it looks like there stopped being Neanderthal bones in Europe about forty thousand years ago, which was around the same time that there started being modern human bones. We know that Neanderthals and humans lived together there for a little while because there are modern humans around now who have a little Neanderthal DNA in their genomes. But modern humans weren't there for very long before the Neanderthals seemed to disappear from the continent.

We don't know if we had anything to do with them going extinct. We may have out-competed them for food, or maybe we even fought wars against them. But maybe they all just caught an illness that they couldn't fight or something like that. There isn't enough evidence in the fossil record to say for sure. It might not have had anything to do with us. We just don't know. But I knew there would be no point in arguing this with Liz.

"We can't undo the past," I said.

"We can." Liz was emphatic. "Now, in this, we can."

She gathered up the plates, brought them into the kitchen and loaded them into the dishwasher. I followed her with the takeout containers and bags.

"Well just promise me you'll tell me before you give this Barlas guy any money."

"Sara, I'm not a child. I can manage my own affairs."

"I don't want him taking advantage of you. I don't trust him, Liz. I'm not sure why you do."

"I'm not sure why you don't. You started from the point of not believing him."

"With good reason. I do know a little something about this kind of thing. This is what I do."

"If he was a biologist from some fancy university and he said he made an embryo using a Neanderthal genome you would believe him."

"I wouldn't!"

"You're holding Theo to a higher standard."

"Of course I am!" I said. "You're my sister. And he says he's making a Neanderthal. You know, extraordinary claims. Extraordinary proof."

Liz took two wine glasses out of the cabinet. She opened a bottle and said, "I don't want to fight about this either."

"Then just promise me you won't give him any money."

"I already told you. I am not giving him a cent until the project is done," she said flatly. "But I want you to promise you'll be supportive."

"Liz, I can't support you getting…scammed."

"I'm not getting scammed!"

"I'm sure you are," I replied.

"Sara, you don't have to believe it's going to work. I just want you to give this the benefit of the doubt."

I didn't have much doubt. Everything I knew about biology, the challenges of synthetic biology, making a mammal out of nothing, told me that this couldn't possibly work. Not in the time frame she was talking about. Not from a tiny lab on Long Island that no one had ever heard of.

"I want you to give them the benefit of the doubt and I want you to be nice to them," she added.

I could see that this was important to her. If I objected I knew that I would not hear from her for months, so I agreed to her terms, and we agreed on a truce that allowed us to get back to being sisters.

Before John got sick we would have gone out to a bar, or maybe dancing. I was hoping we might do that again, someday soon maybe. But the snow was coming down thick and getting a cab would mean standing out in the snow flailing our arms. So we went into the living room and drank our wine as we turned down the lights and watched Achilles chase a little ball around the living room.

Later that night, Liz blogged our visit to Barlas Labs from her bed, and I read it in mine. It went like this:

A Visit to Barlas Labs

Today I had the most amazing experience! We went out to Barlas Labs to meet with Theo Barlas and to tour the laboratory. Theo gave a wonderful presentation about the Neanderthal people. I feel like I know so much more about them now and if possible I am even more excited about the project than I was before. I was so fortunate to have my sister Sara with me as well. As you already know if you read my blog regularly, Sara is a scientist so she was able to discuss many of the technical details of the project with Theo, most of which frankly went a little over my head. LOL.

But the most wonderful part of all was that we were able to meet my baby's surrogate mother, Linda. Linda is such a dear! She was so excited to see us, especially Theo, and I can already tell that her womb will provide the perfect, safe, loving environment for the baby. I feel truly blessed! If you believe that eyes are the windows to the soul like I do then I am sure you would agree – Linda has the most beautiful, gentle eyes I have ever seen. I was just bananas for her!

The project is progressing so well! I am expecting to receive some great news next week, so be sure to check back.

Blessings,
Liz

I set up a fake account to comment:

Linda is a bitch.

But Liz knew it was me. She said it wasn't nice.

chapter six

My little white dog was staring up at me with big black eyes and a mouth full of fur from a golden retriever's ass.

"I'm so sorry," I said to the retriever's owner. "He's a rescue." I was feigning shock, as if this was his first ass and the "rescue" excuse hadn't expired many years ago.

When I got back to Boston I decided there wasn't anything I could do about the Neanderthal project except wait and see how it progressed. So Achilles and I settled into our usual routine, taking our walk around the large reservoir near our home, where he menaced dogs that were bigger than him but had less spunk. We lived in an old apartment in the Brighton part of Boston's student slums. It was a living arrangement born out of necessity rather than choice, the necessity for the dog to pee. I wanted him to have a yard, but yards are expensive and I needed to be near work so I could get home early enough to let him out. When I moved there my salary was too low to afford a classier neighborhood.

It wasn't the nicest place. On the first floor of a large house, it had old windows and an ancient heating system that hissed, rattled, and groaned so it was never the right temperature. It was near many colleges, so the neighbors were students and often loud. We needed regular exterminator appointments to stave off the roaches. Students are also filthy.

But there were some nice things: lots of gumwood molding and yards of built-in bookshelves that seemed anachronistic now that every book I owned was on the computer. I had tolerated the problems by telling myself that it would only be temporary. I had been saying that for years. I guess I expected I would be married by now.

But besides being mistaken for the love interest of a probable con artist by a jealous chimpanzee, my recent love life was pretty bare. It wasn't that I was bad looking. I would say, objectively, that I was probably in the upper thirtieth percentile for women in my age range, looks-wise. According to my doctor, I had a healthy weight for my height, which was only an inch or two shy of average. According to my dentist, I had straight, white teeth in a small, gaggy mouth. My blond hair would have been consistently attractive if I went in for highlights regularly per my hairdresser, and the trainer at the gym said that I had a functional level of cardiovascular fitness but imbalanced muscle tone. She said it very gravely, but I did not think it was a dire enough condition to warrant buying the personal trainer package.

But, while men fell all over Liz, the last time I had even dated a guy was almost a year before. Really, that should say "dated". His name was Angus Gupta. I had known him for years, professionally, but not very well. I had introduced myself to him at a meeting when I was looking for work, and would chat with him at conferences once or twice a year and read his papers. Among the introverts that worked in science this kind of interaction sometimes constituted friendship. But Angus was no introvert. He knew everyone and all their work. He was an excellent scientist. Some thought he might be a contender for a Nobel Prize someday. He was also in reasonably good shape and, though he was probably in his forties, he could have easily passed for thirty-eight. I described him to my sister as being cute enough to be in a Bollywood film. Not as the romantic lead, of course, but he definitely could have played the lead's older cousin.

He even had a Wikipedia article:

> Dr. Gupta's early life began in humble circumstances. He was conceived in India in the last year when its citizens could emigrate freely to the UK. His mother had spent her childhood knotting thread into rugs, and she wanted better for her baby. His father

thought about emigrating, but obtaining the money for a move on their meager wages appeared to be an insurmountable challenge. However, a relative living overseas luckily died tragically, and the Guptas inherited just enough money to move to Scotland. Gupta was born a few weeks after they arrived and was given the most Scottish name his father could think of. (Or the first one on an alphabetical list of Scottish boy names, if the story is told by Gupta's younger brothers Bruce and Cameron.) Gupta was raised in the back apartment of an Indian take-away restaurant. His parents and teachers observed early on that he was both intelligent and hard-working. And so instead of knotting rugs, he went on to attend the University of Edinburgh where he earned both an MD and a PhD in virology.

He was either so well known by then that no one objected to him having an article, or so poorly known that no one noticed he had an article. I was pretty sure he had written it himself, but I didn't think that necessarily detracted from its significance.

Angus became something more than a colleague during the annual meeting of the American Society of Genomicists, a conference for people who study genomes. "Genomes" is just a hoity-toity word for the whole of your DNA. The conference was held in a big hotel and on the last day they had a dinner-dance in one of those function rooms that they use for boring weddings and even more boring corporate Christmas parties. There was a DJ and I love dancing, but Liz told me I shouldn't dance at work functions. She said I dance like a drunken zombie with a bat in his hair. I thought she might have been right and I was trying to develop a better reputation in my field as a serious scientist. So I was concentrating on standing still at the side of the dance floor, lost in the fuzzy mixture of colored disco lights and my gin and tonic, watching the other scientists dance.

Then I looked across the haze and saw Angus. I didn't remember ever having seen him dance before. He still had his conference clothes on and the back of his gray dress shirt was soaked through with sweat. In one moment I saw him grab a partner and loop under their joined hands like a child playing London Bridge, and then in the next moment he was sliding across the floor with his hands on his hips and goading people into joining a conga line. The whole time he mouthed the lyrics to whatever song was playing in an overly dramatic fashion, through a broad smile that never left his face. He was someone actually enjoying himself while everyone else seemed to be self-consciously trying to look like they were enjoying themselves. He danced with an unmitigated joy and enthusiasm that was totally disconnected from the occasion. It was at once so geeky and so primal. I found it mesmerizing.

And then the DJ began playing the Brothers Gibb. Robin sang the opening line from "More Than a Woman," and I could not resist. I jumped into the fray. I grabbed Angus's hand in mine and made him spin me out and in again. It was only the fact that I landed in his strong arms that kept me vertical. I wouldn't say Angus was impressed. In fact, initially I would say that he seemed somewhat alarmed. But since it's the best song ever he was inspired to follow with his cool disco moves until Robin's last croon.

But then the DJ played something too cliché even for me to tolerate, "Brown Eyed Girl" I think it was. I suggested we get a drink. My gin and tonic was missing, and he obliged.

"You dance divinely," I said.

"I liked your talk," he responded, in a strong but not incomprehensible Scottish brogue. I had spoken earlier that day on some research I was doing on viruses. "Will you be getting more samples?" he asked.

"Yes," I said. "Our collaborators are mailing me some frozen rats next week. They're infected."

This is how scientists flirt.

A short time later I was in Angus's arms again, but this time it was in the darkness of my hotel room. I was lucky – I was on a government grant that insisted I share a room with a stranger. We were fully grown professionals, but this was the sort of monasticism society imposed upon us just because we worked in a field that everyone agreed was necessary but nobody wanted to pay for. Fortunately the hotel room was adequate and my roommate did not snore and had gone home early after getting hives, possibly caused by an allergy to the dog hairs on my luggage.

Angus began taking off my clothes. I unbuttoned his shirt. His body was cute. His shoulders were wide. His abs only had a little layer of fat on them. We moved towards the bed, pulling down the abstract floral-patterned bedspread that was coordinated with the generic artwork on the walls. He spoke to me in a soft voice. "What do you like?" he asked. I thought he might call me "lassie" but no such luck.

"Scottish scientists," I replied. He kissed me some more, on my neck and shoulders as the rest of our clothes landed on the floor.

Soon we were horizontal on the bed and he whispered quietly in my ear.

"This is good," he said. "You are so beautiful." His hands wandered all over me. "Would you mind if I tied you up?"

"What?" I asked, sure I had misunderstood his accent.

In a faux voice, one calculated, I thought, to sound sultry, he asked again, "Can I tie you up?"

I was perplexed. Was "tie you up" a Scottish expression for something? Something other than tying me up? "You brought rope?" I asked.

Where would it be? In his bag? He'd been carrying the free beach tote with the American Society of Genomicists conference logo on it.

He reached his hands down off the bed and slipped the canvas belt off his pants. He took both of my wrists in his hands, moving them over my head. I was hesitant at first. "We can have a safe word," he suggested. "How about… ummm… nucleus?"

No one had ever tied me up before. I don't know why. It just had never come up. But I didn't feel unsafe, not with Angus. So I figured I might as well try it. I only hesitated because I couldn't remember if I had shaved my armpits that morning. Sometimes I forgot to pack a razor. "Can we shut off the lights?" I asked.

He shut off the lights in the room, but left the bathroom light on with the door slightly ajar, leaving the room romantically dim. It was a smoother move than I would have expected from Angus, but he was known for his exceptional spatial reasoning skills. I could see him a little when he held my hands over my head, and looped the belt around my wrists. I felt more comfortable when I realized he was too distracted to notice my pits.

He climbed up on top of me with the gleeful expectation of a man who had waited all of his life to tie up a blonde. He began kissing my shoulders and I thought that it seemed like a bit of an odd configuration, lying here with my wrists just bound together like that. I kind of felt like I should be tied *to* something.

This is like that time I bought the mattress, I thought. The store clerks put it on the top of my car for me, but as I drove out of the parking lot it caught the wind and sailed off the top of my car like a seagull in flight. They had wrapped the mattress around and around with rope, but they hadn't tied the ropes to the car. I am the mattress, I thought. I should be bound *to* something. Conventionally, I would guess this would be the headboard.

But Angus was trying his best to be a sadist, bless his heart, so I thought politeness dictated that I at least pretend to be dominated. "Oh Angus," I said with an earnestness I did not feel.

"Shut up!" he barked.

Shut up? Dr. Angus Gupta told me to shut up!

I successfully stifled my first snicker and in the dim light I could just make out a glow on his face that said that this little bit of light bondage was the best thing that had ever happened to him. I thought it was sweet and I was flattered to be inspiring that same unbridled enthusiasm that I had seen on the dance floor. So I tried my best to look scared. "You dirty slut!" he said in a cautious shout, modulated as not to carry beyond this room.

He reached down to his pants again and retrieved a wallet that he began fishing through. In a moment he found what I imagined must have been a very dusty condom and began fumbling with it.

And then my mind wandered back to the mattress. I thought about how the two men who had wrapped it up with so much rope had stepped back, admiring their work, proudly pronouncing, "That ain't going nowhere."

I could not stifle the second snicker, but I managed to make it sound like a cough. A cough leading into something I made a sound like a sharp moan, "Oh Angus!" This was a bit odd since he was still several feet away from me fumbling with his penis, but he wasn't looking for inconsistencies.

Focus, Sara. Focus, I thought. He is the preeminent researcher in your field. You should at least be paying attention.

Once Angus got the condom stretched over his member, he climbed back over me. His voice was loud enough to convey sternness and authority, yet not so loud as to disturb any of the other hotel guests. "I told you to shut up, you bitch!"

And that reminded me of the traffic chaos I had caused at the entrance to the shopping center parking lot. "You bitch!" That was what a woman called me when I blocked her from exiting as I tried to shimmy the mattress back onto the top of my car, the lady with the cigarette hanging out of her mouth and the hair like she'd had it cut by Chewbacca's groomer. This was just like the mattress!

That made me guffaw. And this time he noticed. His face went blank, the tension giving way to confusion.

"I'm sorry," I said quickly.

"Is this funny to you?" he asked, his Scottish becoming thicker in proportion to his agitation.

"I was just thinking about something else. It's great. I mean it's really scary. Awful, scary." I was trying to sound scared, but I giggled. Because you will of course giggle, every single time that it is most inappropriate.

In the shadows I could see the light of domination being extinguished from Angus's face, and he looked a little sad. His penis was going from bratwurst to cocktail weenie and the condom was wrinkling around it like a deflated balloon. One of those balloons that clowns use to twist into animals. Deflated.

I couldn't grab him with my arms, so instinctively and ridiculously I wrapped my legs around his waist. "Wait, no," I said, "Don't go."

He got up anyway. "You're clearly not enjoying this as much as I was," he said, with the air of a man protesting inefficient service from his municipal road maintenance department: "That pothole is a bloody disgrace!"

"No, no, I am. I'm sorry," I said. "I didn't mean to laugh. I was just reminded of something. That's all. I can be submissive. I'm really into it." But Angus was already putting his clothes on. When he turned on one of the lamps I could see the disappointment in his face.

"You just try to do something new, once in a while, and everyone laughs at you," he said, scolding me as I lay naked on the bed, my hands still tied together over my head.

"I'm sorry, Angus. That was really…rude," I said. And then a spark went off in my head. "I was really, really bad. I'm naughty. A naughty, naughty woman. You should spank me, Professor Gupta."

He looked at me and hesitated, as if he was going to change his mind, but it was too little too late. He tied his shoes, grabbed his beach tote, and stomped off towards the door.

"Wait!" I insisted. "Don't go! Your belt!"

But the hotel room door banged shut and Angus was gone – one of the world's most respected scientists, a bright shining star and Nobel hopeful, storming down the corridor in droopy trousers.

The next day, when I called my sister Liz to check on my dog, I told her that I had seduced a Scottish Indian guy using my cool disco moves and left out every single detail of how that actually went. She only paid attention to the Indian part, which she thought made me deep and worldly, and by "me" I of course mean "her" because in her head she had banged him by proxy. She asked if we'd had tantric sex. I asked if that meant he ate an order of tandoori chicken off my breasts, because he totally did, and she told me I was being "culturally insensitive and really gross." I told her that it wasn't gross because the chicken was soft and warm, and the sauce only stained hotel sheets, which they really should bleach between guests anyway. This did not make her happy, so I told her that Angus kept a copy of the Kama Sutra in his conference beach tote "because he's really into spiritual sex." Then I asked her if she thought this was peculiar.

She said I shouldn't worry because people view eroticism differently "where he's from." I told her that I *had* heard that before, about people from Glasgow. Then she realized I was making fun of her, and called me something like a bitch but with more pretentious wording that I cannot quite remember. "Exasperating" was part of it. But she ended with telling me that in all seriousness I should give him her contact information in case he was ever in the city because she knows of this really great yoga studio that he would *just love.*

Will do.

After Angus left I managed to wrap myself in some blankets. I spent a few hours trying to undo the belt with my teeth, but eventually sleep prevailed and it was morning when Tina from housekeeping undid my hands for me. "Men, they are so stupid," she said. "You're the third woman I've had to untie since I started working here." I didn't know if she said that just to make me feel less embarrassed. She told me I should give his belt away on Craigslist, to make myself feel better. But nobody wants a used belt.

That was the sum total of my romantic life for the year: a depressing nothingness and a sulky Scottish sadist.

Whatever. It was what it was.

Achilles and I continued our walk around the reservoir. It was always beautiful there. On this day half of the water was frozen and glowing in the sunlight while the other half was covered with sparkly waves that danced in the wind. The sky was a cold blue so deeply colored that I could almost see purple in it. Across the water, off in the distance, I could see all the way downtown to Boston, to the shiny Hancock Tower and her frumpy sister the Prudential.

I should probably start running this walk, I thought. I was beginning to feel like the Prudential. We had all been so devastated when John died. Liz took it the hardest, obviously. But I was sad too. I didn't want to go anywhere, to even leave the house, for months. I was starting to look like someone who didn't leave the house. Being seen in my underwear unexpectedly was a bit of a wakeup call. Achilles reinforced the message. I had given him a bone that morning and then, when I had to take it away from him because it was time to go for a walk, he jumped up to my waist and bit me on my fat roll. He liked those bones too much. Not only did they send him into an aggressive fugue, but maybe Hank was right. Maybe he wasn't just fluffy. "Next time we'll try running around here," I told Achilles.

The snowstorm's remains surrounded the banks of the reservoir. Some of the snow was brown because of the sand that someone put on the path to keep us from slipping. And some of it was pink because during the winter I feed my dog beets. This was my little art project, to use my dog's tendency to mark his territory to turn our neighborhood's snow pastel. I liked how it gave the view a little burst of unexpected color. I took out my phone to take a picture of the lake, not the pee – I already had pictures of that.

chapter seven

I got in to work at the Daltry Institute on Monday morning and opened my e-mail. The contents were as follows:

From my brother Luka, a link to the YouTube channel where he posts his Sunday Masses so we can both pretend that I watch them, so we can both pretend that I go to church. He never added a personal message, just the link. I usually let them run in the background with the sound off so the hit count would increase to two. My mother had learned to use e-mail so she would increase it to one. I do not know if he bothered sending them to Liz. The hit count never seemed to get to three.

From the American Society of Genomicists, a reminder that abstract submissions were due for their next meeting. I was thinking of writing something about my work on viruses. My latest results were good enough that I might be chosen to give a talk. If I got accepted that would be fantastic – two talks in two years! Or I guess you could say two talks in ten years, depending on how you wanted to count them.

From Theo Barlas, an "invitation to join my online professional network."

You've got to be kidding me, I thought. It was bad enough that Liz had so frequently referred to the authority of her sister the scientist in all those blogs she wrote when John was sick, but being associated with Barlas Labs, even on an Internet site? Yikes.

I opened the e-mail so I could decline the invitation. It said, "Dear Sara," not Dr. Nicoletta, Sara.

Dear Sara,

I very much enjoyed meeting you last week at Barlas Labs. Liz speaks very highly of you and we are all so pleased that you will be supporting her during her adoption process. It will surely be a joyful but emotional journey for her.

I hope you are feeling better.

I would like to add you to my professional network.

Sincerely,
Theo Barlas
Co-Founder, Barlas Labs

p.s. Nice underwear

I think "nice" may have been said sarcastically.

I clicked through to his profile. He had worked at a lot of jobs, but nowhere for very long. Most of them had impressive-sounding titles including acronyms that I did not know the meaning of. I was surprised to see that Barlas Labs seemed to be his first foray into biotech. All of the other jobs were related to some type of sales or business venture. His undergraduate degree was in finance, and there was a fairly recent three-month stint as a student at a language school in Shanghai. That must have been how he met his co-founder.

Under hobbies he listed hiking and cycling which confirmed my suspicions about how his butt became so rounded. Those hobbies sound healthy. People never list "drinking and watching porn" as hobbies even though I expect it would often be more accurate.

His contact list was long: over five hundred people, and surprisingly rich. I knew the names of many of them: scientists, philanthropists, recruiters. As I said, I was trying to improve my professional reputation so there was no way I was going to run the risk of having my colleagues think I was involved with making Neanderthal babies, even though Theo and Liz seemed to think I was.

His profile linked to a Twitter account where he posted insipid articles telling entrepreneurs how to get rich, links to terrible music, and pictures of his supper.

I decided to ignore the request.

I had been working at the Daltry Institute for almost ten years then, as a research scientist. I landed there after a disastrous stint as a post-doc. A post-doc is a job you get when you finish your doctorate. If you do well it can lead to something like a job as a professor or a researcher. Mine went so badly I was lucky to ever work again. In my head I know that I recovered through hard work and perseverance, but I also owed a lot to John.

There aren't too many people in this world who have changed things in everyday life, but John was one of them. Not a lot of things, but enough so that when I went through my day I could pick out little things here and there: a result at work that came out quickly or a weather report accurate for a couple more days out than reports used to be. When I took my first programming course, many years ago, we were taught something called Moore's law. It was a prediction from the early seventies that stated the amount of computing power that can be produced by a one inch computer chip will double every two years. Rules of thumb like that are usually oversimplified, but Moore's law had proven pretty accurate for about half a century.

And then John blew it out of the water.

I first met him a few hours before Liz did. I had come down to New York to visit Liz because I was overwhelmed with job-related stress. After working so hard to get my PhD, my post-doc was blowing up. I'd had some difficulties in the lab and my boss hated me and I could not see a way forward in my career just then. Liz thought a weekend break in the city might do me some good. But, after I drove all the way down there, with a not-quite-completely-housebroken puppy whining in the back seat of my car for five hours, she informed me that she would be ditching me for a date with an English banker who had just asked her out to dinner. She hoped I understood, he was so gorgeous, such a cute accent, last minute, blah blah blah.

So, stuck in New York without anything to do, I found one of those "night out" networking events. A bunch of biologists were going to meet up and talk about work over some beers. Yeah, it didn't sound like a fun night out to me either, but I was spending most of my free time trying to meet people who might help me find a new job, which would be difficult without the benefit of a positive reference from my boss.

There were about five of us sitting on benches around a wooden table. We were in a German beer hall in Brooklyn – a big dark place that sold sausages and French fries that were fatty and salty and came with seven different kinds of mustard to dip them in. It was the kind of food that you knew would put a gentle wind in your sails as you drifted towards a coronary, but you still enjoyed the breeze. And sometimes I dream about their sauerkraut.

John was not a biologist, but he came to the beer hall because he was looking for people with difficult computational problems. I guess most people don't think of biology as being hard on computers because they think of the kind of biology they learned in high school. That paradigm really changed in the nineteen-nineties when DNA sequencing machines started producing datasets that were too large to be processed by eye. By the time I met John the kind of biology I work on was producing some of the largest datasets in the world. There was so much data that once when a lab in England began transferring some of their data to colleagues in the US they used so much bandwidth that they took out the Internet service for the entire town. So John came looking for us.

He was unremarkable looking, neither tall nor short, sandy hair, brown eyes, and a friendly smile. He asked everyone a million questions about themselves and their work, and seemed to take a remarkable amount in, even though biologists are not always the best at talking about their work clearly.

So we talked about each of our research projects for a while. I put the most positive spin on mine, and eventually John got around to telling us that he was developing a very fast processor for computers. We thought that meant something twice or at the outside four times as fast as what was on the market – which would have been totally awesome and we all would've wanted it. If he'd told us the truth – that his prototype was already twenty times faster than the fastest processor available – we would've thought he was drunk. Or lying.

But he didn't go into details because just then Liz walked in with her banker. He had taken her to dinner at some trendy place nearby and I guess she wanted to show me how handsome he was so I wouldn't be as mad at her for ditching me. And really, when I saw him I couldn't blame her. He was over six feet tall and muscular, with thick dark hair that was just starting to get a little gray and big brown eyes. I would have ditched her in a heartbeat as well, but men like that never seemed to notice me.

They sat down as introductions were made, with me failing miserably to remember everyone's name, and Liz asked, "So you're biologists? I know a biology joke."

"No you don't," I said.

"What do you call a cat that's fallen into breadcrumbs?"

This was an example of what my brother and I called a "Liz joke." We had endured them for decades. I blame Mrs. Fuller's third grade talent show. Every year, she made all of the kids, talented and otherwise, get up in front of the class and do a shtick. Most kids played musical instruments or something, but our mom was so busy with three kids and a job that she didn't have time to take us to lessons or stuff like that. But Liz did have a little book of jokes that my father had given her for her fifth birthday, just a year before he died. She memorized about a dozen of these: Why didn't the teddy bear want his supper? Because he was stuffed! What do you get if you cross an apple and a Christmas tree? A pineapple!

Oh how the eight-and-a-half year-olds laughed! And from this moment on Liz was convinced that she was a super-funny person. So much so that she never saw any need to update her act, even when the other kids grew out of that kind of joke and stopped laughing. Instead, their lack of laughter encouraged her. Now not only did she think she was funny, but she was also convinced she was the only person in the world who had any sense of humor.

It went on like this for years. Liz would tell a bad joke, no one would laugh.

But this time it was a little different.

"An inbred cat!" she said. Five people were sitting around this dark table in the beer hall expressing something between polite grins and audible groans, depending on whether or not they harbored any desire or realistic hopes of getting into Liz's pants. I believe the banker managed to feign a snarf. But one person was laughing. Hard.

"Inbred cat!" John said, "Hahahahahahahaha!"

He was laughing so hard that he was gasping for breath. I stared at him in shock. The rest of the table stared at him in shock. Liz laughed with him. And then he wiped a tear from his eye.

I remember mentally counting the number of drinks he'd had. Only one, I thought. A beer? Could a single beer make him giggly? Was he drunk before he got here? No. As I got to know him better over the years, I learned that John just thought Liz was funny. Really, really funny. And beautiful. And smart. He saw her as she saw herself, or rather he saw her as she wanted to be: the smartest, funniest, prettiest, best possible version of Liz Nicoletta that could possibly exist.

And that was it. The banker was defeated. The woman he'd bought a two hundred dollar dinner for just an hour before had already become someone else's girlfriend. On the basis of an inbred cat. He was rich and gorgeous, and he lost out to a broke computer geek with nothing but a prototype and a terrible sense of humor.

That was John in a nutshell. He just did stuff. There was no fanfare, no drama. He met Liz, he wanted Liz, and she was his. He went from being a complete stranger to becoming a permanent fixture in her life within the space of ten minutes.

Because he was always around Liz, I learned a lot more about John's work and he let me play with a prototype of the Corbit Chip. Then my friend Mei, who was already working at the Daltry, arranged for me to have an interview. No one really seemed that interested in having me work there. Given the problems I was having in my post-doc, I think the interview was only tolerated to keep Mei happy. Then the interviewer made an off-the-cuff remark that he had this particular problem that would be so much easier to solve if he only had a computer that was twenty times more powerful and half the cost. Ha ha ha. Well, I said, I do know a guy…

It wasn't as if I had the power to hold John's technology hostage. It was good enough that it was going to get out no matter what. And the Daltry was good enough that they were going to be among the first to find it, no matter what. I just kind of let them get the impression that I was tuned in and well-networked. It had really been just luck. But they gave me a second look and I've worked there ever since.

Oh, and as for the dreamy banker: I was watching TV one night a few years later when I saw that he had gotten arrested for insider trading during an IPO scandal for a chain of waffle trucks. He did seven years in a federal penitentiary for securities fraud.

Federal prisons don't allow conjugal visits. I checked.

Another thing happened that day when I got back to work. Along with Luka's sermon, the work stuff, and Theo's invitation, there was one more e-mail in my box. It said:

Hey kid!

I'm watching you. Be good! Thanks again for the tacos.

Love,
John

chapter eight

A couple weeks after my visit to Barlas labs, I got a call from my brother Luka.

"So have you seen Liz's blog?" he asked.

"No. Is she writing about hot dogs again?"

"Neanderthals."

I knew that Luka would have an opinion about the project.

Sometimes people ask me how I can be both a Catholic and a scientist, particularly a scientist who, at least for some research, studies evolution.

I tell them that they're confusing us with Evangelicals. Catholics don't have anything against evolution. A literal interpretation of the Bible, the kind that says the earth is six thousand years old, has never been a part of our religion, at least not since Saint Augustine warned against preaching idiocy to pagans in 415 AD. He said that if you tell people they have to believe things they know are not true and that do not matter then they will never believe you when you tell them things that are true and do matter, things about Christ and the resurrection. The Church's friendliness towards science is not to protect science. It is to protect Christianity.

The Catholic Church looks quite favorably on the idea of evolution, even allowing the freedom to speculate on the evolution of the human body as long as God's immediate creation of the human soul remains unquestioned. The Vatican even stated in 1950 that Darwin's theory of evolution and Catholicism are compatible. Then, in 1996, Pope John Paul II said that "evolution is no longer a mere hypothesis." Evolution is, of course, taught in biology classes at Catholic schools.

This is because evolution is only a mechanism. It is not an invisible rope pulling us forward. A giraffe does not have a long neck so that he can reach the leaves on the trees. He reaches the leaves on the tree because he has a long neck.

Evolution tumbles forward randomly, like boulders tumbling down an uneven hill, following the forces of nature but without any idea of where they'e going. Rocks bounce and jostle. Big boulders swallow up smaller ones and then split into two. Stones that fall into bad terrain smash and disintegrate into extinction. Our future, and the future of the next generation, is shaped by all of the bouncing and jostling in our past. Billions of years of tumbling down the hill have left the giraffe with a long neck, the peacock with beautiful feathers, and humans with furless skin. The present exists because of the past. And that is where the beauty of Darwin's theory lies, in its randomness, in its luck.

The Church is also pretty friendly towards genetic engineering, even accepting the inherent morality of modifying a person's genes to cure them of an inherited illness. It is of course not moral to give someone enhancements, superpowers if you will. But it's only right to give someone with an illness normal human functioning if possible.

But there are some things that the Church does not support. Research with human embryos is forbidden. We're supposed to believe that the cell that emerges from the fertilization of an egg is a little person. I don't know if I believe that. I can see the logic in the theology, but if I were to look at an embryo in a microscope it would be hard to think of it as a person. But there are lots of other things I can work on. I do not have to work on embryos, and it would upset my mother and Luka, so I don't. Most other things are sanctioned by the Church, even encouraged as most science is done for the good of humanity.

Just as my religion doesn't preclude me from doing science, no one asked Luka to check his reason at the door when he entered the seminary. I knew he would give Liz's project a reasonable hearing, but I still didn't think he would support it. There were a lot of ethical considerations.

"What does the blog say?" I asked.

"She says they implanted the Neanderthal embryo into a surrogate mother."

"That's what I was expecting, after the meeting," I said. "I don't know if it reassures you, but they say they started with a chimpanzee embryo. They're not using human embryos."

"I don't know that there is too much that could reassure me. Who is this Linda woman?" he asked.

"She's not a woman," I said. "She's a chimpanzee."

"She's a chimpanzee?"

I told him she was, and he replied with words priests probably aren't supposed to use. I asked him which part of the project bothered him the most. "Does the Church have a position on Neanderthals?"

"You mean Genesis?"

"Well, you know. Like an official position. On…hominids. They're not in Genesis, specifically."

"It doesn't come up very often," he said. "Priests' sisters don't generally make Neanderthals. But we have a basic respect for God's creation. Making an extinct animal…"

"Do you think the Neanderthal is an animal?" I said.

"Yes," he said.

"But why?" I asked. "How do we know they weren't human?"

"God made Adam and Eve and he made the animals. If they aren't children of Adam and Eve, they're animals. There isn't a third choice."

"They could have been humans," I said, "depending on when the Garden of Eden was. If it was a million years ago or something, then Adam and Eve could have been the parents of Neanderthals and humans."

"Adam and Eve were humans, Sara. Not *Homo erectus* or something," he said. "That's the whole point of the book."

"The Neanderthals wore clothes," I offered, mainly because I like arguing with my brother.

"So?"

"Adam and Eve didn't wear clothes until they ate the forbidden fruit. They didn't know they were naked. The Neanderthals wore clothes. People have found them, skins and stuff. They knew they were naked. So didn't Neanderthals have to come after the fall?"

"Your dog wears clothes," he said. "You send me pictures of him in his Christmas sweater every year. That doesn't make him human. Adam and Eve weren't cavemen, Sara. Their children were farmers. They were humans, not hominids."

"Humans had children with Neanderthals. We can sequence people of European or Asian descent and find traces of Neanderthal DNA."

"You can think what you want, but it doesn't make this right. Do you think this is moral? Liz is talking about creating a Neanderthal to raise as a child, as if it were a human. That's not a Christian family. She's trying to play God."

"I don't think it's a good idea, Luka. I was just arguing hypothetically. I don't think it's going to work."

"I'm in deep shit if the bishop finds out about this."

"I know," I said. "I'm in the same boat. It's not good for me professionally either."

Despite his vow of poverty Luka had the most career ambition of all of us. Liz hadn't had a job in years. And while I guess I was ambitious by most standards, I wasn't in a league with Luka. I hoped to maybe become a senior research scientist. Luka wanted to be the Pope.

"I don't think there's any chance of them actually doing it."

"What do you mean?"

"It's just too hard. Technically. It's a scam or something."

"Well, she's saying they did it."

"How would she know?" I said. "I don't even know, and this is what I do."

"I hope you're right."

"Even if they did make an embryo of something from that sequence I don't think it has a chance of growing into anything. It's made from DNA that's thirty thousand years old. It's got to be too screwed up to function. Anyway, are we coming down for Easter?" Mom liked us all to watch Luka say Mass.

"If I'm still a priest by then."

"It's early this year, so you should be good," I said. "And you're over-reacting anyway. They don't fire priests for having crazy sisters."

"They've never had a priest with a sister like this."

"They don't fire priests for anything. You're too valuable."

"No, they just send them to tiny little parishes out in the middle of nowhere," he said.

"Idaho's nice," I offered. "You like potatoes."

It was funny to think of Luka as some type of moral authority. Growing up he had just been my brother, doling out insults and the occasional beating like any other brother. I was as surprised as anyone when he joined the seminary.

I asked Luka once if he was gay, if that was the reason he had become a priest. It was Christmas night. He always had to work in the morning so we had an evening dinner at our mother's house. He and I were sitting at her kitchen table, drinking wine into the small hours. "I'm nothing," he said. "Don't like men. Don't like women. Never have. Weird, huh?" People understand gay and straight, he explained. They don't understand being nothing.

chapter nine

I was working late one evening a couple weeks later when I received an e-mail from Theo:

Sara,

I hope you are well. My cofounder Adam told me he saw that one of your papers got published. Just writing to say congratulations!

He says he is looking forward to working with you again.

Hope you and your family had a nice Easter.

Please find, attached, the latest picture of our Neanderthal baby, from the six week ultrasound. Everything is going great!

Theo

I opened the attached file. Yup, I thought, it's an ultrasound. But I couldn't tell what the thing was. It had a round belly, and a head, and things that looked like arms and short little legs sticking out. For all I knew it could have been anything: a chimp, a Neanderthal, a picture of a human baby taken from the Internet. It was what I would have expected to see if there was a Neanderthal growing in the chimp's body, but also if there was no Neanderthal and the whole thing was a con, or if they had made a ridiculous mistake and implanted the wrong embryo or something. The least likely scenario was, of course, that it was an actual Neanderthal, so I decided to ignore it.

The information about Theo's cofounder was odd, though. I did not remember ever working with an Adam Zhao. I searched for myself on PubMed, the service that lists publications in biology, to see if I'd ever published with an A. Zhao but nothing came up. Maybe he has me confused with someone else, I thought.

In the most recent publication I was a co-author on a paper describing a new virus. I wrote Theo back:

> Thanks! In truth, my only contribution to that paper was to say we had tried to sequence a new virus, but our normal techniques did not work very well.
>
> Easter was good except that we went to see Luka say Mass and his sermon was about the Garden of Eden, and how God had set us higher than the animals, and how we all descended from Adam and Eve. It didn't seem to have too much to do with Easter, but quite a lot to do with Neanderthals.
>
> Or anyway, that was how Liz saw it so she stood up in the middle of church and told Luka he was a "passive aggressive asshole" and he should be talking about "Eastery things like Jesus and chocolate bunnies."
>
> God bless,
> Sara

Theo responded:

> Liz said that Luka had some reservations about the project. I hope it did not cause too much of a disruption.

I answered:

> Well a lot of the people in the congregation are recent immigrants without great English so I don't know if they followed everything. But they seemed to know what "asshole" means. I wouldn't say they were pleased.
>
> My mom was really mad at her. She made her sit down right away.

I, on the other hand, nearly split a gut laughing at them. But I didn't want Theo to know I was that immature, so I left that part out. He responded:

> If you don't mind I may talk to Liz about being more discrete where the project is concerned.

I wrote back:

Yeah, good luck with that!

Hey, I had a couple questions about the Neanderthal project. I was wondering what the error rate is on your artificial chromosomes.

It was a technical question, but I didn't think it was a hard one. Errors in copying DNA occur in real cells when they replicate, so some mistakes can be tolerated. But if the artificial chromosome's error rate was much higher than, say, one error in a thousand, then anything made with them might not be viable. In turn, their technology's error rate would determine whether Barlas Labs was viable or not. Error rates in reading DNA, for instance, have largely determined which sequencing companies have succeeded and which have failed. I decided to ask Theo about his error rate so I could get a better feel for what kind of operation Barlas Labs was. Theo replied:

Sorry, I can't tell you that.

I responded:

Oh, come on! You must know the error rate! It determines whether your company sinks or swims.

Theo replied:

I didn't say I didn't know. I just said I couldn't tell you. It's proprietary.

Check your mail tomorrow. You should be getting something from me.

Then he added a smug-looking smiley face emoticon and wished me a good night and good luck with my research.

"That guy's not making a Neanderthal," I said to the dog cuddled up on the couch next to me. I was always impressed by Achilles' capacity to sleep, sometimes up to eighteen hours a day.

Dogs used to work. When the wolves that became dogs began living with humans they helped them hunt and alerted them to predators or enemies lurking nearby. In fact, some people think they helped their humans so much that dogs were one of the reasons that modern humans out-competed Neanderthals for food and resources. They believe that when modern humans left Africa and arrived in Europe it was the domestication of wolves that gave them the advantage in the shared environment.

Others disagree. Dogs started living with humans around thirty thousand years ago, in Europe. Because Neanderthals and humans were both living there at the same time, it is impossible to say who the dogs started living with first. Some people speculate that the Neanderthals were first to live with dogs. I've seen an abstract idea floating around that the Neanderthals were somehow more in-tune with their environment and the animal kingdom. But there have never been any Neanderthal and canine bones found together, as you would expect if dogs were being kept as pets.

Either way, dogs were with us now. And I had one, a fuzzy little white wolf, curled up in a soft warm ball next to me.

chapter ten

During this time, the amount of work I had at the Daltry
was picking up. This was the first year of the Panola virus. It
began on a sunny spring afternoon when a family in Alabama was
sitting on plastic lawn chairs in their back yard, cooking hamburgers
on a grill. A shadow passed over like a cloud and the father, without
looking up, said, "Guess that storm is coming."

Then it started raining sparrows. Small dead birds fell on and
around them, landing on the grass, on the patio, and in their above-
ground swimming pool. And then, as the family scurried into the
house for cover, the whole flock fell out of the sky like huge balls of
hail.

This was only the first birdstorm. The birdstorms, we found, were
caused by a virus, which we named after the area where it was found:
Panola. While some viruses store their information in DNA, like
humans do, Panola stored its genetic material in a sister molecule,
RNA. While it didn't seem to infect people, Panola was distantly
related to avian influenza and appeared to be highly contagious
among birds, quickly infecting an entire flock.

Our working theory was that the virus caused some damage to
the lungs that did not cause symptoms until a bird exerted itself, and
then the bird would experience some sort of fatal attack. Because
the birds usually reached this level of exertion only during longer
flights, which they tended to take as a flock, all of the birds would
reach the same threshold at about the same time, causing the entire
flock to fall out of the sky at once. Gradually, the birdstorms were

moving up the eastern seaboard of the United States, following the spring migration. Starlings fell in Tennessee. Blackbirds fell in North Carolina. Grackles fell from the sky in West Virginia.

It was a big outbreak, and there was too much work for the government surveillance agencies to do alone, so the Daltry was participating in some of the sequencing work. I would get samples in, try to sequence the viral genomes, and then use a computer to compare the RNA sequences from the different samples to one another. I was trying to find some clue about what the virus was doing and where it might be going next. But the samples had proven very hard to sequence. The amount of viral RNA in the samples was unusually low compared to the amount of bird RNA. We would sequence millions of fragments of RNA and only a dozen or so seemed to be from Panola. More troubling was that there was a region of the viral genome that, for some reason, didn't want to be sequenced, a region we had no sequences for, that was invisible to us.

There was no lack of samples. The local health departments usually arrived a few hours after the birdstorms and took samples from the dead birds. In fact, a lot of my work was just organizing the mundane processes of getting all the samples sequenced. The problem was that once they were sequenced, the results were mostly junk.

In that vein, I received a request from a graduate student asking for some of the sequencing data that I had collected but had not yet published.

She was not a usual collaborator, but the amount of analysis I had time to do with the data was cursory at best. Also, she was not looking at anything I was interested in, and it seemed like having the data would help the kid out with her dissertation. So I gathered the material together and was about to send it to her when I thought I should check who she was. I looked up her name on the Internet and found out that she was a graduate student in the lab of Dr. Angus Gupta.

So instead of sending her the data I sent an e-mail to him:

Angus,

Are you fucking kidding me? Tell your graduate student to wait for the data to be published like everybody else.

Sara

And he replied:

Dear Dr. Nicoletta,

I was afraid you might feel that way.

As we both know, the progression of science depends on collaborative efforts between many researchers and institutions. I hope that we would all endeavor to separate our personal lives from our professional lives, to foster an environment of scientific cooperation, not competition.

Therefore, in the interest of open science, and to forward scientific research, I would like to professionally request that you send us your data.

Sincerely,
Angus Gupta, MD, PhD, MSc

I responded:

Angus,

Go fuck yourself.

Sara

Then he tried again:

Dear Dr. Nicoletta,

Julia is a very talented graduate student who could make substantial progress on her graduate research if she had this data. I hope you agree that it would be unethical to delay the progress of her very promising career because of a small personal conflict between ourselves.

If you would be so kind as to send us your data it will provide a significant step forward in her work. As you know, the publication process can be long and time consuming and it will likely be many months before the Panola data becomes publicly available.

I would hope that you would be eager to be supportive of Julia, especially as a fellow woman scientist.

Sincerely,
Angus Gupta, MD, PhD, MSc

I responded:

Small personal conflict? Are you on drugs you arrogant twit?

Go fuck yourself!

He responded:

Dr. Nicoletta

I do not think you are behaving professionally. You are clearly letting your personal feeling cloud your judgment in a most discourteous manner.
And in any case, in this episode anyone reasonable would realize that I was in fact the injured party.

Sincerely,
Angus Gupta, MD, PhD, MSc

I responded:

YOU were the injured party?

You left me TIED UP IN A FUCKING HOTEL ROOM. I had to be untied by the maid. I missed my fucking plane home you asshole.

For the third time: GO FUCK YOURSELF

A few hours later this e-mail arrived:

Dear Sara,

I am so very sorry. It honestly did not occur to me that you would not have been able to get out of the belt.

At the time I was unfortunately carried away by my emotions.

It was a thoughtless and horrible thing to do. I hope you can find it in your heart to forgive me.

Please disregard our request for the Panola data. I had no right to ask you for it and we will happily wait for its publication.

Sincerely,
Angus

I guessed that that was as good an apology as I was going to get and life would be easier without Angus Gupta as an enemy, so I sent Julia the data.

chapter eleven

Many things in life that go badly start with a party invitation. This one came in the mail, the real mail on old-fashioned pastel cardstock. I was cordially invited to attend a baby shower in honor of the Neanderthal.

"Isn't it a bit early?" I asked. "We don't even know what it is yet."

"It's a girl!" my mom said on the other end of the phone.

"A girl what?"

"Sara, stop it. You have to go. This is important to Liz."

I asked my mother why she was suddenly in favor of the Neanderthal project. She said it was because she had raised three kids and thought she deserved at least one grandchild. "And Sara, I'm sorry, but you're almost forty now. This might be my last chance."

"I wouldn't say almost!"

"Sara, honey, let's be realistic. You work too much to…"

"Maybe Luka will knock up a nun."

"Sara!"

I asked her if she even knew what a Neanderthal was.

"A Neanderthal baby is better than no baby," she replied.

I told her that I didn't agree, that I thought the whole thing was unlikely to succeed, that Liz was going to end up crushed and disappointed, and that Barlas Labs may well be a front for Greek mafia money laundering. But she had made up her mind and did not want to hear anything more from me on that topic.

"Does Luka have to go?" I asked.

"He's a priest!" my mom said, as if that settled it.

And she needed a ride to Long Island. The party was being held at the beach house where Theo lived.

So on the appointed day my mother and I took the scenic route down to Theo's house. Liz had warned me that it was not in the most fashionable part of Long Island, as if I knew or cared about such things. It was on the north shore, not very far from the city. To get there, we started at my mother's house in Rhode Island, where the forsythia were ablaze with gold against the dark blue spring sky. We boarded a ferry in Connecticut and crossed Long Island Sound on its sunny top deck. Seagulls played in the harbor amongst the sailboats and a huge boxy building where people built submarines. Then we drove through the island's coastal wine country.

It was a mild day so Achilles sat on my mother's lap with his head out the window, an arrangement that disturbed her hairdo, wrinkled her skirt, and annoyed her slightly. We stopped once to taste some wine and again at a tourist trap of a town for fudge, and then eventually we turned off the main road and meandered our way up a long pebble driveway until we reached Theo's house. It had gray shingles with white trim and an old fashioned wrap-around porch. It was like a Nantucket cottage that had grown tall and obese. Masses of yellow tulips, maybe thousands of them, were shining in the sun all around its foundation.

"Wowwwww," my mom said when it came into view, "it's like a banquet hall."

I parked my car next to a purple minivan with New Jersey plates. I wasn't sure whether or not it would be okay to bring the dog so I hadn't asked. I opened the car door and he sprung out and peed on the flowers.

Theo's doorbell played the chimes of Westminster. He opened the door and feigned surprise. "Well Sara! I didn't know you had two sisters," he said, referring to my mother.

"Oh," my mom gushed. "You flatter me."

"Not me, though," I said. Theo smirked.

The dog jumped up to Theo's knees to say hello and then walked past him, startling a little girl in pigtails who screamed "Dog!" and ran off. Achilles's nails clacked across the black and white tiled floor as he ran off in pursuit.

"Come through to the patio," Theo said. "I'm afraid this is the first time I've hosted a baby shower. It's like a Super Bowl party, right?" He was wearing white linen pants and a white shirt, looking the part of a Long Island party host, or maybe a dandy from a hundred years ago.

We followed him through the hallway past a gaudy staircase with a brass banister and a mural of Dutch farm scenes painted on the walls.

"Look at this place!" my mother whispered, "It's fabulous!"

"Yeah, windmills."

Achilles bolted across the hallway again and ran into another room. A little boy screamed this time. "It took my cheese!"

Good, I thought. I won't have to feed him for a while.

"I didn't realize Theo was so handsome," my mom said, nearly swooning.

"He's alright," I whispered back.

"Oh, he's gorgeous!" my mom insisted. "Look at that ass!"

Theo looked over his shoulder and caught my eye with a cocked eyebrow as my mother peered into a small library. Her whispering had gotten a lot louder since her hearing started going.

We stepped to the back of the house where a large open kitchen and living room stretched across the width of the house. All of the fixtures and furniture were white. The living room was decorated with nautical tchotchkes and the back wall was an array of glass doors and windows. I knew Theo lived in a beach house, but that still didn't prepare me for the view that I saw through the windows: the wide expanse of thick green lawn, the rocky shore, and then the sea, stretching out to the horizon, dotted with small whitecaps, and topped by the spring sky.

These sweeping views of the shore were familiar to me from my childhood in Rhode Island, but ones I had only ever experienced as a tourist visiting public beaches or the mansions of Newport. The ocean was Theo's back yard, and there was no one there except the people he had invited. And I, because of this strange thing that my sister was doing, was one of them. I have always loved the ocean. When I see it I have a compulsive desire to jump into the water, to be enveloped in the cold waves, and it taunted me that there was this private bit of rocky shore but it was not yet warm enough to swim.

Theo ushered us outside. Liz was there with her guests. There were half a dozen women I did not recognize sitting on the patio's outdoor sofas. They were all dressed in colorful spring party dresses that went down to their ankles. It was the fashion that year to look like you had gotten tangled up in a parachute. I had never met any of them before, or even heard their names mentioned. I wondered who they were and why they were at this party. There were a few empty chairs and I tried to sit in the one facing the sea, but my mother took that one and I was left facing the house.

There was one familiar face among the guests, but unfortunately it belonged to Liz's friend Billy. "Oh, you came," he said unenthusiastically when he saw me. He was sitting next to a chiseled slab of granite that he introduced as his boyfriend, Anton. Other names were exchanged and cheeks were kissed.

"We were just discussing the baby's room," Liz said. "Billy is going to help me find a decorator."

"I saw a really nice nursery last week," Billy said.

"He's in real estate," Liz explained.

"What color are you going to do it?" Anton asked.

"It has to be pink!" my mother insisted.

A large woman named Paula objected. "Oh you can't do it pink, Liz!" She was next to Anton. Her voice was deep like Lauren Bacall's and her fleshy softness contrasted with his sharp features, the top of her bosom nearly spilling out of her flowery dress. "You don't want to force her into gender stereotypes at so young an age."

"But she's a girl," my mother countered.

A redheaded woman named Stacey, who smelled of patchouli oil and had a bindi on her forehead, said that having a pink nursery can cause a girl to grow up with negative feelings of inferiority towards boys.

"We don't want our children to grow up feeling they have to be constrained by society's arbitrary expectations of them," Paula stated, taking a puff from her electronic cigarette before blowing out a big cloud of steam.

I had only just arrived and I realized that I was already halfway down the road to feminist scorn. The problem was my shower gift. My mom had insisted that I had to buy a present so I decided to pick out some clothes that I thought would look good on a baby chimpanzee, because if anything was growing in Linda's belly I figured it was probably a chimp. So I went to Old Navy and pictured all the baby clothes on a chimpanzee. Nothing looks bad on a baby chimp, but pink is so flattering to dark brown fur. I bought five little dresses and every one of them was pink.

"I don't know," I said thoughtfully. "I used a beautiful pink as the background color on my conference poster on computational methods in viral genome sequencing. I didn't feel disempowered." But no one was interested in that.

"Why just the other day I was buying a sandwich at this cute little café near my house and I could barely get my mouth around it. And I was thinking, this whole world is designed for men!" Stacey said.

"Ohhh, Stacey, I'm so sorry you felt marginalized by your sandwich," Liz said sympathetically.

"It's something no man will ever understand," offered Billy.

"Oh and you know you have to be careful about the paint, don't you, Liz?" said Judy, a bony Asian woman. "Our Jinnie has chemical sensitivity syndrome. I don't like to complain, but she is so difficult to live with when she has an attack. Last week she dumped a plate of spaghetti on the cat."

"Because of the paint?" my mom asked incredulously.

"I read that on your blog," Liz said. "It sounded awful, her shouting like that!"

"It can be difficult, but I can't complain, of course. Things *have* gotten a little quieter now that we repainted the whole house with organic paints."

"I'm just so lucky to have you moms around to give me advice!" Liz gushed.

"Yes, it's all different now than when you kids were little," my mom said. "I wouldn't know where to start. If one of you kids dropped a plate of spaghetti on the cat…well, we never had cats. Luka's allergic…but still…"

"Yeah, and like the Neanderthal baby might be even more sensitive to chemicals than other kids," said Stacey.

"I don't think we should make assumptions about her abilities just because she's differently evolved, Stacey," said Judy.

"No, but I mean, Neanderthals are just so much more natural, you know."

"Yes, but we have to be careful in our language," Paula insisted. "We don't want people to think that a previously extinct child will somehow be more fragile."

"Stacey didn't mean that the baby will be more fragile," said Liz. "But she will be different. That's one of the reasons why we all can't wait to meet her, isn't it! She'll be so…real."

"Yes, I mean real is stronger, not fragile-er," Stacey said. "She just wouldn't be used to all those terrible chemicals."

I wasn't sure that in the time scale of evolution, the half dozen or so generations that modern humans have been exposed to industrial chemicals would make much difference to how well we tolerated them. You might, for example, expect a trait like genetic immunity to a particular infection to become more prevalent in the population over a small number of generations if the infection killed everyone who did not have immunity. In that situation, only people with immunity could live long enough to have kids and pass on their good genes, and then everyone in the population could have immunity by the next generation. But environmental chemicals, while they may of course be bad for one's health, were not killing young people at rates high enough to cause a genetic change on the kind of scale Stacey was describing. I doubted that a modern human baby would be any more sensitive than the hypothetical Neanderthal baby.

"We do have an expert at the table," my mother said. I thought momentarily that she might be referring to me, the biologist, but that was silly. "What do you think, Theo? Will the baby have this chemical sensitivity thing?"

"I think your granddaughter is going to be a very unique and beautiful person. Just like her grandmother," he said in the tone of someone accustomed to closing deals on a golf course. "Now, would anyone like some more drinks? Mimosas? Coffee?"

Stacey asked if the coffee was fair trade. Theo told her it was Kona coffee and she continued to wait for an answer. He clarified that Kona is in Hawaii and she continued to wait for an answer. Anton pointed out that Hawaii is a state with a pride that suggested that this was recently acquired knowledge. Stacey decided to have a seltzer.

The women went on to talk more about chemical-free paint in a way that made me pretty sure none of them knew anything about chemistry. Then they moved on to their children's allergies and food intolerances. I did not have a spreadsheet handy to keep them all straight, but after hearing about them the fact that Theo's lunch menu consisted solely of organic fruit salad made more sense.

Meanwhile, the children darted in and out of the house, slamming the remarkably sturdy French doors each time they passed through. At one point, Achilles shot out of the house carrying a shoe in his mouth while a little girl limped after him, followed by her army of bigger children. The braver amongst them played tug-of-war with Achilles while he growled like an idling Vespa and everyone won except the shoe. Then they circled the lawn while their mothers shouted at them to stay back from the flowers and the rocks and the sea.

At one point I wondered idly how many children there were, but as the day wore on they began to shed layers of clothes which made it difficult to take an accurate tally. Overall, though, they appeared to be quite robust considering their catalog of maladies.

As I ate my fruit salad the dog ran across the patio and a boy came darting out behind him pointing a Nerf gun.

"Hey, kid, you're not shooting my dog are you?" I asked.

"Okay," he said, and ran off again after the dog.

Paula leaned in. "I'm so sorry. He was circumcised."

"Oh," I responded definitively, more because I sensed that was what was expected rather than from any understanding of what the state of the little boy's penis had to do with him shooting at my dog, or why it would be any of my business.

"It's a common reaction to post-circumcision trauma," she clarified. "Minor cruelties to animals."

"Oh."

"If you want to know more I have a blog called 'The Unkindest Cut.' I like to think of it as a support network for mothers of post-cut boys. It can be so challenging!"

"Oh. Yeah. I'll check that out."

I looked over to see Theo refilling my mother's mimosa glass for the third time. He seemed to enjoy playing host, but when the other mothers started educating Liz on the pros and cons of baby slings, Billy and his boyfriend looked as glazed over as I was. "So what do you do all day, Anton?" I asked.

"I'm a journalist," he said. "I have a column at *Zoss*."

"Oh, *Zoss*," I said. *Zoss* was the tabloid that had ranked Liz as plain wife number seven. "That's great," I said. "I love *Zoss*."

Zoss was the kind of publication that completely ignored the brutal wars in the Middle East but would put out a special issue if an actor got caught getting a hand job off an ugly hooker, so it was enormously popular.

I had seen a few blog posts about the Neanderthal project but only because I had specifically looked for them. Some of them may have been written by these very women on the patio. But the science press had so far ignored it, mainly I think because it was not tied to any scientists that anyone had heard of and the project's obvious technical difficulties made it seem farfetched. There also had not been a word about it in the mainstream press. The pregnancy, or whatever it was, was already supposedly four months along. I had been beginning to hope that the whole thing would blow over before it garnered any real attention.

An article in *Zoss* would change all that. Given that Liz had formerly graced its pages, an article seemed like a possibility.

When Billy went into the house I cornered him outside the bathroom.

"How could you bring a reporter here?" I shout-whispered.

"It's my best friend's baby shower! He's my boyfriend. Of course I'm going to bring him! And he wanted to see the beach house," Billy said. "Isn't it grand! I could sell this…"

"Do you know what a disaster it would be if this Neanderthal nonsense got into the news?"

"We don't know that it's nonsense. I mean I hope it's nonsense…"

"You know what Liz is like with the press."

"Of course I do! I was there, too, Sara."

"Why would you bring a reporter here?"

"Anton writes the fashion column! He's not going to write about Neanderthals. He doesn't even know what one is."

"I gathered that."

"He's not book smart," Billy said.

"You can leave out the word 'book.'"

"Don't be a snob! We talked about it. He's not going to write about it."

I glared.

"Anton and I are in a *re-la-tion-ship*," Billy said. "I know you've never been in a re-la-tion-ship, but FYI that means we can trust each other. Not everyone's dream is to grow old alone and hoard Chihuahuas, Sara."

That wasn't my dream, but I didn't see why having one seventy-pound German shepherd was considered normal but having ten seven-pound Chihuahuas was weird. It's the same amount of dog. Okay, maybe it was my dream a little. But not the growing old alone part.

"Now," he said, "may I please use the bathroom before I wet my trousers? They're from Barney's and I'd rather not pee on them."

chapter twelve

When the party started winding down I was able to escape.

I found a spot for myself, sitting on the grass, staring out at the ocean. It was late afternoon by then. As the tide went out the smell of the ocean grew stronger. It was growing chilly, but my worn-out dog was cuddled up next to me keeping me warm.

The noise of the sea was, in a way, more quiet than silence. The waves drowned out the noise of the families as they loaded children, toys, and leftover cake into their fuel-efficient vehicles. I didn't notice Theo approach until he was standing over me.

"I snuck you a mimosa," he said. He handed me a champagne flute as he sat down on the grass. "Don't worry, it's mostly orange juice."

I was grateful and took a sip. It was so sweet that it had to have been fresh-squeezed. Oranges have gotten better, I thought. It was like drinking a rainbow, an effervescent rainbow sprinkled with sugar.

"How did you know they'd be like that?" I asked.

"The oranges?"

"The women."

"Like what?"

"Like that. Gung ho, like that. That was why you picked them, wasn't it? Those people, to be the next Neanderthal parents." Liz had told me in the kitchen. I asked her how she knew all these women and she said they were Theo's candidates for adopting the next Neanderthal children. It turned out that it wasn't a baby shower so much as an audition.

It had not occurred to me that there was a plan to make more Neanderthal children, but Liz said she didn't want the baby to be all alone. She wanted her to have friends, to maybe marry someone like her if that was what she wanted. So Theo said that he would make more Neanderthals, after this one was born perfectly. These women had expressed interest in the project, either on Liz's blog or directly to him, so he invited them to the shower so Liz could meet them and see what they were like.

"I picked them," he said matter-of-factly, "simply because I thought they might be good parents for the Neanderthal children."

"But the ones you picked – they're cut from the same cloth. Liz asked me who I liked the best. I could barely tell them apart."

"There weren't that many people to choose from. Adopting a Neanderthal baby isn't as popular as you would think," he said. "Not yet. But these families, they already have kids that are different. Atypical. I thought that would make them better able to handle being a Neanderthal parent."

"They all blog about their kids' problems."

"They advocate for their children. The Neanderthal kids are going to need that."

I looked out onto the chopping waves and thought about that for a while. The sun was beginning to go down in the west. On the north shore of Long Island the west was to the left, like on a map. The colors in the sky looked like they were bleeding sideways. This was the same sunset that the Great Gatsby would have watched from his lawn, if he were real, the same view of the waves on Long Island Sound. I couldn't quite see Connecticut.

"Munchausen by blog," I said.

Munchausen by proxy is when someone uses another person's illness to get attention for themselves. The other person is usually their own kid. They say he is sick when he is not, exaggerate or make up symptoms. Then they run to the hospital, feeding off the sympathy of the doctors and nurses. It seemed to be what these women were doing: a blog about their kids that was really about themselves, the supportive comments feeding some need. Theo understood what I was getting at.

"You're judging them harshly," he said. "It's not easy to parent a kid with challenges."

"I know. But every kid has problems. It doesn't help the kids to have them blabbed about all over the Internet. That woman writes about her kid's penis. He's not going to like that when he gets to junior high."

"The Neanderthals are going to need a community. They'll need friends."

"They'll need privacy," I said, as if I knew what a Neanderthal would need.

"Well," Theo said, "if we're going to make Neanderthals then they need to be raised by someone. We could keep them in a lab all their lives. Or we can put them in families. These families will advocate for them. They have what it takes to do this."

Theo was stretched out on the grass, propping himself up on one elbow. It was turning into an argument, but it was a gentle calm one. A discussion. Do people still have discussions?

I didn't know if any family had what it would take to raise a Neanderthal, or any lab for that matter. We didn't know what they would need or what they would be like. Would they be verbal? Would they be violent? We weren't even sure what they would eat. Macaroni and cheese? Gluten-free pizza? Foods that are perfectly fine for us to eat can be poisonous to other species. Chocolate or onions can kill a dog.

But, still, I think that it was at that moment that I realized how smart Theo was. It was a conniving kind of intelligence, so different from the kind of intelligence I possess, but it was there and it was big. He had thought it through. These families were already fighting for the Neanderthal children's very right to exist. They would keep fighting for these children (if there were children) for their entire lives. It was what they did. Whether they did it altruistically or from something else didn't matter. Theo had found a way to make the socially impossible seem feasible. He had found people who could make something that so many would find viscerally repulsive, like Luka did, seem like the cause of the moment, this year's saving of the rainforest. I wondered how Anton would write about it.

I still doubted that Theo really did have a Neanderthal gestating in that chimpanzee. I certainly didn't think there was a viable Neanderthal. It still seemed too fantastic to me. But at the same time, it almost didn't matter. He had raised an army and was gearing up to fight the fight as if he had. He had come so far in so short a time, just by not being afraid to do it. That was what he had, that thing about him that would keep my mind wandering back to our time together. I had finally put my finger on it. It was sheer, unadulterated chutzpah. The world I lived in was so full of anxiety, being afraid someone would publish your findings before you or that someone would point out a mistake in your calculations. Theo wasn't afraid of anything. I didn't know if that was good, but it sure was something.

"How did you know there were people like that?" I asked. "You don't have kids. I didn't really know people like that existed before today."

"My dad's third wife had a couple kids. I was a lot older than them. She and her friends were a little like that."

"You're a big brother?"

"I was, for about a decade."

"Your dad doesn't seem to have a very good success rate with women."

"Maybe he just never found his soul mate."

"Do you believe in that?" I laughed.

"Don't you?" he replied, smiling wryly.

"Sometimes I'm not even sure I believe in souls."

"I think my dad found his soul mate now."

"On his fourth try?"

"He took her back to Greece with him for a while, enjoying his retirement."

"Is this his house?" I asked.

"It's our family's home," Theo said. "That's how Greeks think of it. But I guess technically it's his. It'll be mine someday."

"When he dies? That's terrible."

"He doesn't see it that way. It is what he's been planning for since I was born. He came from Greece with nothing in his pocket and he made all this," Theo said, waving his arm around at the estate.

"Do you feel like you have to top him?"

"Top him?"

"People always want to do better than their parents. He set a high bar. Is that why you're doing this?"

"I'm not competitive with him. But he is a role model. Not for making a Neanderthal, but for building Barlas Labs. Building something, anyway."

"John built something. Not from absolutely nothing, but like that. John and Liz, really."

"Were you close?"

"To John? Yeah…he was a good friend to me. More than a brother-in-law. It was such a huge loss," I said, lying back in the grass and looking up at the darkening sky. "But the money…there's a ton of it. I guess I would inherit some of it if something happened to Liz. But I never think about that."

"No. It'll go to her daughter."

"Would it?" I wondered. "Or would I just inherit a Neanderthal?"

I guess that was another thing I hadn't considered. But of course. My mom's too old and Luka wouldn't do it. If anything happened to Liz, would I be in charge of…whatever it was?

"Our lawyers say it depends on whether the law defines the Neanderthals as human or not. But there's no legal precedent. The technology is ahead of the law," he said, almost with a sense of pride.

"It always is."

"I'm surprised Liz hasn't discussed this with you yet. Our lawyers have already started drawing up some contracts to send you."

Liz hadn't mentioned it. "I guess if there was a Neanderthal, hypothetically speaking," I said, "I could set up some sort of trust or something. I wouldn't have to raise it."

"You wouldn't have to raise her, but you would," Theo countered, flatly, as if it were self-evident. "You wouldn't leave her in an institution."

I looked down at the dog cuddled against my leg and gave him a scratch on his head. The rescued dog. Theo was probably right, I thought. I'd have a dog and a Neanderthal if anything happened to Liz. I guess I'd need Liz's money too, to buy a bigger place. I wondered what kind of care a Neanderthal would need. Maybe it would be better off by itself, wandering the woods like Sasquatch or something. Liz was planning to raise it in the city. I could do things differently.

"It probably won't come up," Theo said.

No, there'd have to be a Neanderthal for me to inherit a Neanderthal. I looked at him, a little startled, as if he had made some type of confession.

But that wasn't what he meant. "Liz is going to live to be a thousand," he said, "with all those organic twigs and berries she eats."

"I think she and my mom are more interested in preserving themselves in ethanol today."

"I didn't even know I had peppermint schnapps."

"You don't anymore. Are they still inside?" I asked.

"They're cleaning my kitchen for me."

"First rule of party-hosting, Theo. Don't ever let drunk people empty your dishwasher. It'll be months before you find your forks."

The ocean wind was strong, blowing my hair around. Achilles woke up, looked around, and toddled his way over to a hedge of saltspray roses. We watched him lift his leg to pee and blow over onto his side.

"I don't really believe you're making a Neanderthal," I told Theo.

"I know," he said, grinning.

"I know Liz is just a flakey socialite to most people, but she's my sister. She is really looking forward to this. I don't want her getting hurt."

"She won't. You'll see, in about five months."

"She has been through a lot. She's more fragile than people think she is. Most people don't see it, but I do."

"You don't have to worry," Theo insisted. "It will all work out like she hopes." He sounded sincere, but of course he was intending to.

"Why did you pick Liz?" I asked. "Just because she has a lot of money? She's not like the others. She blogs and stuff but she isn't really like them."

"I didn't pick Liz. She picked me."

I sat up and looked at him, surprised. "What do you mean?"

Theo took a handful of my hair and pushed it out of my face. It was a hopeless effort. The breeze was too strong, my hair too straggly, but I could smell his cologne again, this time mixing with the sea air.

"You'll have to ask Liz," he said.

"You can't just say something like that and then not tell me what you mean."

"I can," he said with a laugh.

Then he stood up and walked back to the house, leaving me alone with the dog and Gatsby's sunset.

chapter thirteen

"**I**t's way too small back here for three people," Liz complained.

"Four if you count Liz's handbag," Billy said.

"Where did you ever find it?" Anton asked.

"The car? It was John's idea of a joke," my mom offered.

"It wasn't a joke!" I said. "I love it!"

"No, I meant the handbag," Anton responded. "It's lovely. Just rather large."

My mom and I were spending the night at Liz's and I was dropping Anton and Billy off at the station so they could catch a train to the Hamptons.

"I got it made at this little shop in Flushing. Remember Sara, how lost we got?"

It was a long time ago, before John got sick. We got off at the wrong train stop and walked for miles before we found the place. "I remember the noodles we had," I said.

"Sara's mental map of the world is landmarked by food," Liz said. "Tell her a place and she'll tell you what she ate there! Do the British Islands."

"Please don't," Billy insisted.

"Newcastle!" I said, "Baked potatoes stuffed with egg salad."

"Remember that curry we had in Glasgow," Liz said, "how spicy it was?"

"Must you two always play this game? It bores everyone else." We would never be too old for our mother to scold us.

"Liz is the only one who appreciates my talent," I said. My memory has always been better than hers. Once she thanked me for remembering her life for her, and only a little sarcastically.

It was a short drive to the train station. As we drove away from the beach house I had seen Theo in the rearview mirror, watching my car as we left. In a little while I got a text from him: *You're right. Not a fork in sight.* Part of me wanted to go back to help him look. His company, when he chose to stop performing, was so pleasant. But I reminded myself what he was doing, the position he was putting my sister in. Maybe he never stopped performing, I thought. Maybe he just changed the act to fit the audience.

I already knew he changed his costume. When I was in the bathroom at his house I noticed that he had left his black-rimmed glasses sitting on a shelf. I wondered what they were for, distance or reading. I put them on to see how they looked on me. Nothing changed. The lenses were perfectly clear. They were not for vision. They were a prop to make him look more intellectual, I guess. I wondered what else about him was and was not real.

We dropped Billy and Anton off at the station and drove west. The towns on Long Island became less quaint as we headed towards the city and more and more like the dense suburbia I had grown up in. Then we crossed Queens and went under the East River into the city. When we got to the Upper West Side I received conflicting advice on what to do with the car.

"Sara," Liz said, "the lot's on 78th."

"It's forty dollars!" my mom objected. "Circle again, Sara."

"Mom, I'll pay," Liz said. "I've got millions."

"Save it."

"For what?" Liz asked.

"A wooly mammoth?" I suggested.

"Look, there's a space!" my mom said.

"Fire hydrant."

And so it went.

People complain about New York City parking, but the Upper West Side is not that bad. Before she lived there Liz was in Brooklyn Heights, and I can tell you the parking in that neighborhood was a real nightmare. She and John shared a small studio apartment there before they were married. They moved in together when Liz had only a small income as an entry-level graphic designer and John did not have any income at all because he was building Corbit Chips. Their place was in an art deco building that had been made rent control in the forties and hadn't been updated since. It still had its original cork floors, tin cabinets in the galley kitchen, and yards of white subway tile in the bathroom. All of the paint was peeling. White chips fell from the ceiling like autumn leaves. When I stayed there the dog and I slept on a blow-up mattress in the same room as them.

Liz complained about how small it was all the time, so as soon as she got back from their honeymoon, she quit her job and began looking for a new place to live. It became like her job. She claimed at the time that it was perfectly reasonable to focus on this because it was such a large investment. But in reality John had just closed a humongous deal, leaving them with more than enough money for both of them, so she really just couldn't be bothered going into work every day.

She found Billy, a sometime actor who sold real estate to wealthy women. They dragged each other around the city until they saw an ad for a "Rare opportunity to combine two adjacent apartments to create a sprawling home in a prime Upper West Side location." They went to the open house, which was staffed by an emaciated woman dripping in semi-precious stones who set the stage for the showing by blasting Frank Sinatra. "Send in the Clowns" was playing when they walked in. It was kind of a buzz-kill, but Billy saw the potential for the place and convinced Liz and John to buy it. The combining part was only estimated to take a few months, so they stayed in the Heights. But Liz fussed over every mundane detail, dragging the thing out, harrying the builders, and annoying their studio apartment's property manager, who kept showing the place expecting them to move out only to be told at the last moment that they would need another month.

The new building's aging doorman became fed up with working on a construction site. He liked order and the constant stream of Liz's construction workers coming in and out, using the wrong doors and elevators, disturbed his serenity. He decided it was time to retire to a quiet life in Florida. People who owned units in the building got a stack of resumes from people vying to be his replacement. John made an enemy at his first co-op board meeting when he insisted that they hire a man who had served our country rather than a third floor resident's hairdresser's husband. Liz said at the time that she thought John was acting weird about it. He had gone around and personally spoken to each of the residents in the building to get their vote. "It's not like we know this Hank guy," she said. "We don't even live there yet."

The expense of the renovation was at once nothing and everything, meaning that Liz bought exactly what she liked and rationalized every penny as an "investment".

"Sara, of course I *need* a $7000 stove! Every kitchen on this block has one. People expect it. Billy says we'd never be able to sell the apartment again without one."

I said, "They only installed theirs because they thought you'd expect it. And they don't cook the food any better." It was true. They didn't. I read that in *Consumer Reports*.

But my sister had joined the trophy wife's circle of consumption. I watched the money bleed. More than I made in a month to retile the bathrooms. More than I made in a year to buy kitchen appliances. More than I made in a decade to put pictures on the walls. "Do you know how many viruses I could sequence with the cost of that rug?" I said.

She paid two thousand dollars for a spiritual consultant to rid the space of negative energy. Luka said he could have performed a real exorcism for free, but only if Liz herself were demonically possessed. Priests do not do real estate work.

"Have you had a loss of appetite?" he asked. "Headaches? Vomiting or obsessive thoughts?"

"Has your head been spinning around unexpectedly?" I queried.

My mother told her to never underestimate the value of having a brother in a trade.

Finally, when the painters were putting the finishing touches on the new place, and the furniture was due to be delivered, Liz and John started packing up their little studio, sorting out what remnants of their old existence they would bring to their new life and moving boxes around. "I thought you said you bought a dolly for this," John had said. "No, I said I bought a Dalí," she answered. "It's a signed print, for the guest bedroom."

Liz teased John that she could pick up bigger boxes than he could. She attributed her comparative strength to the training schedule she had taken up. Two hours at the gym, four days a week, with a personal trainer and vegan protein shakes. But the truth was that John had not been feeling well for a while. Maybe Liz had noticed and thought it was nothing, or maybe she saw him so little and was so wrapped up in the renovations that she hadn't noticed his growing weakness and clumsiness. She didn't know, but by then he had already seen his doctor, and then a specialist, and then another. The news was bad. And when he looked at her face smiling at him, as she showed off her biceps, he knew he couldn't put off telling her any longer.

The housewarming party that Liz had planned was abruptly cancelled. The caterers were notified, the invitations retracted with an excuse that the apartment wasn't ready yet. "You know what contractors are like!" We all drove down to New York of course. But there really wasn't anything to do.

"I feel fine," John said, "Go home."

Liz considered staying in their familiar studio apartment "until this thing passed" but then decided they would move into the new place. She said it would be a more comfortable environment for John to get better in, with better energy. From the beginning the doctors didn't offer much hope, but Liz grasped at every shred of it.

We all did.

The renovations Liz had obsessed over were done and Liz's job now became managing John's health. She took him to doctors' appointments, kept track of his medications, and cooked him healthy meals at home. She ran interference between John and Corbit Chips, playing the demanding wife, pretending to drag him to charity luncheons when he was really going for yet more lab work. She read everything about his illness, from all sorts of sources, and would often call me to ask a biology question and I would do my best to explain.

She also read everything that people were writing about John. At the beginning of his illness, he lost some muscle mass and rumors started spreading on the business blogs, cloaked first in the most polite language, saying things like, "The latest iteration of CorbitChip has clearly worn out founder John Corbit…" But as he became less and less vigorous the tone of the rumors became more alarmed. Eventually, a reporter got up the nerve to ask him about his health, and John was quoted as saying, "Hey, it took me six years to get Liz to marry me. I'm not going to die on her now."

No one outside of John's closest circle had been thinking about death at that point. No one within our inner circle had yet spoken of the possibility out loud. John was only thirty-six, and people still thought of him as the tireless, vigorous person he had been throughout his twenties. The possibility of him dying so young seemed impossible, like Superman dying of a cold. But John was living in his body and he was feeling the ravages of the disease. He knew what it was doing, and what it had the power to do. And I think he was ready for all of us to stop avoiding the conversations we didn't want to have.

Then a few weeks later a secretary at his doctor's office was fired for stealing painkillers from the samples cabinet. In retaliation, and for money to buy drugs, she sold the story of John's diagnosis to a newspaper.

The news caused shock waves within the technology world. An avalanche of bloggers began shaking their heads and saying they were sure he'd get better soon: "My Uncle Lou had the same thing thirty years ago and he's out fishing today…," "The technological advances we have made in medicine…," "The most important thing is to remain positive…" There was no substance to anything these people were saying. They knew virtually nothing about the disease, but they collectively produced a massive body of writing, one that was nothing more than a mixture of good manners and wishful thinking.

It had no value, of course, except in lessening the terror that Liz felt as the likely progression of John's disease became harder and harder to deny. She would read these blogs in the late afternoon or when she could not sleep at night, at those times of the day when a wife faced with a similar situation a generation ago may have smoked a cigarette or drank a tumbler of brandy, to find relief or escape from the reality of what she was facing. The blogs were her soma. Each mindless click yielded a repeated reassurance that everything would be all right.

Then, one day, Liz stumbled onto a blog where a tech writer had used John as an example of why businesses need to have adequate succession plans in the event of the loss of a company's founder. Corbit Chips had a responsibility to its stakeholders to be adequately positioned if something should happen to John. It was solid cautionary advice that would bore most readers.

But not if it is talking about your own husband, the man whom you desperately, more than anything, do not want to die.

That was the day when Liz began blogging herself, in a fit of rage that arose from a primal urge to protect John and sheer terror that the writer was only speaking an obvious truth.

Liz called her blog "A Bit of the Core".

It was almost a counter-blog, talking about how great John was doing, with an optimistic new blog post for each new treatment John began.

It started as John was exhausting traditional treatments:

November

Today John and I had a lovely walk around Central Park. I don't know if it is the unusually warm weather, but John walked for almost a mile today! He loves his new physical therapist.
We are planning to begin a new medication next week and we are hopeful that the holidays will bring some real improvement!

<u>February</u>

We are so glad we are coming to the end of winter! While we have not seen much improvement with this last treatment, we are hoping that the doctors will be able to adjust John's dose...

And continued as he switched to the experimental...

<u>June</u>

Today John and I visited my sister in Boston, and met with Dr. Stewart at Harvard Medical School. We are so excited that John will be enrolling in a clinical trial of his new treatment...

And then to the alternative...

<u>August</u>

John's doctors decided to stop his participation in the clinical trial today because the side effects of the medication have become worse than the illness itself! We have put John on high doses of vitamin E and alpha lipoic acid...

It was like that. Each new treatment began with a hopeful post. Each ended with the expectation that the next one will be the one that works.

Towards the end, her blog started getting comments from a bottomless pit of uninformed commenters ("My cousin cured himself with hibiscus tea..."). It also became a magnet for a carnival of charlatans wanting to be the guru that healed the mighty John Corbit. His life was their brass ring and outlandish claims on Liz's blog were the means of grabbing it:

Relaxative meditation led by spiritual guru Hansu Hansu...

Berries grown only on my father's estate in the Andes, known only to our indigenous people for centuries...

We want to teach you to pray to our healing goddess Zinca...

Conspiracy theories abounded, about the monopoly of big pharma, the toxins poisoning John's nervous system, the medical community's denial of treatments that they KNOW work, just to preserve their own status quo. And the scientists, often in quotes—"scientists"—were alternately mindless slaves to the conspirators, utter failures, or omniscient and omnipotent: people who could have cured the disease if they wanted to but callously chose to let people die, the Wizard of Oz refusing Dorothy a ride home in his balloon for no reason at all.

If any of these proposed treatments had a hint of credibility, I would receive a phone call, hearing Liz's voice in the middle of the night asking, "Sara, could you look this up for me? It says it's based on a study…" I would stumble into PubMed and spend the next few hours trying to make sense of whatever shreds of science I could find. At best there would be an article in a small journal that no one read and any quack could publish in if they paid the $500 publication fee. The article would be an anecdotal report of a single patient (or maybe only a single mouse) who had made some kind of recovery from something that might have been remotely related to John's illness.

I guess we both knew nothing was going to work. But each time I would say, "Well, it looks like there might be something there…" because how could I not? Liz would write on her blog that her sister the biologist had reviewed the literature and so John was starting… whatever. It was our sisterly *folie a deux*.

The problem was, this made me seem like a quack. At some point a science writer read one of Liz's blogs and went on the offensive against what she called "junk science." Any time Liz wrote that I had vetted a new diet, Dr. Charlotte would re-vet it and then write a whole blog, in the shrillest language possible, about how I was wrong because God forbid a dying man might be eating a blueberry for the wrong reasons. This Dr. Charlotte had left science to become a professional blogger in order to call attention to the problem of women leaving science, but she occasionally mixed things up with other topics of exasperation. She was Cruella Deville but more educated and not as sweet.

I e-mailed her once and asked her why she was doing this. She responded that it was unethical to promote treatments that gave people false hope. But without false hope Liz would have no hope, and we were not meant to face death without a fight. Before science your odds were worse, but there was always hope.

Through all of this Liz never gave up on John and John never gave up on Liz. He dutifully followed each progressively wackier regimen Liz brought him. I remember all the awful crap he ate, diets that were little better than twigs and tart berries, spinach and beet slurries. I don't think he ate anything remotely tasty for a full year. Then he told me one day, when Liz was at the pharmacy, that he knew the diets wouldn't work. I never thought they would, but I had not said anything because I thought it gave him hope. I asked him why he tolerated it. He said he could not bear to make Liz unhappy. He felt like he was letting her down, disappointing her by dying. She had planned a long life together with him. He wanted to give her all that and he was failing miserably.

So I came down every week after that, like clockwork, the dog and I driving down on Saturday morning, ostensibly so Liz could take a break. She did not trust the nurses – she was paranoid they would give John a load of junk food the minute she stepped onto the elevator. So she never left. For the whole week she would be there, every day all day except for maybe a short errand here or there.

But when I was there Liz would go to the gym and maybe out to dinner with Billy. John's illness made people uncomfortable. Many of their friends had fallen away, but Billy was as loyal to Liz as a bulldog and stuck around even after John got sick.

I would stay with John. And the minute Liz stepped onto the elevator I would give him a load of junk food.

The first night I snuck him some burnt caramel gelato I had packed in dry ice and smuggled down from Toscanini's ice cream shop in Boston. It was always his favorite when they came to visit me. Its rich sweetness fills your mouth like a blanket of sugar on your tongue. We sat there eating it, giggling like naughty children.

The next week I brought pizza, then burgers and shakes. But what really did it for us were tacos, cheap fast food tacos. When Saturday

Taco Night started John could still eat anything if I cut it up into small enough bites. The soft tacos were the easiest. John and Liz had eaten them when they first got married because they were too broke for wholesome food. Now we ate them because they were good.

Hank stumbled in on us one night when he came up to check if we needed anything (as he did most nights). "Liz is NOT going to like this!" he warned. And then he came up every Saturday night after, even if he wasn't working. He just came to the building because he liked John and tacos. Usually Hank would bring his son and sometimes one of his friends. John still had the best computers and they would sit around playing video games that were, by their 11-year-old boy accounts, better than anything anyone else had. The dog ran around and the apartment was filled with a joyful noise that lifted the cloud of sadness and worry, if only until we received a text from Billy that Liz was on her way home.

And then one Saturday afternoon Hank brought up a package. Liz looked at it for a minute, contemplating the box that took up most of the kitchen table. She began unwrapping it and wouldn't look at us.

"I ordered it," she said, taking a breath. "It's a blender. The nurse said we should probably start pureeing John's food so he won't choke." He had choked on something earlier in the week, causing a few moments of intense worry. "So only pureed food for now, okay guys?"

She took it out of the box and placed it on the counter. With a very forced smile she showed it to us.

"It's a MegaNinja3000. I got the best one. All the TV chefs use it. It's got 900 watts."

I looked at John, he glanced at me. Hank looked at both of us. The dog tilted his head. And in an instant, wordlessly, an unspoken understanding passed between us. We all knew exactly what this blender meant.

It meant that Saturday Taco Night was about to go from *good* to *great*.

Because if you've never seen a crunchy bean taco whirling around in a 900 watt MegaNinja3000 blender, you really don't know what you're missing.

And so Saturday Taco Night became Saturday Blended Taco Night. I would plan for it all week, tweaking the taco recipe: a little more salsa, removing a little lettuce, determining precisely the amount of time to whirl the taco. I trekked around the specialty food shops of Boston looking for the right salsa because I needed quite a bit to get a good whirl and once you fill your handbag with about fifty of those little packets of sauce the evening shift starts to give you the stink eye. I tried spicier and spicier ones. John was eating so much flavorless, healthy food I thought the hotness might wake up his senses a little. His whole life was so controlled by Liz and the nurses. The spices seemed reckless and daring, a release, more like the John he used to be than the one who was confined to a wheelchair. When I heard of peppers that were hotter than the ones you can get in the grocery store I started planting chili pepper seeds on my windowsill. And I bought Tiki glasses to serve the blended tacos in.

Then one day things went a bit wrong. We were in the kitchen, blasting old school punk rock music loud enough to drown out the roar of the blender. John and I both loved it. We made tacos while I danced around to the Ramones and John bopped around inside his head. The dog spun around on his hind legs for treats, and he kept jumping up onto John's lap and then off again. And so Achilles didn't warn us when the elevator doors opened. And he didn't hear when Liz walked into the kitchen. And he didn't notice when she was standing in back of us as the blender zoomed.

None of us noticed until she shouted, "Sara! How could you!"

She went on a rant, about how she trusted me and how I had betrayed her, how John was supposed to eat this and not that, how I had ruined all of her hard work. She was so mad you would have thought she had walked in on me going down on him.

"It's just a taco!" I said.

"John is on a special diet!"

It wasn't a diet from his doctor. It was a diet from the Internet, involving some mixture of pureed roots.

"It's one taco," I said. "One taco! It's good! He likes it."

John was going to say something, but it was kind of hard for him to speak now at the best of times, never mind interrupting two shouting sisters.

"How could you!" she screamed again. "I can't be around you right now!"

She spun around and stormed out of the kitchen and through the living room. She hit the button to call the elevator. The doors immediately opened up. Unfortunately, Hank was standing inside the elevator holding a big bag which said in bright letters, "Doughnut Plant."

"You!" she shouted.

They switched positions, the doors closed on her furious face, and she was gone.

I was annoyed. I thought she was being controlling and I resented what she was putting John through, making him eat these horrible foods when he had so little time left. I was angry. Her anger seemed so disproportionate, and in the moment I didn't understand it at all.

But, later that night, after the night nurse had come in to make sure John was safe in bed, Hank and I sat in the kitchen while we waited for Liz to come home.

"Go easy on her," he said.

"She's being such a bitch," I said.

"Listen, Nicoletta," he said, grabbing a beer from the fridge, "let me tell you a little story, from when I was in Iraq. We were out on patrol once. There was a kid with us, Joe. It was his first deployment. We went over a small explosive device and then we came under fire. It was bad, but we managed to find cover and call for help. We had enough firepower to keep the enemy at bay for a while, but we needed rescuing. And then I saw Joe drinking all his water. I told him he'd better save some. It could be a while before they got to us. He said he didn't care. He didn't think we'd get out. So what the hell? It was hot. He was thirsty. Might as well drink the water."

"She thinks we're drinking the water?"

"Yup."

"What happened?" I asked.

"I'm here, aren't I?" he said.

"What happened to Joe?"

"He got thirsty. Learned his lesson. He was driving a UPS truck in Wisconsin last I heard."

"That's a good job," I said. "He'll be in the union."

"Yup."

Might as well drink the water. Might as well eat the tacos. Liz was mad because she thought I had given up. I had, of course. We all had, every one of us except her.

So I guess, in hindsight, it was really insensitive of us to eat all the tacos.

And the doughnuts.

chapter fourteen

The following appeared on *Zoss* a few weeks after the baby shower:

The Latest Accessories for Ladies Who Lunch: Neanderthal Babies
By Anton Cooper

Anyone who knows me will tell you that I've dated a few Neanderthals in my life. But for the first time I actually attended a baby shower for one.

What kind of harebrained party theme is that, you ask? It wasn't a party theme at all. It was an actual baby shower for an actual baby.

Now before I attended this soirée, I thought Neanderthals were just something that came about by accident or poor parenting. But no, this one is being born on purpose. It seems Neanderthals are the latest breeder craze in designer babies. And why not? Designer clothes, designer pets. Why not genetically modified designer babies?

This Neanderthal is the first. It was made by some process involving DNA and now it's growing just like a regular baby, except it's in some chimp's uterus. But you don't read my column because you were good at science so I'll tell you more about the party. This baby's mamma, the queen bee of the baby shower, is none other than New York's tragic widow Liz Nicoletta-Corbit. It was held at the seaside estate of one Mr. Theo Barlas. Or, rather, at his family's estate. Mr. Barlas is rumored to be the sole heir to the Barlas family fortune, but until that ship comes in he is running the biotech company that is hawking Neander Babies.

Why would John Corbit's widow be associating with Theo Barlas? Are they an item? Does she want them to be? One never can tell for certain but in this reporter's opinion, NO. Neandermom Liz was mostly interested in cooing over Neanderthal baby clothes, and frankly Mr. Barlas seemed more interested in Liz's frumpy sister. That lady scientist spent the day scowling, but there's no accounting for taste.

Who else attended? A gaggle of female breeder types, all dressed in this season's Kate Vu sun dresses (of course!). Paula Roche was typical of them. She is known locally among the good people of Westchester County for repeatedly petitioning her town's public school system to ban wheat from the cafeteria in support of children with gluten insensitivity. What was her take on the Neanderthal baby? "Having any child is difficult but so rewarding, particularly when the child has special needs."

Ms. Roche's own child suffers from behavioral problems, she said, which she attributes to the traumatic early experience of being circumcised at the hands of her now former husband, a professional mohel. And did we ever observe a horde of children with behavioral problems! They buzzed around the place chasing a yappy dog with no regard at all to my sensitive ears.

Stacey Maris from Oakland, California was there. "You know, we're all special," she said as she offered an ample bosom to a hungry kindergartener. Ms. Maris suggested the widow Corbit might try to nurse the Neanderbaby. "Feeding your child with formula – it's just not natural."

That comment put Neandermom's sister in a tizzy. "Not natural? She's an extinct genetically engineered baby gestating in the belly of a chimpanzee. Supposedly." A man at the party who shall remain nameless on the grounds that he's a cheating bastard to whom I've already given far too much of my attention suggested the lady scientist calm herself with a glass of champagne, but

NeanderGrandma, five mimosas down herself, vetoed that idea on the grounds that NeanderAunt was also NeanderChauffeur.

I wouldn't necessarily want a little Neanderthal chomping at my nipples and Mrs. Corbit didn't seem too keen on this idea either, though they pointed out that there are contraptions available to run tubes to your nipples, in case you can't actually make your own stash. "You can get donated breast milk now," suggested a Mrs. Leung-Sheehan from Maryland.

"It is such a lovely gift to give someone, a part of yourself," said Ms. Maris. "I want to do it when my children are ready to be weaned." In this man's opinion, they were ready a good five years ago, but the nursing does seem to be keeping Ms. Maris thin. Or there is a possibility, as the Neanderaunt pointed out, that she could be a drug addict. "I don't mean you're a drug addict," she clarified as Ms. Maris did the Lululemon shopper's equivalent of getting all up in her face. "I mean any donor could be a drug addict. Or a slut. You know, someone you don't want your baby sucking milk out of. Not that you're a slut. You don't seem slutty. But if you sleep around, you know, that's a lifestyle choice." Nice save, auntie.

So what do I make of this idea of breeders making Neanderthals? And what would one wear? Will her head fit into standard hat sizes? Will her stockiness be mitigated by Spanx? Will her joints be too knobby for a classic knee-length pencil skirt?

I couldn't care less, but the baby cake was gorgeous.

He did have that right. The cake was gorgeous. My mom made it. It was neither organic, nor gluten free, and thanks to artificial food dye it was mostly pink. I had a big sloppy piece.

chapter fifteen

As I expected, the article in *Zoss* ignited a fire. I first heard it in my car on my way to work, on one of the few remaining morning radio shows that still had DJs. "Hippy-dippy socialite Liz Nicoletta-Corbit is trying to make a Neanderthal man…well how about that," followed by laughter. Then I heard it again from the late night comics. There was no serious discussion, just a string of caveman jokes:

How many Neanderthals does it take to screw in a light bulb? None, it has the maid do it!

Liz had once been the tragic widow and now she was the wacky socialite. They were two separate caricatures of Liz, each about the same distance from the truth, but in the latest version the little restraint they had shown towards the grieving widow was untethered. This latest caricature was cruel.

I thought I would hear something from Theo during all of this. "Mr. Barlas seemed more interested in Liz's frumpy sister." It seemed farfetched. A man like Theo would be with the sort of woman who spent a lot of time shopping and putting on her makeup, not someone like me. And that, I told myself, was fine. I checked my e-mail every morning expecting at least a snarky comment about what Anton had written, but there was nothing. I wondered if he was embarrassed, but that did not seem possible. Maybe he didn't want to embarrass me with an unsolicited rejection. I wondered if I should contact him, laugh it off. All in all I thought about it too much.

The press coverage annoyed Liz and after the first week she convinced Theo that we needed to have an emergency strategy meeting to deal with the media blitz. I was summoned. "Why don't you just hire a publicist?" I asked. She did not believe in publicists because John's company had one when he got sick and Liz thought she was useless. "Hire a good publicist," I suggested, but Liz said she wanted to handle it herself. "Can't I just Skype in?" I asked. "Noooo! I was on *Inside Edition*. And not favorably. They're calling me the Neanderkook. I need you here. You can't telecommute to being my sister."

In a way, I was happy she was fighting back, or at least being active. The fire that would flash up in her when John was sick and something peeved her had been extinguished for too long. So I loaded the dog into the car and we drove down. Again.

The meeting was held at Barlas Labs. Since it was the weekend, I brought Achilles in with me. I rang the office door and was a bit taken aback when a woman answered.

"Hellooooo!" she said, with a thick accent that I later learned was Dutch. She immediately dropped to her knees. "You must be Achilles. Theo told me you might come down. Your mommy made you take a very long car ride, didn't she?"

"He loves the car," I said.

"Your toenails need clipping," she said disapprovingly. "Let me take care of that for you, little Achilles. Hold still…"

"Do you work here?" I asked the top of her head, as the bulky blonde whipped a clipper out of her pocket and began sending the dog's toenails all over the office.

"You need to cut his nails more regularly," she said. "It's very simple. Just make sure you don't cut into the quick of the nail. That will hurt him."

Achilles ate it up, sitting politely on the scratchy office carpet, handing her one paw after another.

She was a young woman, towering over me when she finally stood up, and very big-boned with short hair. She wore a green cotton button-down shirt tucked into khaki pants. Even I could tell they were unflattering.

"Do you work here?" I repeated.

"Well, yes, I suppose you could say that. I am Katarina. I'm Theo's little sister. Or I was, before his father left my mother for that other woman. He was looking for his soul mate, he said. It was odd. But I guess humans don't mate for life. Anyway, I am here to take care of Linda."

"Oh!" I said. "Have you been here long?"

"A couple weeks. I just finished my veterinarian qualification at home in the Netherlands. So I came back to help Theo. You must want to visit Linda before the meeting? She and Liz get on so well."

"No," I said, "Linda doesn't really like me."

"She doesn't?" Katarina seemed alarmed.

"No. I don't want to upset her."

"Yes, she is quite far along now. It is good you worry about her."

I didn't.

Katarina directed me to the conference room and then Achilles whined a little bit when she left to tend to Linda. Theo, Billy, and Hank were already waiting. Liz was on the phone. Achilles sniffed at her shoes. Theo was playing with his phone and barely acknowledged me. Anton must have been wrong, I thought. He had just been treating me like he treated my mother, trying to ingratiate himself to our family. Now he wasn't even bothering with that. I thought about all the mental energy I had expended wondering how I would handle something that did not exist. I felt like such a dork.

I looked around for a distraction.

"Jesus Christ, Billy," I said.

"It wasn't my fault!"

"How in hell is this not your fault?" asked Hank.

Hank's wife had left him for their son's gym teacher when he was in Iraq so cheating was a sore point for him. He did not blame her very much. It would be hard for any woman, he said, to be young and have her spouse overseas for months at a time like that. I did not blame her, either, because I could not imagine the stress she was under. But then I met her and it turned out she was kind of a floozy. She ended up leaving the teacher for a pharmacist, and the teacher only worked down the block.

"Hank," Billy said, "just because you're a war hero doesn't mean you have to be so holier-than-thou all the time. How was I supposed to know he was that into croquet?"

Theo finally looked up from his phone. "Hold on. You're a cheating bastard at *croquet*?" he asked.

"I wouldn't say bastard! I moved the ball *a little tiny bit* when we were out in the Hamptons. I was just having a little fun. He totally blew a gasket. Why, what did you think I did?"

"You were dating a gamer?" I asked.

"People hide things, Sara. You'll learn that when you start dating."

Meanwhile, Liz held the phone with one hand and with the other she pushed the dog off her leg. "Okay, don't rush," she said. "See you soon."

"Who's that?" I asked, taking the same seat at the conference table that I had used the first time I was there.

"Xiao."

"Xiao?"

"My cofounder," Theo said. "Running late as usual."

"I thought your cofounder was named Adam," I said.

"That's his American name," Liz said. "I like to use his authentic name. Xiao Zhou."

"Xiao Zhou?" I asked.

"Xiao Zhou."

"Theo's cofounder is Xiao Zhou?"

"Yeah, Xiao Zhou. Xiao Zhou. How many times do you want me to say it?" she answered.

Xioa Zhou. I had not heard that name in a decade. The biology community was small, even on an international scale. But still, it was possible that he was a different Xiao Zhou. Both Xiao and Zhou are common names. "Do you have a picture?" I asked.

"A picture? I do, actually. He joined my Facebook. He posted the funniest joke last week," she said. "What do you call a cow that doesn't make milk?"

"Liz!"

"Alright. You have no sense of humor." She took out her phone. "That's him, why?"

"That's Xiao Zhou," I said.

"Yeah, Xiao Zhou. We've been over this."

"That's him," I said. "That's the graduate student."

"What graduate student?" she asked.

"*That* graduate student," I answered.

⌒

Xiao Zhou was the reason my post-doc blew up.

I was working in Marshall Greene's lab. He was an older scientist who had some early success in his career and expected the people in his lab to see him as a sort of demigod. I did when I started.

But I quickly realized that Marshall liked to delegate most of the actual biology in his lab to his post-docs so he could concentrate on going to conferences, particularly those held near golf courses, where he mainly focused on drinking beer with his cronies. I was left in charge of supervising Xiao. In the beginning I liked the idea of being someone's mentor. I still harbored hopes of a career in academia then, of becoming a professor, and I thought it would be good experience.

The career path was competitive. Each professor would, in his lifetime, train dozens of students, all of whom would have to compete for the one position he would leave open when he retired. It was a huge pyramid scheme, so you had to do a lot of work to set yourself apart from the masses. I was concentrating on my own experiments so I did not keep track of everything Xiao did.

And in truth Xiao was not the easiest person to mentor. He would use a hundred micrograms of a reagent in an experiment when I told him one hundred fifty. He wouldn't finish papers or put away lab equipment. He was clearly smart, but didn't seem cut out for laboratory work. And I never really knew where he was. He would skulk into the lab at random times of the day, and then suddenly appear at his lab bench when I hadn't seen him come in. It was like supervising a cat.

I noticed, over the months, that some lab reagents were missing. I attributed this to our lab manager's poor recordkeeping. I also noticed that Xiao was spending a lot of time in the lab at hours when no one else was around. I never saw him before noon, but no matter how late I left—and I regularly left at ten or eleven o'clock at night—he always seemed to be there.

Rarely I would take an evening off. One Saturday night my friend Mei was celebrating her birthday, so I went to a party at a dance club. I was dancing when my phone went off. It was Marshall.

"Nicoletta, get your ass down to the lab!" he said.

I had downed a few gin and tonics, so I was confused, but I managed to find a cab and stumble into the lab. Marshall was there alone. I didn't ask him why he was there so late on a Saturday because I already knew. I had heard rumors that he was having an affair with a Renaissance literature professor. Some women in our department were in a froth over it, mostly because he'd chosen a mistress from the humanities. I didn't give it much credence until I had the unfortunate experience of seeing a used condom in the hazardous waste disposal box.

"What happened?" I asked.

"You were supposed to be supervising him!" Marshall shouted.

"Xiao? What did he do?" I was expecting that he had left the refrigerator open again, destroying someone's experiment, something like that. Which would have been bad enough. You could lose years of work that way.

Marshall looked at me and walked over and shut off the lights. In my gin haze and panic I hadn't noticed the box on the floor. Marshall turned on a black light and shined it into the box. I looked down.

At once I pictured what had happened. Marshall and the professor stumbled into the dark lab in a twisted embrace, intending to be alone without having to spring for a hotel room, but instead they walked in on Xiao holding a black light. It would have been awkward at first, Marshall caught in the midst of a tryst by his diligent grad student burning the midnight oil. But Xiao would have looked shocked, like *he* was the guilty one. Sins are, after all, relative.

I saw what Marshall and his lover saw under the black light: a box of puppies. Puppies that glowed in the dark.

Green, red, yellow. Shining colors, tumbling puppies, glowing under the black light.

Apparently Xiao had a side project. The dogs had been genetically modified.

We had no use for glowing dogs in the lab. I guess he thought he could sell them. We already had zebrafish modified to glow in different colors under an aquarium light. The artist Eduardo Kac had made a glow-in-the dark bunny that was kept at a research facility. Glowing cats were used in HIV research. But dogs as pets, that could run away, those were something else. To me it seemed environmentally dangerous and probably illegal. Evidently Xiao disagreed.

I never got to ask him about any of this. Before I arrived Marshall had fired him from the lab, thereby revoking his visa, and effectively sending him back to China. This would not, of course, happen immediately, but it would detract from his credibility should he decide to inform Mrs. Greene that her husband also had a side project.

Marshall had called me in to clean up the mess. Specifically, he had called me in to sacrifice the dogs.

This research had not been approved by the university. If anyone found out about a rogue project in the lab involving animals, specifically glow-in-the-dark dogs, Marshall would look very bad. And if Marshall looked bad, we all looked bad. Taking the dogs out of the lab was illegal. Keeping the dogs in the lab was impossible.

"This is your fault, Nicoletta," he said. "You were supposed to be supervising him. I don't want any trace of this, this…experiment by morning."

He left me alone in the lab with the dogs.

I sacrificed frogs during undergraduate physiology class, and even a rat. All the students did. I understood that even if we did not ultimately do animal research, this was part of being a biologist, something we needed for our education.

And Marshall was right. The dogs were made without the proper institutional approval required for animal research. It would destroy the lab's reputation if anyone found out. The dogs would have to be put down by someone, if not by me.

But who could kill a puppy? They tumbled all over one another, playing in their little box, looking up at me now and then with their big black eyes set in their furry white faces.

I better get on with this, I thought.

I turned on the black light to convince myself. On closer inspection, I noticed two of the pups didn't glow at all. I shined the light on them, turned them over and over. They looked perfectly normal. Maybe Xiao hadn't modified these. Maybe they were controls, or maybe the genetic modification didn't take.

The third dog, the only male, wiggled to the top of the puppy heap. His whole body, except his left rear paw, glowed not just one color, but several. Xiao must have added green, red, and yellow fluorescent proteins to his cells. With so many bright colors and so much movement, in a room that was still spinning a little from the gin, I had thought all the puppies glowed.

We used glowing proteins in the lab all the time. They had originally been isolated from sea corals and jellyfish. We put the genes that made these proteins into cells to tag other proteins, to follow them under a microscope as they moved from cell compartment to cell compartment. Xiao must have added the glowing proteins when the dog was in an early stage of development, just a ball of a few cells. He added a different gene for each fluorescent protein into different cells. The gene made the protein, and the protein glowed under black light, big splotches of color that made the puppy look tie-dyed.

I realized it was very late and I was still a little drunk. I can't do this now, I thought. I didn't really know how. It's hard to sacrifice an animal, to do it properly. If I did it wrong, the puppies would suffer.

I decided not to do it now, but to tell Marshall that I did. I would come back tomorrow night and do it after a good night's sleep, when I was completely sober. That was my plan.

I texted Marshall. "It's done."

Then I went out, found a cab, and took the box of puppies home with me.

On the way home I stopped and bought some puppy treats. "Sorry, dogs. I'll have to kill you in the morning, but you can enjoy tonight." It seemed profound at the time.

The next morning I woke up confused by the sound of puppies yipping. I rolled over to the box, reached down, and pulled them up onto the bed. They jumped all over me. Thinking more clearly, or so

I told myself, I decided that two of them definitely did not glow. I didn't have to sacrifice all three. Two were probably normal. I could drop them off somewhere. Everybody wants a puppy. They were cute. They would have a chance.

I bought a black light at the local smoke shop to tell them apart. When it was dark I drove to a no-kill dog shelter. I left the box with two of the puppies on the doorstep and I sped away so I wouldn't get caught. It was warm enough, of course, and I lined the box with newspaper and left them a blanket and some water and food. I didn't want to answer questions and figured the shelter would think I was just too cheap to pay the surrender fee, which I also was.

By then it was late and it didn't seem right to sacrifice the one that was left, especially on a Sunday. I gave him some food. He seemed lonely without his sisters so I let him sleep on the bed. "Sorry, glowy dog. Sleep well. I'll most likely kill you in the morning." He cuddled up against me with his little head sharing my pillow.

"It's been ten years," Liz said. "You can't still be mad."

"Ten years of running home every night to let him out. Ten years of no dog walker, no kennel, no doggy daycare. Ten years of driving to New York every time I need to go out of town because the only people who know about him are in this room and I can't leave him in a kennel."

"Honey, that's not because of Xiao! That's because you're neurotic."

"If they found out about him he would be put down!"

"Sweetie, who has a black light?" she said.

"I live in Brighton, Liz! They're students. Everybody has a black light."

"Nobody cares if your stupid dog glows in the dark, Sara," Billy said.

"What?" Theo asked.

We did not answer him because just then the office door opened.

The strategy meeting was not very productive after that because Theo and Xiao spent the rest of the afternoon at the hospital getting the tip of Xiao's ear sewn back on.

I don't know what Xiao did to Achilles that he still remembered him ten years later, but as soon as he saw him Achilles sprang up like a fuzzy white demon from hell. He bounced onto a chair, sprang across the conference table, and then, I swear, he flew, right up to Xiao's head. Xiao turned at the last moment to protect his face but Achilles managed to make contact with part of Xiao's ear and chomp down.

Hank jumped up and deftly began administering first aid.

It was not very pleasant to have to fish that thing out of Achilles's mouth. He was determined to swallow it so I had to pry open his snarling teeth and stick my finger down his throat to rescue it, at which point he bit me, and then I had to put the bloody thing into Katarina's lunch container with some ice while Liz yelled at me not to get blood on Theo's carpet.

"You were supposed to sacrifice them!" Xiao shouted.

"You were supposed to do your fucking experiments!" I shouted back, holding a growling Achilles by his collar to prevent him taking off the other ear. "Instead you made glow-in-the-fucking-dark dogs!"

"People would have loved them!"

There was a disagreement at the emergency room about why the tip of Xiao's ear was in a plastic sandwich box rather than attached to Xiao's head. Xiao said that his injury was caused by a dog bite. Theo, mindful that people who treat dog bites usually have a few questions for the dog, insisted that Xiao was delirious and his injury was definitely not caused by a dog bite. Theo was better at convincing people of things than Xiao was and so he protected my dog.

A few people recognized Theo as the "Neanderthal Dad," so the disagreement, which I guess became quite animated, led to all kinds of wild speculation, though none of it was wild enough to involve a glow-in-the dark dog with a chip on his shoulder. There was even one photo of Theo leaving the hospital with his bandaged co-founder and the headline, "Is this man harboring a Neanderthal cannibal?"

"Well," my mom said when she heard about it, "everybody likes Chinese food."

Liz told her she was being racist.

chapter sixteen

Over the next few days, news coverage of the Neanderthal project increased. When they were done making fun of Liz it seemed to increase ratings to discuss the project with experts of varying qualifications. Geneticists, anthropologists, and bioethicists weighed in briefly, but most of the conversation was dominated by celebrity pundits with a distinct emphasis on strong rather than informed opinions. One woman confused genetic engineering with embryonic research but they kept inviting her back. And a man on the street objected because he had heard the term *Homo neanderthalensis* and thought the whole project was part of the gay agenda.

Then Theo started doing interviews. I was listening to NPR in my office:

Host: Resurrecting the Neanderthal species from ancient DNA. Could we? Should we? Technology has advanced. Has the Neanderthal man's time finally come? Again? We're here with the man at the center of the controversy, Barlas Lab's CEO and co-founder, Mr. Theodoros Barlas. Mr. Barlas, welcome.

Theo: Thank you for having me.

Host: Now, tell us, Theo, straight off, why are you making a Neanderthal?

Theo: At Barlas Labs we strive to push the boundaries of biotechnology. We have developed, in our labs, the ability to make very large artificial chromosomes, chromosomes that can be used as the genetic template for any living thing. So we asked ourselves, what project can we do that will significantly change the world for the better? What project would demonstrate Barlas Lab's ability to alter the course of history? Because that is what this technology does. And the answer seemed obvious. What species is more worthy of a second chance at life than our closest relative, the Neanderthal? We have the technology. We have the capability to build the world's first resurrected Neanderthal man. So that is what we are doing.

Host: You're changing history, but, is it a change for the better? You certainly seem to think so. Let's take some calls and see what our listeners think. We have Michael from San Diego on the line. Michael, what do you have to say?

Michael: Making a Neanderthal! This is so *bleep*ing cool! To start from...

Host: Michael, we get it. Theo, Michael is in favor of your project.

Theo: Well thank you Michael for your kind words. I just...

Host: Another call. We have Nicole, on the line from Storm Mountain, West Virgina. Nicole, what do you think?

Nicole: Yes, thanks for having me. I just want to say that I am unequivocally opposed to using genetic technology to create new species. We have so many existing species here that need to be helped and...

Host: Theo! What do you say to that? You have some pretty powerful technology there. Is this the best use of it?

Theo: Well certainly there are many, many projects where our technology could be invaluable, and not just in de-extinction efforts. This kind of synthetic biology has wide applications in medical research and agriculture. Working on the Neanderthal project does not exclude our technology from also being used for other purposes. Our goal is to continue pushing the boundaries of biotechnology.

Host: Do you have plans to make other extinct animals?

Theo: No, not at this time. We are focusing solely on the Neanderthal project.

Host: Another caller. Andrea, from Arlington, Virginia. What do you have to say?

Andrea: This project is an abomination. God made all of the creatures great and small at Creation. We didn't evolve from *monkeys*. It is not the job of man to go around willy-nilly playing God, messing with His creation...

Host: We get it. Religious implications aside, do you have any ethical reservations about de-extinction?

Theo: No, on the contrary...

Host: I'm afraid I have to stop you there because we need to take a brief break. When we come back, more with Theo Barlas, quite possibly the creator of the modern world's first resurrected Neanderthal person.

I shut off the radio.

chapter seventeen

During the third week of the media frenzy they came for me. That Dr. Charlotte woman wrote a long blog saying I was a quack, that I had a track record of supporting questionable science, and that it was not surprising I would be involved in something like this. She objected to the project on the basis that she did not think it could really happen and it was another example of the media over-hyping junk science. This distracted from real science and blurred the lines between fact and fiction in the public's consciousness.

Writers in the low stakes world of science blogging can be quite competitive. If one person writes something nasty about someone, a bunch of the other bloggers try to write something nastier. By the end of the week, twenty-six bloggers had regurgitated Dr. Charlotte's blog, each one using more inflammatory language than the last. One of them was by Dr. Charlotte's protégé, a twenty-three-year-old graduate student from Pasadena. She was an earnest dingbat who called me a quisling to the field she had loyally dedicated almost eight whole months of her life to. I had to look up quisling (it means someone who collaborates with their country's enemies) so I was pretty sure she had used a thesaurus. Dr. Charlotte's original post got picked up by a couple aggregator sites so a few people who were neither graduate students nor Dr. Charlotte's immediate family members read it.

And then it got worse. I saw it on the morning news, one that pretends to be a real newscast.

"Now to get some more insight into the family that is adopting the Neanderthal baby, we have with us Tina Gil. Miss Gil has become an avid defender of one member of the Neanderthal family. Tell us Miss Gil, when did you first meet Sara Nicoletta, the Neanderthal mother's sister?"

"I first met Dr. Nicoletta when I was working the morning shift at a hotel here in Phoenix."

"You're a maid there?"

"I'm the housekeeping shift supervisor. I went into the room where Dr. Nicoletta was staying to change the beds. That is how we met. And I came on TV today because I want to say that what they say about her in the media is not true."

"So you went in to clean Sara's room and she was there?"

"Yes. She is a very nice lady. We get so many customers. Mean. But Dr. Nicoletta, she is a very nice lady. She is not the kind of person these people are saying. She even sent me an Edible Arrangement the next day."

"Just for cleaning her room?"

"Yes. And because I helped her with her belt. Some customers, they don't even say 'Hi' when they pass you in the hall. Like we are invisible. And Dr. Nicoletta, she sends me chocolate covered strawberries. She treats people nice. She did not have to do that."

"I'm sorry, you helped her with her belt?"

"Yes. I helped her get out of her belt."

"I see, Miss Gil. Now was the belt around her waist?"

"What? I do not want to talk about that. I came to say she is one nice, classy lady. Her sister is the crazy one. She is the one making a Neanderthal baby," she said with disgust, "not Dr. Nicoletta. Everybody's sister does things they don't agree with. My sister, she has a pet capybara. Do you know what that is? It's a hundred pound guinea pig. You want to wake up on the guest sofa with that thing staring at you? It's a crazy thing to have inside a house and it bites. But I can't control that. And if Dr. Nicoletta's sister wants a Neanderthal in the house, she can't control that either."

"Now isn't it true, Miss Gil, didn't you tell our producer last night that the belt was actually around Sara's wrists?"

Tina looked into the camera with a shocked expression on her face.

"And that, when you went into the room, Sara was naked except for a blanket?"

"Dr. Nicoletta is a very nice lady. She just had a little trouble with her boyfriend. No big deal. It has happened many times that I have untied naked women. And once a naked man tied up with a garden hose. Dr. Nicoletta is the only one that ever sent me a thank you. And she said nice things about me on Yelp. My supervisor was very happy. That's going to be in my annual review."

"And isn't it true, isn't it true Miss Gil, that you advised her, you advised her to sell this belt on Craigslist?"

"No. I told her she should give it away. Dr. Nicoletta would never sell someone else's belt. Even though he had it coming."

The camera focused on the anchor as he gazed seriously into the camera.

"Our investigative journalists have been working on this story, and they found this ad. Do we have a screenshot? There it is. This appeared on the Boston edition of Craigslist. You may remember that Boston is where Sara Nicoletta lives. What is interesting about this ad is that it was posted shortly after a biology conference held in Phoenix, a conference that Nicoletta attended. Men's canvas belt, brown. Good condition. Appears to be of average size. Free. Can deliver to areas within 10 miles of Boston."

The camera panned out so that we could see both the anchor and his over-coiffed co-host. "Wow," she said gravely, "someone really must have wanted to get rid of that belt."

I found out months later that Tina's local station had aired a nasty editorial about me, about my responsibility to the public as a scientist, a regurgitation of Dr. Charlotte's point of view. She had called their response line to complain. Because she said that she had met me, a young producer took her to a Russian bar (on speculation, I guess) and bought her shots of blackberry-flavored vodka until she spilled the beans on my bondage problem and then threw up in the producer's handbag.

I was watching again in the evening when the news station interrupted programming with a late-breaking update. "This is Erin Brooks standing outside the Equinox gym on 8th Avenue in New York City. Just moments ago we caught up with a close personal friend of Liz Nicoletta-Corbit to ask him to comment on the allegations that Liz's sister, the Neanderthal Aunt, was found bound and gagged in a Phoenix hotel room."

They cut to footage of Billy, his gym bag swung jauntily over his shoulder and a small sweatband circling his head. "What? That's ridiculous," he said, with his lip curled up in disbelief. "Sara doesn't have sex. Oh my God! Did someone steal her wallet?"

I turned off the television.

After dinner I got a phone message from Liz. "Sorry, I've been trying to call you, but I guess you are…TIED…UP. Hahahahaha-hahahaha! Did you hear that Billy, TIED UP! Oh, I'm just kidding, honey. Was it the Indian guy? I guess he was reading the Karma Suture!!!! Hahahahahaha! Get it?" I didn't. "Karma…Suture? Call me, sweetie!"

And then my mom called because she wanted to make sure I had remembered to cancel my credit cards after my wallet got stolen.

And then Luka called to offer to take my confession. "It's not encouraged to take confession from family members, but it still counts. But it doesn't count over the phone so you'll have to come down and tell me about it. All about it, Sara. All about it."

As if.

An e-mail from Theo just said, "So…"

chapter eighteen

In the late spring my apartment became very noisy. A paparazzo loitered outside on a regular basis. I understood the public's curiosity about the Neanderthal project, but not why anyone would want to see a photo of me leaving for work. But I suppose if you are going to be a paparazzo and don't want to move out of Boston, this is what you have to put up with. There are only so many pictures you can take of our local celebrity couple Tom and Gisele, and no one is going to pay good money for a photo of Noam Chomsky. Well I would, but no one with good money.

On the first morning he parked against the sidewalk opposite my place. Achilles noticed him and barked until I went outside in huge dark sunglasses and a pink Red Sox hat, like I had seen celebrities do in *People*, and asked him to go away because he was upsetting my dog.

"I got a right to be here," he said, but he left when he realized I wasn't going to do anything his readers would find interesting, like wear a Prada dress with suboptimal shoes or take a stegosaurus for a walk around the block.

The next day he came back and Achilles barked again. By the weekend the dog was sitting on the top of the couch so he could stare out the window. When the paparazzo came he jumped down to the floor, sprinted over to the window, and propped himself up on his hind legs with his front paws on the sill. He was as tall as a toddler, with just enough height to see out the window, but he had the soul of a wolf, stalking his prey. First he let out a low growl, warning me something was suspicious. Then he barked sharply, "ARF! ARF! ARF!" He looked over his shoulder at me, asking me to come over to look out the window, too. There was something I had to see.

The first few times I got down on my knees on the floor next to him, looking out the window as well. "Yes, you found the bad man. Good dog." But the paparazzo didn't seem to have anywhere better to go so the barking went on and on and on.

"Shut up, Achilles," I said. Instead he barked more vigorously because clearly I didn't understand there was A MAN OUT THERE. A MAN! I closed the curtains, but he stuck his head under them. I tried distracting him with a bone, but bones gave him the runs and we were still working on our fitness routine and I didn't want him getting fat again.

Achilles's new arch enemy tried to evade detection, parking down the street and hiding behind different trees. Achilles learned his stench and would start barking in his general direction the moment we went outside.

"Hey, that thing better not bite me," the paparazzo said. "I got rights, you know."

"He's an attack bichon," I warned, but he didn't know what a bichon was and I didn't think he'd be able to spell it correctly to look it up.

The noisy student neighbors complained about the noise, but Achilles didn't work nights and I didn't feel too bad about waking them up at eight a.m. when they regularly woke me up at three. So they took their annoyance out on the paparazzo. Late at night I heard them drunkenly telling him which of their body parts he should take a picture of. Then they started showing him.

Why on earth was he there? Did he think I'd come staggering back from a bar in the middle of the night? I wish. He had spent too much time stalking celebrities. Scientists, if they are not still working, are tucked safely in bed in the wee hours of the night.

In the midst of this I received an e-mail:

Dear Sara,

I will be in Boston giving a talk next week. If you are around on Thursday night perhaps we could meet for a drink?

Sincerely,
Angus

I should have just told him to go away, I know, but I was sad about the media coverage and sad that I had been thinking about Theo but nothing had materialized there. I felt lonely and friendless so I wrote him back:

Hi Angus,

Thank you for the invitation, but it is difficult for me to go out at the moment. Perhaps you have seen some of the news coverage about the Neanderthal project? That's my sister.

Would you like to come here for supper instead? I have to warn you that sometimes there are paparazzi outside my apartment.

Sara

Angus was, in his heart, kind of an attention whore so I think the paparazzi actually made the invitation more enticing. He agreed to come, but I clarified a few things:

No bondage! There's no maid service here. If you leave me tied up the dog will eat my face off before anyone finds me.

Angus responded:

Well that's a shame, but I'd still like to see you as long as there is no inappropriate giggling!

I told him I couldn't promise that, but he shouldn't take it personally. He asked how I felt about spanking. I replied:

You've got one coming.

Angus responded with a smiley face. I'm not sure he realized I was kidding, but his flirting made it seem like a real date or something.

On the designated night I cooked a Turkish feast. I roasted a chicken, and prepared *turlu*, a vegetable stew made with eggplant, zucchini, and tomatoes. I got some *halloumi*, a hard, salty cheese made from a mixture of goat and sheep's milk. I pan-grilled it until the outside developed a light brown crust while the inside was still pure white, soft and creamy. There was fresh, soft flatbread from the Middle Eastern bakery near me.

For the appetizer, I thought I would make something a little spicier. I gently roasted round red chili peppers until they were soft, and when they were cool I stuffed them with chopped arugula and spinach. To give it a little kick, I added a bit of chopped Bhut Jolokia, the ghost pepper, an Indian chili that is the hottest pepper known to man. They are too hot to be sold in the grocery store, but I had some plants that I had grown from seed on my windowsill and there were two ripe peppers on it that night.

I kept the food warm and the apartment smelled of the warm spices.

Angus arrived on time. The doorbell rang. The dog howled. I opened the door and Angus handed me a big bouquet of flowers. They were my favorite, two dozen gerbera daisies in red, yellow, and orange – simple but bright and cheerful.

He looked as good as he had the year before. He was, I thought, exactly the type of man that I should be attracted to.

"It's so good to see you," he said.

"How was your talk?" I asked.

"Great, you should've come."

"Was it all clinical stuff?" I asked. "I might have been bored."

Most of what Angus did was what is called translational research. His lab took the kind of science I did and made it useful to patients by developing medicines and things like that. His work could not exist without mine, and my work would be useless without his. We talked a bit about his latest findings, and the silly question one of our colleagues asked, and how the guy got all red in the face when he didn't like the answer. I offered Angus a drink and we sat down on my couch.

"This is quite a place you've got here," he observed.

I guess it was. I didn't have enough books to fill the yards of gumwood bookshelves so Luka had started procuring knick knacks for me from members his congregation: a conch shell from Haiti, a wooden statue of the Madonna from the Philippines, a Day of the Dead mask from Mexico. He had even managed to find a taxidermied peacock with almost all of its feathers. Liz said my apartment was beginning to look like a natural history museum, but I had gotten used to it and I didn't think about it unless people came over, which wasn't very often.

"How is this Neanderthal project going?" Angus asked.

"I don't know. They say the pregnancy is progressing," I said.

"They say? You don't believe them?" he asked.

"No! Why, do you?"

"I don't know as much about it as you, but I think it's plausible," he replied. "If they can make the long chromosomes. You know, we have received some promotional material from Barlas Labs claiming they can, for research purposes. We ordered a few to evaluate them."

This was the first I had heard about Barlas Labs marketing their chromosomes. But of course it made sense. If you can make a Neanderthal chromosome you can make anything. Theo was diversifying, and leveraging the publicity of the Neanderthal project. Everyone had now heard of Barlas Labs.

"But making a chromosome is very different from making an embryo," I said. "They won't even tell me how the epigenetics works." Epigenetics is the other stuff, besides the DNA strand, that makes the chromosome work. It includes, for example, the placement of the nucleosomes, complexes of proteins that the DNA wraps around to give it structure.

"Maybe it just works," Angus said.

"What do you mean?"

"You've read the paper from the Venter Institute when they made the bacteria from the artificial chromosome? They didn't do anything special to the bacteria. They added the chromosome to a lot of empty bacteria and some of them just worked."

"Yeah, but it's a lot easier in bacteria than in a mammal."

"But maybe it's the same principle," he said. "Maybe it just works."

"They don't have that many chimp embryos to work with, to use a brute force approach. And anyway, I used to work with their chief scientist. He's not exactly a rock star."

"So? It's a private company. They don't have to figure everything out themselves. They can buy other people's intellectual property. They just have to be good at writing checks."

He was right, of course. That was another thing I had not thought of. Just because they had the technology for making long chromosomes did not mean Xiao had figured out how to make long chromosomes. He may have just figured out who had the technology and how much to pay for it.

"I didn't invite you over here to talk about Neanderthals," I said. Quite the opposite. I had invited him over to avoid thinking about Neanderthals and Barlas Labs.

Angus got a smile across his face. "Oh no?" he said.

Men are easy to distract when you don't want to talk about something. All I had to do was lean in a little closer.

He took me in his arms. A few months earlier I had been so mad at him, but he was still undeniably hot. He was still so smart, still so good-looking. My feelings were not necessarily a burning flame, but he was definitely a flicker of light in the joyless drudgery that my life had become and feeling his warm body near me certainly perked up my mood.

He kissed me. I kissed him back. After a little while I remembered the food, went into the kitchen, and brought the appetizers out as if I were a geisha or something. I placed the tray on the coffee table in front of the couch. I switched down the living room lamp. I sat down next to him and, wordlessly, unbuttoned his pants and pulled down his zipper.

It would be going too far to say that I thought his stellar publication record made Angus deserving of a blow job. No one ever in the history the world has thought that, despite what men with good publication records but bad cars might hope. But I will admit that my admiration for his professional competence did contribute at least slightly to my attraction to him. And maybe I was trying to impress him a little, to redeem myself as having at least some competency in the bedroom after the last time we were together.

I got down on my knees, leaned in closer towards him, and watched his face as I took him in my mouth. He grinned at first, in the moments before my lips touched him, and then smiled broadly, joyfully as I wrapped my mouth around him. "Oh that's so good," he said. I kept watching his face as I began going up and down on him. Then in a few seconds his face took on an expression that I did not quite understand at first. Was it passion? Was it joy? Ecstasy? It was more intense than that.

Then I realized what it really looked like was alarm. Alarm with a good chunk of pain thrown in.

And at that moment a very recent memory flashed into my mind. I was in the kitchen arranging the dishes to set on the table, and …

"Wash it off!" I shouted.

"What?"

"The peppers! I ate one of the peppers. Wash it off. It's going to burn your penis." More. It's going to burn your penis more because it did appear to be burning his penis quite a lot already. The ghost pepper. The hottest pepper known to mankind. Just seconds before I had brought the appetizers into the living room I had stuffed one of the peppers into my mouth, a whole mouthful of a chili pepper, tepid by comparison, stuffed with the ghost pepper. I had to wear gloves preparing them and now I had bathed the remnants of the ghost pepper all over Angus's manhood.

Oh, poor Angus. He jumped up off the couch and scurried to the bathroom, his pants halfway down around his thighs, muttering, "God damn it, woman."

I hadn't felt this panicked since I set my glove on fire during organic chemistry lab. Maybe it was flashing back to that memory that summoned the chemical properties of chili peppers to my head. The chemical that makes peppers hot is capsaicin. I could hear the rush of the shower coming from the bathroom, but water is polar protic so it does not do much to dissolve capsaicin. Other things, like milk and alcohol, can wash it off. I did not have any real milk, only soy. Liz had badgered me about the hormones in milk so I converted. I wasn't sure what chemical properties soy milk had, so I grabbed the bottle of champagne that I was chilling for later.

The dog, meanwhile, sensed the excitement and began running around the apartment, diving under chairs, jumping up on the couch, barking, and growling.

In my panic I popped the cork too fast. It went flying off, and hit the light fixture in the kitchen. Crash! A large shard of glass cracked off and fell to the floor. I left it there and ran into the bathroom to help Angus.

Half in the shower with him, I poured the fifty-dollar bottle of bubbly over Angus's now shrunken penis.

He stepped back from it, throwing his arms wide. "Jesus, Sara!"

Jesus? I thought he was Hindu.

"It's polar aprotic," I said meekly.

"It's fucking freezing!"

He obviously was not as impressed by my recollection of organic chemistry as I was, and it did not really seem to have high enough alcohol content to improve things much.

"Does it still sting?" I asked.

"Yes!"

"Maybe use more soap," I suggested.

Then I heard it: a loud, shrill yelp coming from the kitchen.

It was not barking. It was unmistakably a yelp of pain. Awful, terrible pain. I ran into the kitchen. There was bright red blood on the floor, a shiny red pool of so much more blood than should come out of a tiny dog. Achilles had sliced his leg on the glass shard on the floor.

"Oh God!" I picked him up and carried him into the bathroom, blood draining onto my clothes. I wrapped his wounded leg in a towel and shouted over the sound of the shower. "Achilles cut himself."

Angus looked out from behind the curtain and saw the blood.

"I'm sorry," I said. "I have to get him to the vet. Now."

"Go!" he said, "Go, go!"

I left, jumping in my car, hysterically speeding off towards the veterinary hospital, the little dog in the seat next to me. I could not believe what was happening. In the course of five minutes I'd gone from the dream of a romantic evening to the nightmare of my little dog bleeding next to me. Be okay. Be okay, I thought and then whispered, over and over again.

When we got to the hospital I knew it was bad because they immediately whisked him away from me, before they even asked me how I would pay. I had never been separated from him like that, leaving him with strangers. Owners were not allowed in the treatment area, only their pets.

I sat down on the bench in the waiting room, the one for dog owners, separated by a low wall from the bench for cat owners. I texted Liz. "Achilles in the hospital."

I thought about how much Achilles and I had shared: the walks around the reservoir and in the woods, the drives back and forth to New York, him sleeping in a ball at the end of John's bed. He wasn't a good dog. He was a stubborn, rambunctious, naughty dog. But he loved me. Some evolutionary biologists say that dogs only pretend to love you, so you will feed them. But then nature would have had to invent two things, invented love and then invented something that looked like love. It was easier, if your dog was going to act like he loved you, for him to just love you. I didn't pretend to love him so he would bark to warn me of paparazzi. I just loved him.

Liz called me. I could not answer. I was too scared to speak. Sick dogs and cats came through and waited their turns: a Siamese with a scratch in her meow, a big dopey black lab who had swallowed a sock. I tried to watch the TV but couldn't concentrate. A vet tech came out periodically to say they were working on him. It felt like an eternity. I looked at the magazines. There was a tabloid. Neandermom was on its cover, with a picture of Liz coming out of a frozen yogurt shop. I already knew about that.

At last the door opened and miraculously a veterinarian emerged with a little white dog on a leash. The dog had one leg wrapped in bandages and a big white cone around his neck. He looked up at me as if to say, "Where have you been?"

Achilles was okay, the vet told me. She listed all of the technical procedures they had performed on him, the transfusion they had given him, the dollar amounts they would cost me. Hundreds. Many hundreds but I did not care. She preferred to keep him overnight, but if I wanted to go home, we could.

"There was one thing," said the vet, hesitantly.

Oh God, I thought. They have a black light. "What is it?" I said, as casually as I could.

"Are you that Neanderthal woman's sister?"

"No," I said. "No, I'm not."

Achilles sat in the passenger seat as I drove back to Brighton. Then I carried him in. He was tired, a rare moment when his fluffy, warm body was limp in my arms.

The apartment was empty. The dishes had been washed. The broken glass was cleaned off the floor.

There was a handwritten note on my table.

Dear Sara,

I hope your dog is OK.

I know this is an inopportune moment, but it is unhealthy to prolong things in situations like this. I do not think this relationship is working out. I would like to say we are just incompatible but I think maybe you just might not be the sort of person who can be very good at this. In fairness to you, I have not had very many lovers so this should not be regarded as a statistically significant observation. You should not let it trouble you too much.

In any case, I respect you as a professional colleague, but to avoid future emotional and physical injury I think it would be best if we keep our relationship strictly platonic.

You do not need to be concerned about my penis as the stinging has stopped.

Good luck with your Neanderthal niece. Please let me know how that turns out. Also, please tell me how your dog is. He seems like a reasonably good dog.

I will see you at the ASG conference. We accepted your talk, by the way. I recused myself from the committee. All was on the up and up.

Your (now strictly platonic) respectful colleague,
Angus Gupta, MD, PhD

And that was the end of that.

Later a tabloid ran a photo of an internationally renowned scientist leaving my apartment building in soaking wet pants. He smiled for the camera but no one who reads tabloids knew who he was, and no one who knew who he was reads tabloids.

At least my dog was okay.

chapter nineteen

The next day I stood in my kitchen looking at the injurious peppers ripening on the window sill. The ghost pepper, the hottest pepper known to mankind. No wonder Angus's penis stung. This was my fourth crop. I got more than one a year with the help of heat mats and grow lights. The first crop was for John, for taco night. I told John when I planted them and he was excited even though at that point eating them would have been completely impractical. The seed packet said they would take ninety days to become peppers. John only lived for seventy-three. When he died they were tiny little white flowers, not searing hot peppers, but beautiful in their own way.

When John's body gave up on him, it was good that he and Liz had moved into the bigger apartment. They had room for nurses and all of us to gather around. They had the money for a private doctor, and whatever equipment John needed, so he didn't have to be in the hospital. Achilles was permitted in the bed, curling up in a ball at John's feet. Luka came bringing prayers. Our mother turned up with Italian wedding soup by the gallon, in an array of versions cooked to whatever dietary restrictions Liz imposed: vegan meatballs, gluten-free pasta, kale instead of escarole. Liz would remind Mom that she's Irish.

"I'm Italian by marriage," Mom said, "and boiled cabbage never made anyone feel better. Just makes them feel gassy."

And there was Hank. He did everything for Liz when John was sick: sent the laundry out, kept the nurses on schedule, shooed reporters from the front of the building aggressively enough that he never saw the same one twice. John had become more famous in his dying than he had been when he was healthy, in part because of Liz's blog. But Hank had stood guard in Iraq during the war, against people who made even the most aggressive paparazzi seem effete by comparison. They were completely outclassed.

Near the end Hank called up every evening just to make sure Liz had remembered to eat her supper. On the very last night Hank called and when she did not answer he went up to find her. John had told Liz that it was time. She had sent the nurses home. She wanted to be alone with him. I was worried that she would not be able to pull herself together when the time came, but she did. She told Hank to call me and I would bring Luka and my mother down to New York. Then Hank helped Liz call the ambulance, and John was transported to the hospital.

She could have just kept hoping for him to last a few more hours, but then it would have been too late. Instead, she let John die in the hospital like he wanted, so his heart would keep beating in another man's body. His spinal cord and brain were extracted and frozen so that they could be used for research so others might not suffer the way he did. John and I had even chosen the researcher who would receive them. My friend Mei was working on his disease and she was so wonderful. She treated his tissue as sacred, because it was. It must have been so hard for Liz. I don't know if she would have been able to do it without Hank, but she did it and I am proud of her for that.

In the morning Hank took us to his brother's funeral home to sort out the arrangements. To an outsider this might have looked like nepotism, even corruption on the part of the doorman, funneling business to his family from his building's wealthy and bereaved tenants. There was even an article in the gossip section of some rag, passing itself off as investigative journalism, making that accusation. What a thing to say, I thought, about a man who had fought for his country, by people who were so devoid of decency that they could not even recognize it when they saw it in someone else.

But the vultures were miffed, so they said all kinds of things. They had been denied their spectacle. There were no pictures of the casket, no photos of the grieving family to publish. Hank's brother's funeral home was located on the eastern edge of Queens, in an area more accustomed to burying tradesmen than tycoons, and the paparazzi, lacking imagination, were all staking out the grander funeral homes in Manhattan.

The arrangements were not made public. I only told John's family and a small band of friends who had liked him when he was poor and had bothered to visit him when he was sick. To keep the press from trailing Liz to the funeral, Hank arranged for her to be spirited out the back door of the building the evening before. She spent the night with Hank's mother, in the same bed that Hank had slept in as a child. "All the hotels have stoolies," he said, as if he were Humphrey Bogart in 1940 and he did this sort of thing all the time. "And my mom's cooking is better than any hotel."

My brother Luka said Mass at a nearby chapel. Hank's son sang a hymn with a voice that teetered so close to the precipice of manhood that it may have been the very last day in his life when he could still sing like an angel. Hank's sister-in-law did the flowers – huge bouquets of white lilies, just like the ones Liz and John had at their wedding only a few years before.

Of course Hank was among the six pall bearers who carried John's body out of the church. He had been John's true friend and his protector, both during his life and after his death. He protected all of us. He was a guard, in the same way that I was a scientist and Luka was a priest. It was more than what he did. It was who he was. And we all wanted Hank, in that moment, to be there next to John, to guard him and to carry him.

It was as perfect as the funeral for a thirty-eight year old man could possibly be.

John was so broken down at the end. He could not move. He could barely speak. There was so little left of him and yet the void that was left when he finally took that last step was enormous.

Leaving the funeral, I thought about the last time I had seen him, saying goodbye that past Sunday afternoon. I thought that was the last time I would ever hear from him.

But it wasn't.

A few weeks later I got an e-mail from a new e-mail address, jcorbit_in_heaven. I thought it was a scam, but it really was from John. It said:

Hey kid,

Thanks for coming to visit me!

I thought you might be sad that I'm gone so I got you a little present to cheer you up.

It's in your mom's shed. Keep an eye on my Liz.

Love,
John

So on the following Saturday, on my way down to New York to visit Liz, I stopped at my mother's house. She had a big old wooden shed in her back yard. In the past it had served as both a chicken coop and a woodworking shop.

"I don't know," she said, "some man came last week and said he had a delivery for Sara Nicoletta. Wanted to put it in the shed. I didn't look at what it was. I was meeting Jeanie next door for lunch. You should see her son. He turned out so good looking."

"The son sentenced to home confinement?" I asked.

"It's only for a few more months. You need to think long-term. He helped me mow the lawn. Or half of it. The right side was more than two hundred feet from Jeanie's front door so that alarm thing went off…what a nuisance…but the left side looked lovely! Here's the key."

We opened the shed, expecting a package, maybe some books or another exotic knick-knack for my apartment.

"Oh, John!" my mom moaned, staring up at heaven as I started jumping up and down.

Inside the shed was a shiny, canary yellow, mint condition, 1989 IROC-Z.

Convertible.

To truly appreciate what a wonderful gift this was, you have to understand something about my high school years. In Rhode Island in the early nineties, girls would line up in front of the bathroom mirror armed with aerosol cans full of extra-hold hairspray and complain that their permed, perpendicular hair was too flat. They wore short skirts and white high-heeled ankle boots, with a leather fringe. Boys doused themselves with enough Drakkar Noire to set off the smoke alarms.

In this world, an IROC-Z was the most coveted possession. It was the "it" car, a top-of-the-line Corvette. There were at least five in the parking lot. The lucky owners, the offspring of landfill owners and crooked real estate developers, would show them off by circling the school at high speeds, burning the rubber off their tires. It was such a distraction that when the janitor destroyed eight classroom windows by washing them with an abrasive cleaner, they decided to cover half of them with bricks to spoil the view.

The teen culture was tacky but I didn't know it then, and I felt like a reject because I was on the outside looking in. My family came from the right town in Italy and we had lived near the school for three generations, but I was bookish. My mom wouldn't pay the forty dollars for me to get a perm. She told me acid washed jeans were a waste of money. There was no hope of any car, much less a cool car.

Life was easier for Liz. She wore black from head to toe with her art friends and she was not socially cursed by being a remarkable student. To her, our high school in Rhode Island was something to forget. But I needed a do-over. And that was what John gave me.

Sure, the car was impractical. It was too small for the passengers. It had no air bags. It predated CDs and the tape deck was jammed with a Triumph album that still played but wouldn't come out.

But it was an IROC. An IROC!

And it went really, really fast.

It was fabulous.

chapter twenty

Theo and Liz were not alone in their public support of the Neanderthal project. Like-minded people organized by blogging, promoting Twitter tags (#NeanderNow, #EvoBelieveYo), tacking signs on community bulletin boards, and asking people to sign petitions in front of organic supermarkets. Judy and Stacey, whom I'd met at the baby shower, started a charity walk to raise money for resurrecting and raising the Neanderthals. They also tried to start a paisley ribbon campaign to raise awareness of Neanderthal acceptance. They chose paisley because all the colored ribbons were already being used to raise awareness of different types of cancer. But it turned out paisley was already being used for thyroid disease so they switched to an abstract floral pattern. It didn't really catch on.

Paula Roche summed up their general philosophy in her popular blog:

Five Reasons Why We Must Embrace Phylo-Diversity
By Paula Roche of "The Unkindest Cut"

A person's phylogeny is defined as the history of how she has evolved, the natural history of her evolutionary descent that makes a person who she is.

We are entering an era of technological advancement where it has become important that we recognize the need to not only accept but also celebrate that members of our human family will begin to have a wider diversity of phylogenic origins. Some of us, the *Homo sapiens sapiens* (HSS), will have evolved continuously over millennia. Others, such as the *Homos sapiens Neanderthalis* (HSN), will have had an interrupted history.

In a few months we will welcome the first of these phylo-diverse children into the world. Unfortunately we expect that these children will probably experience the kind of prejudice that is all too commonly witnessed against anyone who is slightly different. We have already seen it manifesting itself in people protesting the HSN's very right to exist.

Of course there are always going to be closed-minded people who hold onto their bigotries. These people will never be convinced.

For the rest of you particularly those who may be on the fence about the prudence of creating Neanderthal people or who will encounter phylogenically diverse children in the future I offer you just a few of the reasons why it benefits all of humanity to embrace phylo-diversity:

Reason 1

We have an obligation to rescue the HSNs from extinction. Imagine if turned out that the Sasquatch legends were true and Sasquatch was just a Neanderthal who had survived for many years longer than people realized. Wouldn't we feel obligated to let him live in peace? Of course we would! Wouldn't we make sure he had enough food? Wouldn't we make sure he had proper medical care? Now that we have the technical ability to rescue the HSN from extinction do we not have the same moral obligation to undo their extinction as we would have to prevent it, to let them live in peace? Of course we do! The answer is obvious. We cannot continue to abuse our environment our planet and other living things the way we have been. We must make every effort to preserve what we can and fix what we could not preserve.

Reason 2

Embracing Phylo-Diversity makes it easier for people to appreciate all diversity. We expect HSN people to have some superficial difference from HSS people. But when you get to know them you will realize that inside they are just like everybody else. Having the opportunity to get to know different kinds of people makes us all more tolerant of people with all kinds of diversities.

Reason 3

Neanderthal art is likely to add substantial depth to our culture. We know that they made jewelry and painted in caves. They had musical instruments. Imagine the transcendental beauty of hearing an HSN playing a bone tusk tuba!

Reason 4

Some HSSs assume that the HSNs might not be as smart as us. Indeed the word "Neanderthal" has been used as a bigoted slur for unintelligent and misogynistic people for years. But we must remember that there are different kinds of intelligence. The HSNs were a highly successful species living for hundreds of thousands of years through the inhospitable climate of the ice age. They may be more intelligent than us, better able to make substantial contributions in science math or medicine. They may be more in tune with their environment. Imagine them guiding us towards understanding our ecology. They may be more imaginative. Imagine them being able to solve problems with new ways of thinking we cannot understand yet.

Reason 5

HSNs probably develop in a different pattern than HSSs. Allowing children to be in a classroom of students with different socially mixed abilities, modeling different good behaviors and achievement, gives children an opportunity to learn and teach one another that would not be available in a phylogeny segregated classroom. Imagine your little HSSs coming home and telling you about the HSN girl or boy in her class! Wouldn't this be so exciting! Imagine the birthday parties!

The comments section was largely supportive, for example:

Well said, Paula! It surprises me that there has been so much opposition to this project, especially from people who I had previously considered educated and intelligent. The amount of knowledge that we could gain from recreating a Neanderthal should make anyone with even the most minimal amount of intellectual curiosity supportive of this project. Some scientists have speculated, for example, that the Neanderthal could communicate telepathically. Surely anyone with any kind of intellectual rigor would want to investigate that.

With a few exceptions:

It is just a matter of time before these Neanderthals come over from the past and start taking all of the good jobs from hard working HSSs. HSSs have got rights too, you know. You don't see us going into the past and taking all of their jobs. Just how are our millennium's laborers supposed to compete with guys who can lift a three hundred pound weight? You can call me a bigot all you want but this is a matter of simple economics.

And at least one challenge to Paula's grammar from someone who liked to complain:

I hate to complain but your underuse of commas is really distracting.

As his army started mobilizing, Theo became less and less involved with the press coverage of the Neanderthal project himself. He had defenders now. He no longer needed to defend himself.

chapter twenty-one

The American Society of Genomicists conference convened in June. I was speaking on the first day of the conference, giving the last talk in the afternoon session before we broke for dinner. Each session had a chair, a scientist who is an expert on the subject and helps pick who is going to give the talks.

Angus Gupta was the chair of my session.

I had given talks before, but this one was probably the most important. I was outlining the information that we knew on the Panola virus and the data I had assembled from the birdstorms. I was representing the consortium. Normally data on a new virus that was taking such a toll on the continent's birds would be of great interest to the scientists in the room. This year, nothing was normal.

When I was done Angus said, "We will take a few questions from the audience," and called on a German scientist.

"Dr. Nicoletta," he said, "what evidence have you seen that there actually is a Neanderthal gestating in the womb of that chimpanzee?"

I looked over to Angus. He did not say anything so I said, "I would prefer to answer questions about my own work, not someone else's."

"Yes, but you have been to Barlas Labs. Surely you were shown something there."

"That is my sister's project. I can only comment on my own research," I said.

"Yes, yes, I understand, but you are here as a scientist. As a scientist…"

Here Angus interrupted, speaking into the microphone. "Dr. Nicoletta is here to discuss the work that they have done on Panola. Could we please confine our questions to that topic?" and he called on someone else in the room.

"Perhaps just one question on the Neanderthal. One question. Have you had a chance to analyze the sequence of the artificial Neanderthal chromosome? For the error rate?"

"I have not. I honestly don't have any special knowledge about the Neanderthal project beyond what has already been reported in the press," I replied.

"But have you seen any evidence of the fetal development?"

I had seen the early ultrasound, of course, but I did not know how to read ultrasounds. "None that I have sufficient expertise to evaluate," I said.

"Do you know how the epigenetics works, within the cells?" shouted someone else.

"No," I said.

There were more questions. People were talking over one another now. Had I seen the chimpanzee? Did I watch the fertilization? When would the artificial chromosomes be available? Did Neanderthal development follow the pattern of human growth? These were the questions I could pick out as they were shouted at me, one over another. There were more. The auditorium had erupted into a cacophony of men's and women's voices. The Academy was in disarray.

"I have nothing to say on the Neanderthal project," I said.

Then someone shouted out from the room, "She can't talk about it. Her hands are tied."

The auditorium erupted in snickers.

I looked over to Angus, the man who had tied up my hands, the man who was in charge of preserving order here, hoping for him to save me. He looked stunned, angry even, but he did not move. I turned from the podium and fled from the room, my face hot with anger and embarrassment. Fuck the Academy, I thought. Fuck them.

I walked quickly to the elevator and pounded on the buttons. Why had I bothered? I worked so hard, for so many years, to build a reputation as a serious scientist. I had worked so hard on that project, to add to our knowledge of Panola, to stop it before it wiped out our bird population and possibly even crossed into humans. I wanted to show it off, to show the progress we had made, to show the progress I had made as a scientist, and it came to this. I wasn't a scientist any more. I was a slut whose sister was making a Neanderthal baby. Dr. Nicoletta did not exist. I was just Sara, Liz Nicoletta's little sister.

Up on my floor I fought tears as I fiddled with my door's key card. Once in my room I lay prostrate on the bed, burying my head in the freshly bleached pillowcase. Why, Liz? Why was she doing this to us? I hadn't started any of this but it overwhelmed my life.

A few minutes later there was a knock at my door. I didn't answer.

A deep Scottish voice said, "Sara, please let me in."

It was Angus. I tried to be silent enough to pretend I wasn't in the room.

"Sara, I want to apologize. Please let me in. I know you're in there. I'm not leaving until I speak with you."

He said it like he meant it so I opened the door.

"I'm sorry I let that happen," he said. "Your talk was very good. I shouldn't have let them take it over like that. I was just…so…so…stunned."

"It's been all over the news for weeks here, Angus. I should have known this would happen," I said, then collapsed on the bed, my head on my knees, tears streaming from my eyes. "I should have asked someone else to give the talk."

"Sara, I'm sorry…"

"Could you please just go? I want to be alone."

He did not leave. He stood in the room silently, for a good five minutes just watching me cry. And then he said, "Here, let me make you a cup of tea."

He walked over to the in-room beverage service tray and found the kettle. He took it into the bathroom and filled it with water. As the water boiled he said optimistically, "It's a difficult thing, one's sister making a Neanderthal, aye, it is. But there's nothing in life that can't be made at least a little better with a good cup of tea."

"A cup of tea? Angus, my career is a disaster. My sister's gone off the rails. And the whole world thinks I'm a slut because you left me tied up in a hotel room."

He looked at me, pausing for a moment. I didn't want to make him feel guilty again. What he did was bad, but it wasn't his fault it ended up in the news. No one would have cared if it hadn't been for the Neanderthal project. But my reputation was in tatters. I saw that now. Even in the closed confines of the Academy, among my colleagues and the people whom I respected most, I was a laughingstock.

Angus responded sincerely, "There's biscuits, too."

I looked at him, stunned, and then I couldn't help but laugh.

He sat down on the bed next to me and gently put his arm around my shoulder. "I know things look bleak now, but your work is good. It speaks for itself. And the Neanderthal project is out of your control. All you can do is worry about yourself. Keep doing your research and in the end, everybody will forget the other stuff."

That was the scientist's answer for everything. Work harder. It was our ethical code, the only real philosophy we had. Search for the truth, and if the thing you did failed, try something else.

"Look," Angus said, "I know this will sound pollyannaish but it's true: science is a meritocracy. You get ahead by putting your nose to the grindstone. Scientists have politics and drama, like everyone else, but if you put out good papers, and stay honest, you will be successful. Your findings are correct. That's all you need."

We sat silently on the bed for a while. It was a hard pep talk to swallow after what had just happened.

"I know you don't believe me but no one cares about your personal life. Yes, this afternoon for a few minutes they were curious. A Neanderthal baby—of course they are interested. But when your paper comes out, they will argue about your statistical approach and biases in your sequence preparation and the robustness of your conclusions, just like always. You can be whoever you want if you're a scientist. Just do good science."

"What about you?" I asked.

"Me?"

"You should find a girl who wants you to tie her up. I've been thinking about that."

"You've been thinking about that? That was just one time, Sara. Don't overthink it."

"No, it wasn't. It's who you are. I don't think it's wrong. That's why you asked me, right? Because you knew I wouldn't think it was wrong. It's just not my thing. You should find a woman who likes that. On the Internet or something."

"I'll take that under advisement," he said, grinning.

"I'm serious. It's important for you to be true to who you are."

"So I can't be self-actualized if I'm not tying someone up?" he said, slightly mockingly.

"I'm not saying that." I thought for a minute. "But I guess that's the point I'm trying to make."

"Okay, I'll find a girl and you'll finish your Panola paper." He stood up. His work in my hotel room was finished and this time he wasn't leaving in a huff. "Don't worry about them."

"Thanks for coming up," I said, sincerely.

"Have dinner with me."

"No, I think I'll get room service."

"It won't do you any good to ostracize yourself. And my student Julia wants to meet you. We want you to be on the examination committee for her PhD thesis defense."

"Really?" I asked. Being on someone's examination committee was a big deal. No one had ever asked me before. "But wouldn't I be a distraction?"

"Not at all. Your work on Panola is superb, and it's close enough to Julia's. No one else would do a better job."

He really said that, and I don't think it was just to make me feel better. It meant a lot, coming from Angus Gupta. He was, despite all his peculiarities, a really, really good scientist.

"Okay," I said. "I guess I wouldn't mind a glass of wine."

"Aye, I could do with a lager myself."

"Maybe a Scotch."

"Aye, now you're talking, lassie. Now you're talking."

And then we had a very pleasant dinner of the hotel's dry chicken and salty string beans almondine while we talked about viruses and Angus didn't let anyone bring up Neanderthals.

chapter twenty-two

AS the baby's birth neared, Liz's blog posts focused less on defending the decision to have a Neanderthal baby and more on the birth itself. She discussed her plans for feeding the baby. She had heard that some adoptive mothers breastfed their children using a contraption with tubes to pipe milk from a container to Liz's nipples, to trick the baby into thinking she was breastfeeding.

She discussed what the baby would eat when she got bigger. I don't know why rich kids cannot eat anything, but all of Liz's friends' children had food intolerances so Liz was expecting the Neanderthal to have them as well.

While the kids' problems seemed to originate from their neurotic mothers, a Neanderthal's intolerances would be the result of her genetics. For starters, a Neanderthal would almost certainly be lactose intolerant. Most humans are. Lactase, the enzyme that breaks down the lactose sugar in milk, is produced in infants' guts so they can digest the milk they nurse from their mothers. But its production tapers off after the baby is weaned. If lactase is not present in your gut and you drink milk, you will become very gassy and uncomfortable. When Northern Europeans and others began domesticating cattle, long after the Neanderthal went extinct, a change occurred in their genomes. A couple mutations arose that kept the lactase gene on.

These mutations stayed in their descendant's DNA. Perhaps it was sexual selection: people did not want to mate with gassy people. It kills the mood. More likely, the people who were able to properly digest milk were better able to survive the cold winters of northern

Europe. When the Neanderthal genome was sequenced the researchers checked to see which version of the gene the Neanderthal had. As expected, they found that the Neanderthal has the lactose intolerant version.

Liz pondered whether she should compromise her (intermittent) vegan principles and raise a carnivorous child. Neanderthals mostly ate large game, and there are conflicting views on whether they ate any vegetation at all. While Liz claimed to abhor the idea of meat, she also wanted to give her child an authentic diet. That would actually be pretty easy, even in Manhattan. She already had an enormous freezer. She just needed a friend with a gun and a hunting license and that thing could be packed with venison year round.

But I wondered how Liz's dinner parties would go if everyone else was eating organic barley and seitan pilaf and a Neanderthal child was at the table tucking into a deer's liver. They might get jealous.

Mostly Liz made plans for the Neanderthal's birth. She wrote many blog posts on her birth plan. This one was typical:

Afterbirthing Plan

Greetings all!

The baby's birth is quickly approaching so I have been spending most of my time working on a birth plan.

Many of you have asked what my plans are for the baby's placenta. I have, of course, been giving this a lot of thought.

As most of you probably know, it is becoming more common for mothers to save their baby's placenta. Some women have embraced the traditional practice of burying it in the yard, using its high nutrient value to nourish the ground, perhaps planting a commemorative tree over it. While this is such a beautiful practice, there is an increasing amount of knowledge about the health benefits of eating baby's placenta.

I know this may be a jarring idea at first if you have never heard of it. This just shows how much we have medicalized birth in our culture.

In fact, eating the placenta is very common. All other mammals that produce a placenta eat it shortly after birth. And so many women have begun eating the afterbirth and have reported that it helps ward off postpartum depression, increases milk production, and contributes to the overall well-being of the mother. And, of course, it is a beautiful way of bonding between mother and child.

But, as our baby will be born to a surrogate, I have been deliberating whether or not I should eat the placenta, or if it rightfully belongs to Linda, our surrogate. She, after all, is doing quite a lot of the physical labor!

Luckily, my sister, the scientist, came through with an answer. She explained to me that a placenta is the boundary that both separates and joins the bodies of the mother and child. So, genetically, one half is like the mother and one half is like the baby.

I have decided therefore that the only logical solution is to separate the placenta into two. Linda will be able to have the half that is like Linda, and I will have the half that is like the baby.

In many ways, the division of the placenta between Linda and myself symbolizes the separation of the baby from her birth mother, and the joining of the baby with me, her real mother. Of course we expect that this will be a bittersweet transition for Linda, which is why we have to be so careful to make sure the birth process happens with openness and love. And I do hope that by participating in her tradition of eating placenta we will help Linda realize just how much we do truly love her and will always regard her warmly as an integral part of the baby's life.

So, with that settled, my only decision now is to decide how to eat my half! My friend Judy had her baby's placenta ground up and made into caplets. Stacey had hers sliced and rolled with rice into sushi. But here in New York we have access to Brooklyn's finest artisanal placenta butchers, so really my possibilities are limitless!!

I must admit that since becoming a vegan there are things that I really do miss! This seems like a once-in-a-lifetime opportunity to enjoy meat without incurring the moral burden of sacrificing another living being. All this week I have been toying with the idea of having it sliced into pieces and baked into a vegan quiche Lorraine. Or two! How big will this baby get, anyway! LOL! Linda seems to think she is quite big enough!

What have you all done? I'd love to know your thoughts so please do leave a comment below.

Namastae,
Liz

And so Liz had decided to go natural by turning the whole thing into a bourgeoisie culinary adventure. Luka responded to the blog:

Liz, don't be such a pussy. If you're going to eat a placenta, eat a placenta. Slice that puppy up, slam it inside a sesame seed bun, and take a nice big bloody bite. Really tuck into it. Let the placenta juices ooze out of the corners of your mouth. Breathe in its smell. Embrace the natural experience of eating a gooey chunk of raw innards, just like every other mammal does: fork free! There is no need to involve someone else. Do it yourself! You're an awesome cook. And save a little bit for me. I'd like to try it with a little Sriracha sauce and maybe just a dab of that breast milk, if you get that going. Wait! I just had a brilliant idea! If there's enough milk maybe we could make some breast milk mozzarella and turn the whole thing into a big sloppy Philly cheese placenta! Doesn't that sound yummy! Mmmmm! I can't wait!

She deleted that. And she got a little mad.

For the record, all she asked me was what the placenta was made out of. I did not actually recommend that she eat the thing. I'd like to add that my professional opinion as a biologist is that I am actually 100% in favor of placentaphagy, transgenic and otherwise, in certain specific circumstances. The mothers of all non-human mammals eat their placentas because they're hungry and they do not want the smell of afterbirth to attract a predator to eat their babies. So, if you happen to give birth while you are out alone on safari, you are in the proximity of a pride of lions, and your broken-down Range Rover has neither a loaded gun nor a cooler full of food, nor doors, then I would say that eating your placenta is certainly a good idea.

chapter twenty-three

In the background of all the Neanderthal drama, the weather that year was strange. Of course it had been strange for several years, so much so that normal (snow in the winter, hot sun in the summer) was beginning to feel like an artifact, something that only existed in old paintings and movies. The end of May was so cold that puddles froze. We were expecting Panola to come north with the birds, but the migrations were disrupted by the cold weather. The beginning of summer was cool and dull and cloudy. Then the weather shifted and July ended with the worst heat wave we had ever seen, humid and sultry with a full week of hundred degree days, made so much more difficult to endure because it was the first time in months that the temperature climbed out of the seventies.

My Brighton apartment was unbearable. There was little cross-breeze and when I tried to put in a window air conditioner it crashed onto the sidewalk and did not work after that. I nearly bought a new one. I was at the big hardware store when a shipment was being unloaded and I managed to hoist the very last unit into my cart, gleefully, but then I heard a very old lady ask the worker if there were any left. I was afraid she might keel over in the heat so I hoisted it again into her cart, the opposite of gleefully.

The Daltry Institute was air conditioned, but poor Achilles was stuck at home all day. I shaved him practically to his pink skin to help him survive the heat. In the mornings he still begged to go out for a run, but after a block he would find a shady tree and stretch out with his belly on the dewy grass. He was like a lawn ornament:

eighteen pounds as stiff as concrete. I would pick him up and carry him home sweating, even that early in the morning, and he would spend the rest of the day stretched out on the cool concrete floor of the basement laundry room with his legs splayed behind him.

My only prospect for relief came in the form of an invitation addressed to both Liz and me. The greeting said, "Girls."

Girls,

Come down to the house this weekend. The swimming will be fine.

Theo

In that heat an invitation to a private beach, regardless of its source, sounded like a dream. I was still reeling from the disastrous conference, and I had not been outside much that spring. Everywhere I went I got stares. It added anxiety and hassle to the idea of leaving the house, so I did not go out much except for our runs.

When the weekend came we took the quick and ugly way down to Long Island: over the Throgs Neck Bridge, along the highway, and up Theo's pebble driveway. It was definitely top-down weather and not entirely because my car's air conditioning had lost most of its vitality around the turn of the century.

I had added a little dieting to my running, so when I was in Theo's bathroom changing into my bathing suit I thought I looked good, or at least better. My fat roll had mostly gone away. My bathing suit was a one piece, red with a halter top, like the kind a nineteen-fifties pinup model would have worn. It was pretty. I felt pretty in it, like Marilyn Monroe.

I walked out onto the grass. And then I saw Liz, taller than me, long and lank in a red bikini, the product of thousands of dollars in yoga instruction, holistic nutritionists, and personal trainers. As if that wasn't bad enough, she was accompanied by a very chiseled and mostly nude Billy. They were so fit they looked like super heroes. I suddenly felt frumpy, like their older aunt covered in a swimming burka.

"How about a swim?" Theo suggested.

Liz and Billy declined. Their embracing of natural living did not extend to actual nature. They liked swimming pools, preferably ones perched atop five-star hotels, with attractive cocktail waiters who brought them organic fruit, blended with ice and vodka. And Achilles did not enjoy a doggy paddle.

"Just you and me then, Sara," Theo said.

Theo took off his shirt. To my surprise, he was cut with muscular abs, defined biceps, and wide shoulders. He was already brown from the sun. He walked barefoot across the grass towards the shore.

I took a breath, unwrapped myself from my towel and followed.

Theo crossed the wet rocks with the certainty of someone who had crossed those rocks hundreds of times before. He reached where the rocks ended and the water began, pushed further out, and all at once dove into the ocean, swimming.

"Is it cold?" I asked.

"It's fine!" he said, lying back, treading water in the gentle waves.

Theo's eyes were on me like the sun. He was making me feel hot, making me aware of every inch of exposed skin.

I stepped across the rocks, not with his certainty, not leaping like a gazelle, but slowly and cautiously making my way to the sea. The rocks were wet and slippery and I did not want to fall. The cold waves splashed at my feet. The sea air filled my lungs.

"Dimethyl sulfide," I said.

"Dimethyl what?"

"Dimethyl sulfide. It's what the ocean smells like, that tangy smell. Bacteria make it when they eat seaweed and plankton."

"You're quite a fountain of knowledge, Sara," he said, still treading water.

"I know," I said. "I can't help it. I think it might be weird."

"Very."

"I always thought everyone remembered everything, but I guess not." I reached the last rock, and stepped onto sand and into water that was up to my knees.

"It's cold!" I shrieked.

"Don't be a sissy!" he said, splashing me with a huge wave of water.

I shrieked again. He did it again.

I liked that. I mean, I hated that, but I liked that he treated me as an equal, not as a fragile woman. I felt chilly in that water, but I was not fragile. Frigid sea water was my natural habitat.

I grew up in New England so I knew what I had to do. We learned as kids, in the water at Scarborough Beach. It was never warm, not even at the end of August. Liz would dare me to go in. She would egg me on, or tell me we were racing in and then stand on the sand barely dipping her toes in as I raced into the water. Luka would just pick me up and throw me in. But that was how you had to do it, the way Theo did, go in as abruptly as possible. Take all the cold at once.

I stepped across the rocky sea floor and plowed my way through the waves. The water came up to my thighs, skimming the bottom of my bathing suit, and then up to my waist, saturating my bathing suit to a deeper red, and then I dove under. It was bracing, stimulating, and intense. It was instantly cooling, fantastic.

I swam out towards Theo. I did not open my eyes under the water so I did not realize that when I stood up I was only inches away from him. I looked at him, he looked at me. We were both surprised. I leaned back in the water and swam.

"You grew up swimming here?" I asked.

"Yup. All summer."

"It's awesome. We swam at the state beach."

"The state beach was probably more fun."

"I doubt it. With all the traffic and the crowds? And the public changing rooms and the kids peeing in the water?"

"You were there. It would have been fun."

"We did have fun," I said.

We loved it, when we were kids: the sand and the waves and the hot dogs and frozen lemonade. My mom sat in a beach chair and read and ignored us for the entire day. It was a wonder we did not drown. She worked so hard when we were kids, after our dad died. It was her chance to relax and she did. Once, Luka got fished out by the lifeguard. Well, twice actually. Both times were on the same day. It was particularly choppy and he was feeling rebelliously daring.

"You're so nice," Theo said, for no reason at all.

"What do you mean?" I asked.

"To your sister. And people."

"Everyone's nice," I said.

"No, they're not."

"I'm not that nice," I said. Then to prove my point I splashed him with a huge wave of water.

Theo and I swam a bit more, but mostly waded. I guess no one really swims much at the ocean, unless they're doing a triathlon or something.

When the cold water began to chill our bones we clambered back onto the rocks, across the lawn, and to our lounge chairs on the patio. Liz and Billy had not moved since we went down to the water. Achilles was still stretched out under my chair and didn't even look up.

"Theo," I asked, "Could you put some sunscreen on my back?"

He sat on the edge of my chair and massaged the lotion onto my back. I have always loved the smell of coconuts.

"What's this on your shoulder?" he asked. "Did you get burned?"

I laughed a little. I saw the back of my shoulder so rarely I sometimes forgot what was there.

"Something like that," I said.

"Sara…" Liz said.

"No, wait, what is it?" he asked. "It looks like…It looks like a badly drawn butterfly."

I laughed again, looking at Liz.

"It *is* a badly drawn butterfly!" I said.

"Sara!"

"Well I have to tell him now."

"Nooooo!" she said.

"When Liz was in high school, she thought she might want to be a tattoo artist. I was her first client."

Theo laughed.

"You squirmed. Do you have to keep telling that story?" Liz said, without lifting her head off the chair.

"It goes with the tattoo," I said.

"I told her I'd pay to get it removed. She keeps it to spite me."

"I wouldn't say spite. Maybe mock," I replied. "It hurt enough going on. I can't imagine what it would feel like coming off. Anyway, it reminds me of you."

"It's your own fault," Billy said. "Who lets their sister give them a tattoo?"

"She's usually pretty artsy," I said.

"I'm not artsy."

"You are too," I insisted. "You made me go to that poetry night."

"Fifteen years ago she spent ten minutes watching a half-naked man…"

"It was the bottom half!" I interrupted. "That's not half-naked. That's just naked."

"Alright, she spent ten minutes watching a *naked* man peeling string cheese. She didn't understand the symbolism," she appealed to Theo, "and I've had to hear about it ever since!"

"I'm just saying she's artsy," I said.

"I'm not artsy. I'm an artist. I worked as a graphic designer for years, Theo."

Billy concurred, "She did all the best menus. When she quit, some of the city's top chefs cried."

That was true, actually. She was kind of a legend in New York restaurant circles, greatly admired for her tasteful use of curlicues.

"Don't stress me," Liz said. "I'm having a baby."

"The crap-hurling chimp is having a baby," I corrected.

Billy told us to stop bickering, for the sake of the baby. "Judy says that adoptive mothers should be treated just like biological mothers. You wouldn't be bringing up your ugly tattoo if Liz were pregnant in the traditional sense. You should treat Liz like she's pregnant. It will help us all prepare for the birth."

"I think that sounds like a good idea," Theo said, probably also annoyed by the bickering.

"Yes, we should all meditate on how beautiful the ocean sounds. Silently," suggested Liz to everyone, but she was looking at me when she said it.

I was happy to sit and relax under the summer sun. I lay back in my chair and let my jaw soften, my muscles sink into the lounge chair. I tried to keep my abdominal muscles a little contracted, though. I did not want to completely slob out on Theo's patio. And I made sure not to fart. Even though we were outside, and Achilles and I had stopped for tacos on the way down.

Achilles was stretched out in the shade under my chair. He was farting up a storm. I was hoping I wouldn't be blamed. Eventually the summer heat cooked all five of us into a divine laziness. The stresses of the last few months left our bodies as the sun's heat entered. The press coverage, what people thought, the national argument about de-extinction, did not matter.

"Somebody make me a piña colada," Liz finally said.

I struck her with my invisible magic wand. "Poof. You're a piña colada."

"Somebody make me a piña colada to drink."

Billy struck her with his invisible magic wand "Poof. You're a piña colada to drink."

"Theooooooo…" she tried.

"You can't drink," he said. "You're pregnant."

I guffawed.

"And I don't have any coconuts," he added. Liz's whining continued, though, and she was still the client.

As a consolation, Theo offered to drive to town to get some ice cream and far be it from me to refuse ice cream. Billy asked for nonfat, stevia-sweetened, iced soy milk, but Theo told him it wasn't permitted on the premises. Only Achilles offered to join him, but it was too hot for him to be left in the car.

Billy watched Theo go into the house and the minute the door shut said in a false falsetto, "Theo, could you put some sunscreen on my back?"

Liz laughed. "Awww…Don't make fun of Sara. That's just how she puts the moves on someone."

"I didn't want to get burned!" I insisted.

"She put the moves on him like a fourteen-year-old virgin? Are you a virgin?" Billy asked.

"Shut up!" I said, "I'm thirty-seven! I just burn easily. I'm half Irish, you know."

"Our people are pasty," Liz said.

"And you never formally thanked me for publicly defending your honor during that stupid bondage story," he said.

"Yeah. Thanks Billy. Very chivalrous."

"So I guess you don't think Theo's a con artist anymore?" Liz asked.

"No, she just wants to bone him anyway," Billy answered for me.

"I don't want to bone him!" I insisted. "I don't think anything."

"You never stop thinking!" Liz said.

"I don't know what's happening. I don't know if he's a con artist. I don't know what he knows or what he thinks is happening or what Xiao told him. I don't know what's growing in Linda's belly. I don't know why you want to make a Neanderthal. It's completely disrupting everything in my life, but I don't know anything."

"You know you want to bone him," Billy said.

"Shut up!" I said. "I'm suspending my disbelief because I want you to be happy, Liz. I'm trying not to think about the rest of it. I just hope you don't end up disappointed."

"Awww," she said, "you're always so good to me."

Theo took longer than expected but returned with strawberry gelato. As we ate it he asked me to give him a lift to the lab so he could check on things. Katarina was there every day, and was actually sleeping at the lab now, but told Theo she was taking the afternoon off to go to the movies for a Lassie marathon.

"What's wrong with your car?" Liz asked, taking a scoop.

"It's not a yellow IROC," he said. "Plus, my tires were slashed."

"What?" Liz asked. "In the driveway?"

"No, in town. All four. I had it towed and got a cab home."

Some people really hated the Neanderthal project.

chapter twenty-four

Theo drove. I didn't usually let people drive, but I could tell he loved my car as much as I did. However, I did *not* let him change the radio station. There is a right way and a wrong way to do things. If one is driving an IROC on Long Island one must blast house music, not heavy metal. We were not driving a Trans Am in Chicago, although of course that would also be awesome.

We pulled into the Barlas Labs parking lot. It was late on a Saturday afternoon so there was only a handful of cars in the lot. The sun beat down on the asphalt so hotly that the difference in temperature between the air on the ground and the air just above it bent the sun's light like a prism. A mirage of steam came off the parking lot, circled under the parking lot trees and stretched all the way to the woods that edged the office park.

When we got out of the car I noticed Theo peering across to the other side of the lot.

"What's that?" he said.

I followed his eyes and saw a thin man in a blue shirt and plaid shorts pushing a stretcher. The man was heading towards a battered blue van parked alone in the lot. And then I saw it sticking out from under the sheet: a brown furry hand.

"That's Linda!" I said. "He's stealing Linda!"

Theo sprinted across the parking lot. I chased after him, but I wasn't as fast. Then he suddenly stopped short about ten feet in front of the stranger.

The man drew a gun and pointed it directly at Theo. Then at me too, as I halted next to Theo and recognized the man's face. It was sunburned and weathered, filthy with mud, but it was the one that I had been watching on the television news, the one I had seen through the bars on the highway near here. He was Peter Ward, the escaped convict.

"There seems to have been some misunderstanding," Theo said, inching forward and using the calmest voice imaginable. "That chimp you have there, sir, belongs to me."

"Stand back!" he ordered.

"Okay, Mr. Ward," Theo said. "We don't want any trouble. I just want my chimp back. We can forget about this whole thing."

"If you want her you're going to have to pay for her."

"She's pregnant. She needs medical care. You don't know how to take care of her."

"Four million!" he said, looking at me. "That's fair. And it's enough to get me out of here. Tell that rich wacko if she wants to see her Neanderthal baby it will cost her four million cash! And you can have her this afternoon."

Theo implored, "You can't kidnap…"

"It's not kidnapping!" he said. "I'm stealing an animal."

"You can't take her," Theo said. "You don't know how to take care of her. If the baby dies they'll convict you of murder."

"Murder of an animal ain't murder," he said.

It didn't seem to be an appropriate time to get into an argument about the legal status of a Neanderthal person. But that didn't stop Theo.

"We don't know what the law will say yet," he said. "We think she will probably be classed as a human. I wouldn't take that chance if I were you. But, either way, you'd be killing the Neanderthal baby, the first Neanderthal baby in thousands of years. Do you want to risk that? I'm sure you don't want to do that."

"I never hurt no one!" he shouted. "Not in my entire life. And I'm not a stalker! But I'm not going back to prison! Not for nothing! I'm not!"

His eyes were wild. He seemed to be in the throes of madness. He was like a caged animal, threatened and responding to reason with the opposite of reason. He waved the gun towards us as if deciding whom to shoot first. The gun settled on me. I froze with panic. My eyes felt wide, my body stiff, a ray of heat shooting through me from my face to my feet.

Theo lunged, his whole body leaning forward.

The distance between them was short, probably seven feet now, but it was one step too many.

"No!" I shouted, but it was a silent shout. I had no physical voice, only panic inside my head.

And then Peter Ward tumbled to the ground.

Theo had not reached him. What happened? Why was he on the ground?

Then I saw and realized. Panola.

Recently birds had been falling out of the sky, sparrows, finches, starlings, all up the East Coast, birds on spring migration. Today Panola had reached Long Island.

Peter Ward was knocked out cold by a Canada goose.

Theo stopped, perfectly still for a moment, stunned, perplexed, snatched from the clutches of death, not believing his own eyes.

I couldn't believe mine either, but now I could move and Theo couldn't. I grabbed Ward's gun and took the bullets out of it without shooting my face off and stuffed them into my pocket. I checked him for another gun. There wasn't one. I unbuckled his belt, slid it off, and used it to tie his wrists together. He stirred and groaned.

Theo was still immobile, astonished.

Another goose fell between us with a thump. Then I heard a noise like the sound of a thousand vuvuzelas. A flock of geese was flying towards us, but not with their usual grace. There was no elegant V formation. It was a haphazard mess with individual birds suddenly stopping mid-flight and spiraling down to the ground, one by one, a Kamikaze bombardment of waterfowl. Another fell to my side with a thud.

"Get Linda!" I shouted. We lifted her up, pushing her stretcher into the van. We climbed in ourselves and shut the van doors. Out the window I saw Ward stand up and run off into the trees on the edge of the parking lot. I checked Linda's pulse, as if I knew what a normal chimp pulse should feel like. My only assessment was that she had one. She was breathing but seemed thoroughly unconscious. Ward must have drugged her.

"The birdstorms usually only last a few minutes," I said.

He still hadn't said a word.

"That was brave of you," I said.

"Kind of stupid."

"You could have been shot. For a chimp."

"I wasn't thinking about the chimp," he said.

We heard a crash. A goose had smashed into the van's windshield.

"I mean, for the baby," I said.

The light inside the van was dim and the air smelled like the earthy animal odor of the chimpanzee. The noise from outside was a cacophony.

"He was aiming at you," Theo said.

It seemed inconceivable. Theo had been thinking about me. He had almost gotten shot because he was thinking about me.

When I heard his words I felt an overwhelming rush inside of me, the rush of millions of boulders tumbling down a hill. I felt their force like gravity propelling me forward, forward in space, forward into the physical space that Theo occupied, and forward in time, bouncing forward down a hill towards an unknown but inevitable end. These were the forces that had shaped humanity, that had shaped life. These were the boulders that God had tossed and I was rolling with them, tumbling down the hill.

Everything before, everything since, nothing was like that. The world, the universe, was a blur and the small space inside the van, Theo's face, his eyes, his skin, his smell, was clarity. I reached for his hand and took it in mine. Then, finally, I was lying on the floor of the van and Theo was inside of me.

chapter twenty-five

When the birdstorm ended we climbed out of the van without speaking about what had happened. The only thing that didn't overwhelm me was logistics.

"You need to take Linda back to the lab," I said.

Dead geese were strewn around the parking lot. The few cars present had dented roofs, shattered windshields. A dead goose lay splayed across the hood of my car as if it had been airbrushed on. Car alarms blared in the distance and near us.

We looked around. There was no sign of Ward.

"You need to take her back to the lab. I have to process the birds."

Linda was not safe in the parking lot. We had no idea what Ward had given her. She could wake up at any minute, violent and confused. And the parking lot was strewn with virus. It didn't seem to infect humans, but that didn't mean it would not infect a chimpanzee.

I could not go with him. I knew I was the first scientist who had been caught in a birdstorm. There seemed to be something about the virus that made it difficult to isolate, sequence, and study. The Panola research group thought that if samples were taken from the birds more quickly, we might get better results.

"I'm not leaving you alone," he said.

We could hear police sirens coming closer, no doubt responding to the commotion of the birdstorm. "I'll be surrounded by police in a minute and he's not interested in me." He looked doubtful. "I still have the gun," I said.

After some hesitation Theo pushed the stretcher back to the lab and I opened my trunk. In there I had a kit that every scientist working on the project kept, just in case. When they gave us the kits I thought it was ridiculous, that the chance of any of us being caught in a bird storm was too small to bother. The kit included Runcorn field sequencers, the latest technology available for sequencing. They were based on nanopores. The nanopore itself was a tiny hole made by a circle of proteins. The hole was small enough that we could stretch a strand of DNA through it and read its sequence. The sequencer contained millions of nanopores, each reading a different fragment of DNA. Runcorn field sequencers were disposable, handheld devices that could be used to sequence genomes anywhere. Each kit contained a dozen. I thought this was a publicity stunt on the part of the manufacturer, but here I was about to put my kit to use.

The protocol for isolating the viral genome was printed on laminated paper and included in the kit. Our goal was to get samples from four different types of bird tissue (blood, brain, lung, liver) from as many birds as possible, as swiftly as possible. We had to extract the RNA from the tissue and put it on the sequencer. This would, hopefully, give us a decent survey of the virus before its RNA broke down into pieces too small to sequence.

I opened up the dissection kit. The first step on the laminated sheet said to cut off the bird's head. I looked in the kit. There was a teeny-tiny pair of scissors and a delicate little scalpel.

"Crap," I thought. I didn't need to delicately decapitate a little sparrow. I needed to butcher a fucking goose. I didn't know how to butcher a goose.

An entourage of police cars pulled up, sirens screeching. To me they were the cavalry.

The first policeman got out and approached me. I suspected he was about to order me out of the parking lot, while calling me ma'am in a slightly condescending manner, so I interrupted him.

"I'm Dr. Sara Nicoletta of the Panola Virus Task Force. This is a category five birdstorm. I will need assistance in processing the scene. Are any of you hunters?"

It wasn't really called the "Task Force". It was called the "Working Group," but I thought "Task Force" sounded more butch. And the birdstorms didn't have categories. There was work to be done and I was the only one who knew how to do it so I was in charge. It was just a matter of convincing them. They looked at me quizzically, unsure whether to ask for identification. I do not have a scientist card, but I had a bunch of equipment. A young policeman stepped forward.

"Ma'am, I'm Officer Ari Barnes and I do some hunting." He spoke with a drawl that led me to believe he was originally from somewhere a full day's drive south of Long Island.

"Good!" I said. "You can wear the HazMat suit. And also," I added, "we saw Peter Ward. He went that way." I pointed to the woods and handed Ward's gun to the astonished officers. They recognized it as the type of gun that had been reported stolen from a home where they had found Ward's fingerprints.

And so a bunch of police ran off into the woods, bravely, I thought. I deputized the deputy to be a scientist. Officer Barnes, dressed like an orange bee keeper, deftly butchered the first goose for me using a Swiss Army knife that he carried in his pocket, which may or may not have been consistent with police regulations. He handed me each body part so I could sample it, process it, and load it onto the sequencer.

In the meantime more police arrived to join the search for Peter Ward. A helicopter circled overhead. This time the woods were still thick, but the weather was perfect. "We got him!" someone shouted. "We got him!" I barely looked up when they brought Ward through and locked him in a car. Officer Barnes did not look up at all.

My deputy scientist worked so fast that after a couple hours we had complete samples from four different geese, and I was running low on sequencers.

The health department arrived in a big van and wrapped yellow tape around the epicenter of the bird storm. Because I had been taking samples without protective covering, they told me I would have to go into quarantine.

"Panola doesn't infect people!" I argued. "And there are dead birds around for miles. You should put the whole island in quarantine."

But they wanted it how they wanted it and I had to defer. A roll of yellow tape and a truck with writing on it trumps a fake task force. Two weeks in quarantine.

chapter twenty-six

When we finished butchering the geese, Officer Barnes was hosed off with disinfectant and I was quarantined in a room at the local hospital. It was not as nice as Theo's beach house, but I kind of enjoyed it. I had my own room, my own bathroom, one of those beds that go up and down, and someone brought me food. But best of all the paparazzi could not reach me in there. I had nothing to do except analyze the data and look at Panola.

I messaged Theo:

Me: I'm quarantined.

Theo: I heard. How's the food?

Me: Healthy.

That was about as deep as it got. Neither one of us was the sort to talk about our feelings.

Liz had decided that after ten years, and in her condition, someone else should take a turn babysitting Achilles. He was staying at the beach house, dining on a steady diet of fried sausage and breaded chicken cutlets. He obviously preferred this to the organic, vegan kibble he got at Liz's, but Theo complained that he had gotten the runs on his father's antique Persian rug. I suggested he try dog food, even though I knew Achilles would not eat it while he smelled sausage.

We talked a little over Skype. The hot weather had broken and whenever I was on the computer Achilles would jump into Theo's lap.

"He keeps doing this," Theo said.

"It means he owns you."

The clothes I was wearing had been confiscated, along with the ones in the duffle bag inside my car. At first I enjoyed wearing a johnnie all day, but then I decided that if I wore it home I would look like a drug addict who had absconded from an ER before her toxicology screens came back. I texted Liz and asked her if I could borrow some clothes, but she sent Billy out with her credit card instead.

He texted me:

Billy: What size are you? A twelve or a fourteen?

Me: I'm a six.

Billy: Petite?

Me: Yes.

Billy: What about cup size? A or a small B?

Me: 36C! Are you blind?

Billy: It's not my fault you dress in rucksacks. Do you need tampons? They have Super Plus and Ultra.

Me: THOSE AREN'T CLOTHES

Billy: Just trying to be helpful!

Having Billy buy me lingerie was embarrassing, but the health department had also burned my bra, and not in a feminist protest sort of way. The clothes Billy bought were nice. I wished I could afford a personal shopper. It would save so much hassle.

I watched myself in the news coverage of the birdstorm. The local TV station played footage of me sitting on the ground in shorts and a T-shirt taking samples from a dead goose. Officer Barnes was next to me in his HazMat suit and we were surrounded by a parking lot strewn with yellow crime scene tape, shattered glass, and dozens of dead geese.

And that was how I went from being the Neanderthal baby's kinky aunt to being the harbinger of the apocalypse.

Theo was questioned about Peter Ward. I didn't know how much detail he went into about Linda's attempted kidnapping. The police search parties had gone into the conservation land abutting the parking lot. It was not a deep woods by any means, but parts of it were thick with brush and far off the trails. They found a makeshift campsite in one of these areas, across a wide expanse of muddy streams that few casual hikers or dog walkers would have bothered to cross. Ward was living like a hermit, stealing bits and pieces from the surrounding suburbs by night. He had food, clothes, and propane tanks. He hoarded copies of *Us Magazine* and *Zoss*. The news anchor held them up to show that most of the covers featured pictures of his stalking victim, Janice Bowen, on the cover. Some also had pictures of Liz. They even found a large telescope that an amateur astronomer had reported missing from his back yard. He must have been watching the office park from behind some trees, maybe out of a desire for security or just boredom.

It reminded me of when I had seen him in the corrections department car. He was free, for a while, but still looking at the world rather than being a part of it. I suspected he was one of those people who had spent his whole life like that.

I worked and worked and worked, analyzing the output of the sequencers, comparing the sequences here to the pieces of Panola genome we had gotten from the other locations. I had Internet access so I was able to communicate with my colleagues at the Daltry, and even phoned into a few meetings in my johnnie.

On the first Thursday that I was in quarantine I got an e-mail:

Hey kid,

Happy Birthday!

Love,
John

Liz usually made a big fuss on my birthday, but she forgot this year. She later blamed it on "pregnancy brain."

My mom remembered but didn't think I could receive phone calls in quarantine. "Did you think the virus would travel down the phone lines, Mom?" I asked. She still would not use a phone during a lightning storm, even though she has had a cordless since the eighties.

Luka did not pay attention to things like birthdays. I thought about telling Theo, but I didn't want to seem like I was feeling bad for myself.

So it was nice to hear from John. For the first time ever I wrote back:

I miss you.

And he responded:

I miss you too.

I set up an autoreply. Every time he wrote to me I wrote back, "I miss you."

I wondered how long our conversation would go on, how many messages he had told his robot to send me, how long his server would stay active. I wished for eternity or at least a thousand years of him wishing me well and me telling him that I missed him. His robot only had my one e-mail address so I hoped that my e-mail provider would stay in business forever. It might be possible. There is a company in Japan that has been making paper bags for more than a thousand years. I wanted it to last forever, this virtual continuation of a mortal conversation that ended far too soon.

chapter twenty-seven

The next week the health department made a big production out of releasing me from the hospital. I was seen by two different doctors and then a class of medical school students. The teacher-doctor explained to them that, while accidents in science are unavoidable, knowingly exposing yourself to a potentially deadly virus without proper containment was very, very stupid.

"Yeah, don't do what I did, kids," I said. "But it doesn't infect humans."

"It doesn't infect humans *to our knowledge*," the teacher-doctor clarified. Then he waxed on for a while about safe research protocols.

I offered to explain more about Panola to them, about our research approach, and what we had observed about the epidemiology of the virus. But they were more interested in feeling my un-swollen lymph nodes and looking down my not-irritated throat. One student asked about the Neanderthal project, but I told them I was too tired to talk about that, so they wrote "fatigue" on their little charts. I suspected it would be a quiz question.

A nurse handed me a package before I left. The Panola Working Group had sent me a new emergency kit in case I got stuck in another birdstorm. I was shocked that I ran into one, but the project manager who made the kits was excited about it and included a card with flowers on it saying she hoped I was feeling okay and thanking me for my service to science. It was a refreshing change from her usual communications of, "Are you done yet?" and "How about now? Are you done now?" She also said she had revised the contents of the kit to include larger knives and two HazMat suits. I did not think a bigger knife would help much because I still didn't know how to butcher poultry.

The authorities arranged for Officer Barnes to drive me back to my car, which had been sterilized to a degree that shortened the life of its upholstery while presumably lengthening mine. I got to sit in the back of Officer Barnes's cruiser, like a perpetrator, but he wouldn't put the lights on.

"So your sister is the one making that Neanderthal baby," he said.

"They're trying, I guess," I said. "I don't know if they'll succeed."

"What do you think about it?" he asked.

I figured there might be some legal implications if I said I didn't entirely believe they *were* trying to make a Neanderthal and I wasn't exactly in the mood to discuss it with a police officer.

"Not sure. What do you think?" I asked.

"Honestly, I don't think it's right, ma'am," he said.

"Why not?"

"Well, you know, ma'am. My father, he's a preacher. He doesn't believe in evolution," he said. "He taught us not to. When we were taught about Neanderthals at school my dad would take out his books and he would show us how Neanderthals were just humans with bone disease. I think he would say that it wouldn't be right to bring back a human with a bone disease. They are dead. Let them be dead."

"Do you believe in evolution now?" I asked.

"Well, I'm open to it. But I don't reckon it matters. If my dad's right and she's a human, you're just making a sick kid. That's wrong. If my dad's wrong and she's just almost a sick human, well the 'almost' part doesn't seem to make much difference."

I thought about it. It was simple but one of the better arguments against the Neanderthal project that I had heard.

"How did you end up on Long Island?" I asked.

"A woman," he said. "She came up north to be a pop star. I followed. I became a cop and she became Janice Bowen. I guess our lives were too different."

"Wow," I said. I knew then why he had not looked up when Peter Ward was captured. He was not intent on his work. He was seething.

"I was going to join NYPD, like on TV, but my mother was too scared I'd get shot."

"You like it on Long Island?"

"They're good people here, 'cept for making fun of the way I talk. 'Course, the most exciting thing that happened so far is those geese falling out of the sky. But my mamma's happy. She can sleep at night."

"Thanks for your help with the geese. We got some great data."

"You were getting DNA sequences? We learned about that in high school, after the Neanderthals."

"Panola and a lot of viruses store their genetic information in RNA, not DNA. But it's basically the same idea."

"What are you going to do with them?"

"Well, when you sequence the viruses you have to sequence the bird so sometimes you get a lot of bird and not much virus. We got sequences from birdstorms all over, but they didn't have much virus. The ones we got here are the best. I looked at all the sequences and I think one gene is evolving faster than the rest of the virus."

"What's that mean?" he asked.

"It means it has more differences. The sequences of the other genes were mostly the same in all the samples: ACGUCG… like if you copied a page on a Xerox machine and then copied the copy, millions of times. There are slight changes here and there, between the first copy and the last. It blurs, but there aren't many changes. This one gene codes for a protein called neuraminidase. It has more differences between the virus sequences in different samples, like this one gene is being copied by hand, by a half-drunk monk. That might mean when the bird's immune system attacks the virus, copies of the virus with differences in this gene are more able to survive than ones that don't."

"Like it's trying to find its best sequence?"

"Yeah, like that. It makes a lot of copies so it can try a bunch of stuff and sees what works."

"So the sequence it's got for that gene now isn't very good?"

"It looks that way. The protein this gene makes might be a good target for a medicine. But we have to try it in the lab. Not me, someone who specializes in that sort of thing, if I can convince them."

The real worry was that Panola might cross into humans. The virus looked a little like flu. It had not happened yet, and Panola hadn't been seen in other mammals. But just in case we wanted to be ready with a vaccine and a treatment. And we needed to figure out how to stop losing birds. Panola was turning into an environmental disaster.

"We're going to publish a paper on the virus," I said. "I'm going to put you on the author list, if you don't mind."

"I'm not a scientist!" he said.

"You brought a meaningful skill to the project. That qualifies you, by any standard. I couldn't have gotten the samples without you. It's nice to be a published scientist. You go down in the scientific record as having done something. No one can ever take away from you."

"That would be something," he said. "I wonder what my dad is going to think about that."

"He'll think you were doing God's work," I said.

"He already does."

"Well, a different kind of God's work."

Officer Barnes turned into the office lot. My car was parked where I had left it.

"This is where they're making the Neanderthal," I said. I do not know why. I just wanted to be honest with him.

"We kind of figured that when we saw you here. There's going to be trouble," he said.

"There already has been," I said, thinking about Theo's slashed tires and the attempted chimp-napping. "Some of the people who have strong feelings about the project aren't very trustworthy."

"What about this Barlas guy?"

Was he trustworthy? Theo was a lot of things, but I still didn't know the answer to that.

"He's not a criminal," I said, feigning a smile.

"Now you know that ain't the same thing," Officer Barnes said.

"Can you put the siren on, just for a minute?" I asked.

"No, I cannot," he said. He seemed like a bit of a stickler for the rules, but I guess that's why he was a cop. As he opened my door and freed me, the perpetrator, he grinned and said, "And I'm not going to put you in no handcuffs, either."

chapter twenty-eight

Gatsby's sun had nearly set. I was sitting by myself on a small couch on a second story porch, wrapped in a thin blanket, watching the last pink light dim over the horizon. The sound was quiet. The air was growing cool. A few seagulls and one lone sailboat slowly glided by. In a while there would be stars.

How many hours are in a life? I did the arithmetic in my head. Half a million, more or less, depending on your luck. Most of those hours ran into one another. They were nondescript units of time that were used up and forgotten. But some hours were different. These hours existed as our real life, the substantial time that was diluted by everything else. They were the best hours. They were the worst. They were the hours that we experienced with an intensity and a truth that separated them from the rest. How many of those hours are in a life? That was harder to calculate. A few dozen? A hundred? I did not know how many of those hours I would have, but I knew I had just experienced three of them

I had arrived at Theo's house full of doubt. Theo and I hadn't spoken about what happened during the birdstorm, or what would happen next. I was worried. Maybe it had not meant anything to him. Maybe I was just one of the flock, a person he was with in the moment and then moved on from.

Or worse, I thought, maybe *he* was just one of the flock. It was hard to admit that to myself. It was supposed to be against nature. Millions of years of evolutionary selection is supposed to have left women wanting to be protected and cared for, to be built a home and presented with a freshly killed beast and then cuddled in the dark. But that wasn't what I wanted from him. I wanted something more primal, more basic, something older than homes, older than hunting. It was not intellectual. It was not sentimental or romantic. It was instinctual. On the surface I wasn't even sure that I liked him. I wasn't sure what he was doing with his life. I didn't trust him. But none of that mattered. I was attracted to him for no reason that I could understand, but it was stronger than anything I had ever felt before.

Three hours ago, I was standing on Theo's front porch, wearing the expensive lingerie and clothes that had been delivered to me in quarantine and putting on lipstick that was too red for the afternoon light. I did not know what would happen next. Our relationship was strange and complicated. I did not know what he would do. There was the Neanderthal. The project encompassed everything, even more for Theo than for me. All of his decisions would be weighed in the context of what was good for the project.

But more basic than that, there was a contrast between us. He seemed glamorous compared to me. He had grown up wealthy and knew how to do the sort of things that came with that: how to dress, where to eat, how to be charming to people he didn't like. He was nothing like the kind of men who were usually interested in me, nothing like the kind of men that I even usually met. He was shinier. He glistened in the sun and when he gave me any attention it was like being sprinkled with glitter.

If he was not interested in me I knew I would take it hard. His shininess lessened the gloom of my days and made me feel like I existed for my own sake. Not a sister, not a daughter, not a Neanderthal's aunt. I wondered but didn't care if it was contrived, if I was supposed to feel that way because it served his end, if my attraction was a means to silence my protests about the project. And, anyway, the bullets in Ward's gun were real. There was at least that truth. I took a breath. I pushed the button. The bells of Westminster rang out and then I heard Achilles bark.

Theo opened the door wearing a Barlas Labs T-shirt, a bigger and softer-looking version of the one he had given me. I wanted to touch it.

"Hi," he said.

"Hi," I answered.

Achilles skirted past him and jumped up to my knees and howled with joy.

I stepped into the hallway. There was an awkward silence. I didn't really know what to do next. I had called him from the hospital and told him that I would come to his place after I was released from quarantine. He only responded that he would be home. I wondered if he expected me to just pick up my dog and go.

"Thank you for watching Achilles," I said. "Was he good?"

"Sure," Theo said. He didn't kiss my cheek this time, or even touch me. He just stood there with a slight grin on his face.

"So," I asked, as casually as possible, still looking down at Achilles, "do you have plans for tonight?"

"Yes," he said, flatly.

"Oh. Oh, okay," I said, haltingly.

"Don't you?" he asked.

"Well," I stammered, "I need my dog back."

Theo smiled. "Come into the kitchen," he said.

I wanted to stay in the hallway, as stationary as the potted fern in the corner. But I followed him. And then I saw it, on a white plate on the white kitchen counter and I smiled with relief, surprise, joy. "Did you make that?" I asked.

"Is it that obvious?"

It was lopsided and the frosting was oozing off the side. But it was chocolate, and Theo was lighting the candles.

"How did you know?" I asked.

"A little bird told me."

"Liz?"

"Actually it was Hank."

"Hank?" I wondered how he knew and then remembered the reminder e-mail I had received that past November on Hank's birthday. It came from John, his way of keeping us all together forever.

"Are you going to sing?" I asked.

"Do you want me to sing?"

"Can you sing?"

"I can carry a tune," he said. He looked at me smiling. His green eyes were shining. His shirt was tight around his thick shoulders.

At another time I might have wanted to hear him sing. But at that moment I wanted something else.

"Can you sing quickly?" I asked, looking down at the cake.

"Quickly?"

"Quickly," I said.

"I could sing quickly," he said.

"Or we could skip it," I suggested, looking up and touching his blue shirt because I couldn't not.

"I'd hate to skip it."

"No. No, let's skip it," I said.

"Okay," he said. "We can skip it."

Then he lifted me up in his arms. He swept me up, like they say in grocery store romance novels, but it really was like that. He carried me through the hallway and up the gaudy staircase to the master bedroom with the king size bed and the shiny painted white headboard. We left the candles to melt into pools of wax on the cake.

Three hours.

The house could have burned down but didn't.

My heart could have broken from ecstasy but didn't.

Later, sitting on the porch, the moments that had just passed were already memory, a collection of ethereal images seeding themselves in my mind, some to take root, others to become shadows, others to disappear completely. There was Theo's skin, browned by the summer sun and warm to the touch. There were the gentle curves in the muscles on his shoulders. There was the look of desire in his eyes when he was close to me. There was the dust in the air, illuminated by the afternoon sunlight streaming through the windows. There was the smell of the ocean and the gentle sound of the waves. There were the sheets, white and crisp. There were his hands. There were his lips. There was his smell. There was intensity.

And now I was waiting for him on the second-floor deck outside of the master bedroom. I was wearing his shirt. It smelled of his cologne and of him. I could see down below to the grass in the back of the house and Achilles out on the lawn. Theo had let him out. He ran around and came back in. I heard Theo climbing the staircase.

He came out onto the porch. He handed me a piece of my cake and a glass of champagne and then his arm was around me and my face was leaning against his warm chest and we were both wrapped in the blanket.

I took a bite of the cake. It was dense with chocolate so dark it was almost bitter, with raspberries between the layers.

"The sky is so beautiful," I said. "Is it always like this?"

"No," he said. "It's never like this."

Four sets of nails clicked up the staircase and across the bedroom floor. I looked down to see Achilles poking his little white head out onto the porch. Then he bounded onto Theo's lap, circled around, and settled in.

"It's funny he stayed downstairs," I said, scratching the dog's head.

"I put a sock on the door," said Theo.

"A sock?"

"That's our signal when one of us is entertaining a lady."

"I was the third one this week," I said.

"The sixth," he replied, running his hand through my hair. "It was a slow week. Your phone kept making noise. Here, I brought it up."

It was Liz. She texted to say she had called the quarantine and they told her I'd been released. She wanted to know where I was.

"I'll tell her I'm on my way home."

"You don't want her to know you're here?"

"No," I said, "I don't want anyone to know."

"Why not?" he asked.

"I just want it to be us."

He kissed the top of my head. "I want it to be just us, too. But I don't think that's going to happen."

"Why not?" I asked.

"Did you see that sailboat out on the water?"

"God, were they watching?"

Theo was used to the activity on the sound. This had been his home for so long. The boat was lingering for no reason that he could tell. He had a chrome nautical telescope mounted at the windows downstairs. I thought it was for decoration, but it worked. He had seen a paparazzo on the deck of the boat when he went down to take the dog out. They were taking pictures of me on his porch.

"But it's so far away," I said.

"A 600 mm lens, with a doubler. They can get a picture half a mile out."

"Was that half a mile?" I asked.

"Maybe a little farther. It's rocky close to the shore."

"Should we go inside?" I asked.

"They're gone now. And it's getting dark. They don't have a flash that works that far. It would take a searchlight."

I hated it. It was a pointless invasion. After this long summer, I just wanted to be left alone.

"Don't cry," he said. I wasn't really. Just a few tears.

"I wanted it to be just us. Not the whole world."

"I'm not that bad," he said.

"That's not why," I said.

"You could do worse."

"Stop it."

"Some people think I'm pretty good looking."

"Stop it. You're not," I said.

"And charming."

"Who thinks that?"

"And I'm rich."

"Your dad's rich," I said, pushing myself further down under the blanket and closer to him. "That doesn't count. And anyway, scientists aren't motivated by money."

"I'm excellent in bed." He was trying to make me laugh when I felt like crying.

"You're okay," I replied.

"You said phenomenal."

"Are you sure? That sounds like a big word for me."

"Phenomenal."

"I would say, objectively, that you've mastered a small range of techniques…"

"A small range?"

"…with adequate precision…"

"Adequate?"

"…and given sufficient effort and practice it is possible, that in the future…"

"Everyone will think I'm a stud," he said.

"What will people think of me?" I asked. I knew: a whore, again, judged under a prevailing sense of morality that begins and ends with sexual purity.

"They're going to think your hair is a mess," he said.

Memories of the last few hours came rushing in. "That's your fault," I said.

"Then they are going to think that you look beautiful, sitting there under that blanket."

I was glad to preserve at least that modesty.

"They're going to think you could do better than that Barlas guy."

"I should at least try," I said, as if it was possible to have more than everything.

"Then they're going to think that Barlas guy is pretty lucky."

"They'll be right," I said.

"They will be," he said.

I texted Liz that I was spending the night at Theo's house as the light faded out of the sky and the constellations faded in. A crescent moon rose in the east. I found Vega, the brightest of the three stars that formed the summer triangle. How many people, I wondered, had sat wrapped in someone else's arms, looking up at Vega? All of them, I hoped. It seemed like such a basic human activity, so deeply pleasant.

People looked at the stars less these days. I wondered how many people would notice if the stars were all suddenly rearranged, assembled into a constellation of a turtle instead of a fish, an accountant instead of a hunter. Would the people gazing up from Manhattan roof decks and suburban back porches have anything more than a nagging feeling that something wasn't quite right? I wondered, vaguely, if the Neanderthal would have noticed. They saw the stars, but did they read pictures into them like we did? Did they use them for navigation, orienting themselves by Polaris in the north? Would they have noticed?

"Liz texted me back," I said. "She says I should stop throwing myself at you because you're not interested and she doesn't want me to embarrass myself."

"Why do you put up with that?" he asked.

"She means well."

He took my phone and he started texting, "Theo thinks I'm really sexy..."

"Noooooo!" I said.

"...and he is a very tender lover." Then he hit send.

Three hours.

You would think three hours was enough.

But it wasn't.

I didn't bother checking the phone when Liz texted back, "Ha ha."

chapter twenty-nine

The sun was just beginning to stream through the windows when my phone rang, awakening me from a dream.

Theo and I were walking together in a forest. It was autumn. We were on a small mountain that Achilles and I had walked dozens of times. It is a gentle hike past familiar landmarks: a tiny stream traversed by wooden planks laid by earnest Boy Scouts, a grove of birch trees that were ghostly white against the surrounding pines, large boulders that were detritus from the last ice age. Leaves covered the ground, and there was a slight haze around us. We were walking together, not speaking, not hand in hand but next to one another. And then suddenly Theo was gone. I looked everywhere, panicking, twirling to see all around me. And then I looked down and saw the top of his head. He was inside a hole, a round cylinder with a circumference a little wider than his shoulders and brown dirt walls as deep as he was tall. He looked up at me, his neck bent back, and he was smiling.

When I dream I don't realize things incrementally like I do when I am awake. Realizations sweep over and engulf me like a big wave at the beach. That hole, the void, had always been there, I knew, like the stream and the boulders and the birch trees. I had passed it dozens of times, had always known it was there, but I never noticed it until Theo fell into the emptiness.

My subconscious does not operate by subtle nuances.

The noise of the phone was jarring but the barrier between dream and reality was difficult to traverse. At first I tried to ignore the ring-ing, but then Achilles started barking. He was an amplifier for my phone if I accidentally left it on vibrate while I was in the shower. But today it felt like it was very early in the morning and I cursed myself for every, "Good boy!" I had rewarded him with over the years.

"Are you still at Theo's?" Liz asked on the other end.

"It's seven o'clock," I said.

"So you left?"

"What?"

"Did you go to work?"

"I'm in bed."

"Oh good! I was afraid you'd left!" she said. "You can come to the ultrasound!"

"The ultrasound?"

"You can see the baby."

"What? I don't want to go to an ultrasound. I want to sleep." I didn't know if I had a champagne hangover or if I had just stayed up too late, but it felt much earlier than seven o'clock. "Why are you up so early?"

"Have you seen Theo yet today?"

"I can see him now," I said.

Theo didn't open his eyes, but he reached a bare bronze arm out from under the white duvet. I handed him the phone.

"Hi Liz. What's up?" he said. "No, let's reschedule it for a little later. Eleven o'clock? See you there. I can bring Auntie Sara. No, I don't mind. She's not much trouble."

He hung up.

"Not much trouble?" I asked, rolling over to look at him.

"Only a little," he said, rolling towards the windows, still holding my phone.

"Are you texting again? What are you texting?" I tried to grab the phone, but his arms were longer than mine. "Stop it!" I said, but he had already hit send. He handed me the phone and settled back under the covers, grinning and closing his eyes.

"You told Liz you have a big clock," I reported.

"I did? Well I do have a big clock."

"Where?" I said. "In the library?"

"You saw it," he said. "All last night."

"It's not that big," I said.

He didn't open his eyes.

"It's like a hot dog someone's already taken a bite out of."

"No it's not," he said. "It's like a big loukaniko."

"A what?"

"Greek sausage," he said, rolling over so he was facing me, but his eyes were closed again. "They're big, like my clock."

"A killer whale's penis is eight feet long," I said.

"Go get a whale for a boyfriend, then."

"Are you my boyfriend?" I asked.

"Yes," he said, flatly, as if it was self-evident and I had no more say in the matter than if I had asked if it was raining.

I was so flummoxed that all I could come up with for a reply was, "A duck penis is shaped like a corkscrew."

"Go back to sleep Sara," he said.

"That's valuable information. You know, if you ever need to open a bottle of wine by a pond or something."

"Go back to sleep," he said.

He put a warm arm around me, pulling me closer. Having exhausted my knowledge of penises of the animal kingdom, I surrendered to sleep.

chapter thirty

L inda lay on her back on the small twin bed in the back corner of her room. The bed was covered with the kind of paper doctors use to cover the examination table when you're getting a pap smear. Katarina wore latex gloves and rubbed lubricating jelly on Linda's shaved belly. Xiao was acting as the assistant, holding the ultrasound at the ready as Linda nonchalantly fingered the cord that connected the wand to the machine.

Liz, Theo, and I watched the procedure over a camera feed in the lab. One large monitor showed a crisp image of Katarina and Xiao performing the procedure, while another had a video feed of the ultrasound itself.

A wide curtain had been erected across the window that separated Linda's quarters from the lab. It appeared to have been made from several shower curtains fastened together with packing tape. It was wonky so it looked like Xiao's work. Katarina said it was to keep Linda calm during the procedure. I suspected this meant she did not want Linda to see me. I wondered if Theo had let them know I was coming, maybe texting or calling while I was in the shower. I felt like Hester Prynne, wearing a scarlet letter so the whole town knew about my sex life. Maybe Linda would notice a change between Theo and me. Would she still be jealous, now, in her condition? Or was she no longer focused on matters of romance? Or not romance but rather mating or status. In her strange interspecies society, Theo must have seemed like the alpha male. Maybe she would hate me even more.

Not only was Linda's belly strikingly large but a definite bulge kept moving across her belly. First it was on the left side, then it would cross to the right, and then it went back again. This surprised me. It should not have, but after months of talk about the baby in her belly I still did not completely expect to see a baby in her belly.

Katarina began the ultrasound by rubbing the wand across the top of the bulge. "That's her bottom," Katarina said. And there was the baby's butt, or at least something too large to be just a case of terrible indigestion. Theo looked at me. He noticed my surprise. He put his hand on my back and grinned in a way that unequivocally said, "I told you so."

My head was swimming. I felt tired and nauseated. At the time I thought I must have been hung over, though I hadn't drunk that much. Reality seemed like a dream.

Katarina passed the wand over the different parts of the baby as images fluttered by. They were white streaks against a black background. "That's her heart," Xiao said.

"No, it's her liver," Katarina corrected him, smiling sweetly at his ignorance, her voice saying, "Silly boy!" if not her words.

I looked at Theo and he also seemed to realize at that moment that Xiao was banging his sister. He didn't look pleased.

"This is her heart," Katarina announced. "See the four chambers? See how it's beating?"

I found it difficult to make out anything at all, but the white blurs were pulsating rhythmically.

"Why is it so fast?" Liz asked.

"Fetal hearts always beat faster," Katarina said. "And small children's too."

"It's normal?" Liz asked. It was, in a way, a silly question. If this really was a Neanderthal in Linda's belly then this was the only time a Neanderthal fetus's heartbeat had ever been measured. There was no normal. There was only this.

"Oh yes, perfectly normal," Katarina assured.

She moved her wand lower. Linda grinned and made chimpanzee laughing sounds as if she had been tickled. Katarina passed the wand over the baby's head. I thought I made out the profile of a face.

"Oh, look at her!" Liz said.

"The face of the Neanderthal," Theo said. He was glowing.

I saw the face, too, but I couldn't gather any information from it. It just looked like a face. I could see a vague outline of the nose, the mouth. The forehead looked high, but I could not tell if it was as high as a chimp or lower, like a human. The ultrasound seemed like a Rorschach test. Each of us was looking at the same thing and seeing whatever we brought to the experience. I wondered why they were not using the newer, 3D ultrasound. Theo called Barlas Labs a lean start up, but surely a better ultrasound wouldn't be a major cost in the scale of a project like this.

"Sara, that's our baby!" Liz said, so gleeful that it jarred me.

I was experiencing things analytically, as a scientist. Liz was just experiencing. I looked at her, the joy in her eyes. I had not seen that look in a long time. She was looking at the baby with the same look I had seen in her eyes when she looked at John.

The air in the lab suddenly felt very thin.

Katarina said everything looked fine. "And the placenta?" Liz asked. "Is she going to make it to term?"

"It looked okay," Katarina said. "Good enough."

One concern was that the chimpanzee has a shorter gestation time than humans, by a few weeks. We did not know how long a Neanderthal gestation should be, or if Linda's uterus would be strong enough to last as long as it should, or if her body was built to tolerate a chimp pregnancy and not a moment longer.

"We could start giving the baby corticosteroids," Xiao said, "to speed up her lung development, in case she comes too early."

"Oh, do we have to?" Liz turned to Theo. "I want Linda to have a natural pregnancy, like we said in the birth plan."

"Above everything," Katarina said, "we want her to have a safe birth."

They acted as if Liz had veto power, but I wondered how far that went. We were in a lab, discussing things as if we were in a hospital. The oddness of it rushed over me. A natural pregnancy: that boat had sailed long ago. Thirty-thousand years ago.

I realized that I couldn't really see what was happening, not directly. Linda was hidden behind the curtain. There was a feed over video. I suddenly felt distrust, intense distrust. I think this was worsened by Xiao's presence. He deceived me before, pretending to be working on the lab's experiments when in fact he was making dogs. How did I know that what I saw was really what was happening?

They ended the ultrasound and drew blood. Katarina came out from behind the screen. "Today's blood samples," she said, referring to the vials she carried. "Poor dear, every few days. It's not medically necessary, I tell him, but Xiao insists on monitoring everything for the experiment." She put the vials into the lab refrigerator, shut off the monitors, and then disappeared back into Linda's quarters.

The experiment. The words rang in my ears.

"Shall we leave Katarina and Xiao to their patient, then?" Theo said, like an MC announcing that the show was over and it was time to go home. Thanks for coming! It seemed abrupt and added to my anxiety. I was almost shaking, as if I'd had too much coffee.

Liz left first. Theo was waiting for me in the hallway. We were somewhat alone. "Are you coming back to the house?" he asked.

"No," I said, "No, I'll take Liz back to the city."

"Ok," he said. He looked confused and hurt. "Why?"

"I'll take her back. I'm not feeling well," I said.

"So you're going to drive to the city?" he said.

"Yeah, I'll drive Liz back to New York," I said. "I'll sleep at Liz's."

"She can take the train. You don't have to be her chauffeur."

Liz must have opened the conference door just then because I heard her shout from the other side of the office, "Get OFF, Achilles!" and then, "Sara, get my purse for me, will you? I left it in the lab."

Theo was still staring at me, confused by my change in attitude. But he was no more confused than I was. I turned my back to him and headed into the lab.

Liz's enormous handbag was easy to find on the lab bench next to the refrigerator. I was alone, for a moment. The refrigerator was there. I could know, I thought. I could know what was really happening, what was growing inside Linda's belly. I looked around, opened the refrigerator and slipped one of the vials of blood into a pocket in the handbag.

Then I thought about the curtain. How did I even know that they really did an ultrasound? I didn't see it. Maybe it was just a film feed, a production for Liz's benefit and mine.

I went over and peeked behind the curtain.

Through the small gap I saw Linda, still lying on her bed, still playing with the ultrasound wand, now rubbing it on her large belly like Katarina had done, grinning and shrieking, tickling her own belly.

She was ignoring Xiao and Katarina who were standing together on the floor on the other side of the room, kissing.

So that was gross.

chapter thirty-one

The barrier that separates a growing fetus from her mother is imperfect. Nutrients from the mother's blood enter the baby's womb, and sometimes bring unwelcome passengers: alcohol, pesticides, viruses and other germs. Waste from the baby enters her mother's blood supply so that the mother's body can get rid of it for her. When this happens, little bits of the baby come along as well, bits of dead cells that get sloughed off during normal growth. As a side effect of this process, it is possible to sequence DNA found in the mother's blood and learn about the baby growing inside of her.

This technique was new then. People were just beginning to use versions of it to find out, for example, the sex of their babies. The Y chromosome is a strand of DNA that is only found in males. It takes a Y to make a guy, as my high school biology teacher used to say. The mother would not have a Y chromosome in her DNA, so if you found DNA from the Y chromosome in her blood you would know she was having a boy. Similarly, you could count the different chromosomes that were present in the blood. If there was an extra amount of chromosome 21 that meant the baby likely had Down's syndrome, or by its genetic name, trisomy 21 (three chromosome 21's).

In the same way, you could look at the sequence of the DNA in the blood of a chimp and see if some of it belonged to a Neanderthal.

I began sequencing the DNA from Linda's blood at a rest stop on Long Island. Only a year before, this wouldn't have been possible but the Runcorn Sequencers in my Panola kit made it work. Liz had gone in to use the toilet before me and left her purse in the car. I pulled the vial out of the pocket and then, in the handicapped stall in the ladies' room, I put the blood straight onto the sequencer.

The Runcorn worked much quicker than the larger machines, too. Those could take a day to sequence a sample. This one produced a lot less data, but it was enough and the sequencing run was done by the time we got back to Liz's apartment. I started a program to analyze the data in the guest room, while Liz phoned her decorator to complain that the baby's nursery had not been painted the correct shade of beige. The program identified what species the DNA came from by comparing the sequences in the DNA reads to a database that contained the DNA sequences from most of the species that anyone had ever sequenced.

"I'm going to yoga!" Liz shouted from the living room.

I looked at my computer. I excluded all the sequences that were chimpanzee. Those, I figured, probably belonged to Linda.

Among the sequences that remained, the first sequence, the second, the third, all the sequences that weren't chimpanzee, all those that belonged to the baby were listed in a table. The table indicated each sequence and what species it belonged to. I scanned down the species column. It read:

Neanderthal
Neanderthal
Neanderthal

I felt the blood rush from my head. My vision blurred. The first sixty sequences that weren't chimpanzee hit Neanderthal. This can't be right, I thought. I looked again. Was I pointing to the right sequences? I scrolled down the page a little. There was a human sequence next. That could be contamination from me.

Neanderthal
Neanderthal

And then another sequence. The computer couldn't tell what it was. Maybe more contamination or sequencing errors. And then more Neanderthal.

Neanderthal

Neanderthal

Neanderthal

Neanderthal

I stopped scrolling down. This can't be right.

I looked back at my scripts. Had I done the analysis right? Maybe I made a mistake, but the code was pretty straightforward.

This can't be right.

The baby, growing in Linda's belly, was what Theo said it was.

She was a Neanderthal.

Theo had told me this again and again. Liz had told me again and again. It hadn't seemed real. I felt like I was waking up from a dream, but the dream was reality and reality was the dream.

Looking at the sequences made my cheeks burn hot. My understanding of the world was shattered, like a glass window suddenly shattering into ten thousand small pieces, all falling to the ground at once. John's illness, our grief. It had sapped me of all my emotional energy. I had been running on the fumes of denial for a year.

For a moment I doubted myself. How did I know this was Linda's blood? Maybe I was supposed to sequence it. Maybe Theo left a honey pot for me, chimp blood spiked with artificial Neanderthal sequences. That would be easy if you were in the business of making artificial DNA. We were trained, as scientists, to think like that, to explore every possibility. But in the end, if we don't know for sure we have to take the most parsimonious solution, the simplest and most likely to be correct.

The simplest explanation was evident. I had run out of everything now, even denial.

Emotionally exhausted, I shut my computer. I couldn't be near it, near the sequencer, near the blood sample. I left it all and fled.

I left the apartment. I left the building, not even taking Achilles or saying hello to Hank as I left. I needed the air above me and the concrete under my feet, to be by myself among the anonymous faces.

I walked briskly, away. Away from the building, aimlessly.

How? I thought. How could this thing growing in Linda be a Neanderthal? How could Theo have done this? How could Xiao have done this? It was impossible.

I walked. More blocks, north, west, east, without direction around the sidewalks of the Upper West Side, past the cafes and shoe stores, past the yogurt shops and the park. A building stood like a stone cathedral at the corner of 79th and Columbus, with strong walls and verdant grounds. It was the American Museum of Natural History. It was sanctuary.

Dusk was falling when I bought my ticket. The attendant warned me the museum was closing soon. It didn't matter, I told him. I only wanted to see one thing. A vague memory guided me, like the kind that navigates you through a town from your childhood, one where a relative lived for a while. I went through the atrium and the exhibit halls, past the tourists and groups of tired children, to the Hall of Human Origins.

The Hall was a crypt, dark and full of bones. Near the entrance were three skeletons in glass display cases. They weren't real bones. But they had been made from real bones, modeled from casts. A modern human was in the middle. He stood upright and proud, looking straight ahead. Even without his flesh and skin he was familiar. He was us. On the left hunched a chimpanzee, bent over with long arms that touched the ground. I thought of Linda. And then, on the right, there was a Neanderthal man. He was reconstructed from the bones of the relatives of the baby that was kicking in Linda's belly.

Her father would have looked like him.

I peered at him, contemplating his body. The Neanderthal man was not like the chimpanzee. He was like the human. He was a little shorter, it was true. His joints were stockier. His brow was more pronounced. But he was not different, not like the chimpanzee. He stood up. His eyes gazed forward, perhaps not as arrogantly as the modern human but solidly, with pride. I could imagine him covered in skin like mine. If I passed him walking down a crowded sidewalk I might not even notice him. Or if I did notice the small differences, I might think he was a little sick, that he was a human with some sort of bone disease, and I would turn away to be polite.

I wondered what the man in front of me would have been like as the baby's father. Would he have cradled the baby in his arms? Chimpanzee fathers don't bother with their kids. Heck, some human fathers don't bother with their kids, either. But gorilla fathers like to play with their children. Maybe Neanderthals did too. He was so much more like a human than anything else.

I had no doubt the baby's mother would have loved her. She would have picked her up in her arms and fed her. She would have carried her around and protected her. I can't imagine what the baby's mother would have thought to have her child alone in the world, in a world from the future, with strangers. How could she even conceive of this? It would be like having your child ripped out of Heaven itself.

"How could we be doing this?" I thought. I was muddled. My face felt hot again. I looked at the skeletons and wondered if this could be okay. Were the Neanderthal possibly animals?

The differences between the human and the Neanderthal seemed trivial. They wore clothes. They buried their dead. When scientists sequenced the Neanderthal genome they found a sequence for the FOXP gene. This is a gene that we think makes people capable of language. The Neanderthal sequence is the same as the sequence that humans have. So the Neanderthals probably used at least some sort of language. But does that even matter? Some humans do not have language, but they are still human. We still love and value them.

I could not look at the Neanderthal and see him as an animal, as something other than fully human. The idea of being human but not fully human was impossible.

I saw him as us.

And then I saw Liz's project for what it was. They, my sister and Theo, Xiao and Katarina, were experimenting on a child. A baby. A person. They had created a child from dust, a child with no mother and no father, a child whose very existence was based on nothing but an unreliable DNA sequence. Through my blindness, through denial and worry about my sister, I had let it happen.

I had finally opened my eyes and was face to face with the enormity it. And then, like an exhausted child, I fell to my knees and began sobbing in the Hall of Human Origins.

chapter thirty-two

I was back in Liz's apartment, lying supine on the bed under the Dalí print with Achilles at my side. I thought of us as different, but we were the same, Liz and I. We were both capable of such deep denial, her with John's death and me with the Neanderthal's birth. I wondered how it had happened, if it was something in our genetic makeup, or if it was caused by our tumultuous childhood. Nature or nurture, we were the same.

I had shouted at her through tears. "Why, Liz? Why would you do this?"

She told me her story again. About wanting a child, about the Neanderthal, how natural and special she would be.

"Bullshit!" I said. "Why are you doing this?"

She talked about how we owed it to their people, how we had driven them to extinction and we owed this to them.

"Bullshit!" I said again. "Why are you doing this?"

She talked about how spiritual she would be, what a wondrous experience it would be to raise a child like that, how good it would be for our family.

It was everything she had said before. And then I recalled something else she had said, that Theo had said. I asked a different question.

"When will the experiment be done?"

"It'll be done when it's done," she said.

"You said you'll only pay Theo when the project is done. When will it be done?"

"It's done when it's done," she said.

I thought about what Angus had said. If you can make a Neanderthal, you can make anything.

"It's not done when the Neanderthal is born, is it? There's going to be another child, isn't there?"

She pursed her lips and looked down. I was screaming, now, shouting.

"What have you done?" I asked.

"It's not wrong," she said. "People have children for all kinds of reasons."

"She's a prototype!"

"She's not a prototype. She's a sister. Like you're a sister."

"She's a prototype! You couldn't start with a real child, so you started with one who's not quite real?"

She wasn't sitting any more. She was standing by the fireplace that she never bothered to light. Her face, finally, looked aged. "Theo's lawyer said we would go to jail if we started with a human child."

"But she is human, Liz. She's real!"

"We had to make sure it would work," she said quietly. "We thought starting with a chimp would take too long, and not be convincing enough. And then I remembered an article I read about making a Neanderthal man. The lawyers thought it would be close enough to a human to convince authorities that the method is safe but not so close that we would be prosecuted. We had to prove it would work."

"It did work!" I said.

"That's good!" she said.

I collapsed into her couch, folded over with my head in my hands. "Does Mom know? Billy?"

"Yes."

"Hank?"

"Luka doesn't know," she said.

They had all so quickly and strangely acquiesced. I'd been living in a dream, an illusion, a con perpetrated by everyone closest to me. I felt like vomiting.

"We didn't think you would understand," she said.

She crossed her antique rug and sat down on the beige couch next to me, putting her hand on my back.

"You didn't think I would agree. That's not the same thing as not understanding. I understand just fine! I am the only one who understands. What kind of life is she going to have? This child?"

"She is going to have a lovely life! We are making friends for her…"

"Rolling them off the assembly line…"

"And I am going to raise her, Sara, like she was my real child."

"She is a real child, Liz!"

"I know! She's my baby. I love her."

"She's human!" I said.

"She's a Neanderthal human. I know."

"No!" I said. "She's human, Liz. There aren't different types of humans. There aren't regular humans and Neanderthal humans. There are just humans."

Liz calmed down. "Now you're just being silly."

I began sobbing again, this time with my head in my hands. Achilles was worried. He jumped up next to me and nuzzled his head onto my lap.

"I made her because I want her, Sara," Liz said calmly, sitting next to me. "I want to be the mother of a Neanderthal child. Just like I've said, over and over again. We are going to raise her. She will be part of our family. She'll be like a big sister to the other children."

"She'll be like the dog!" I shouted.

"She's not!"

"Part child, part pet, depending on how she turns out."

"She's not like the dog! How can you say that?"

"You can't just make a child as a prototype, Liz!" I said.

"I'm not!" she said. "It's not wrong. People have children for all sorts of reasons. Mom said she had me because she had too many mimosas at Auntie Carol's wedding, and Daddy looked good in his polyester suit."

"That's hardly the same thing!" I said.

"And she had you because she was afraid that Luka and I would fight too much if there were just two of us. The reason we are born isn't sacred, Sara. People have kids so their brothers can have bone marrow donors. It doesn't make them less valuable."

"This is different," I said.

"Why?" she asked. "The baby will be loved. You know she will be. I have the means to give her the best care possible."

"John would never have wanted this. He wouldn't have wanted this. You know he wouldn't have wanted this!" I said, through more tears. But even as I said it I was not sure it was true. John was an ethical man in all things: his technology, his business. But he had loved Liz so much, so blindly. He would have wanted anything she wanted.

"He told me he wanted it," Liz said curtly.

"You must have misunderstood," I answered.

She stood up and paced the room again, calming herself. "He always wanted children. He just didn't want to pass on his disease. Now we can make our children but with no disease," she said. "It is what he would have wanted, Sara. You must realize that!"

We did not know what caused John's disease in everyone, but she was right. We knew what caused the disease in John. I sequenced John's DNA when he first got sick. I sequenced his mother and his father. His parents were not sick so we compared his genome to theirs, with the idea that however he differed from both of them might be the cause of the disease. But nothing made sense and we did not have enough time to figure out what the mutations he had were doing. But because he gave us his spinal cord and his brain when he died, and because we sequenced the genomes of hundreds of others who had the same disease, we figured it out. Mei discovered three mutations in John's genome that had made him susceptible to the disease. She mapped the pathway, from his DNA to the rest of his cells, and showed the effect of the mutations on his neurons. She was even in the process of making a mouse with John's disease, by changing the mouse's DNA in the same place that John's DNA had mutations, to create John's murine avatar.

Even if we had known the cause of John's disease when he was alive, we would have been powerless to treat it. There was no medicine, no surgery. In the race between science and the illness, the illness won by many, many years. This wasn't uncommon. The same was true for other diseases. For instance, we had known the genetic sequence that caused Huntington's disease for decades, but we didn't have a cure. We knew the mutation that caused Familial Fatal Insomnia but did not have any treatments yet.

But if the Barlas Lab's artificial chromosomes worked, it would be easy to change John's DNA in the spots that had caused his disease, to make DNA with a sequence that was John's everywhere except in those three spots. Then making the genome of a baby that was John and Liz's would just require taking a chromosome from each of them, like in a regular baby. It could be done.

"I want you to be happy for us!" she said, earnestly.

There was, of course, no us anymore. There was just her.

"This baby…you don't even know if she will be healthy," I said.

"She will!" she said. "The baby is doing great! You saw her yourself."

"You shouldn't be doing this," I said. "It's not right."

"It is! It's wonderful."

"Liz, there's a difference between right and wrong. There is an absolute, incontrovertible difference between right and wrong. And this is wrong."

It was an impasse that would not be breached.

I went to the guest room and sobbed on the bed until I felt nauseated and then slept for a few hours.

I woke up thinking about the formal ethical training scientists had. We're taught, first and foremost, that we cannot experiment on humans as if they were animals. We cannot call someone an "other," define them as not-quite-human just because they look a little different than us. Every year I had to fill out a quiz on the computer to prove that I understood that. Everyone at the Daltry did: the director, the scientists, the woman who works in the lunchroom, and people who deliver the mail. We are so vigilant because it has happened before. Scientists, trying to understand a disease or do something that they told themselves was really important, have in the past convinced themselves that someone was an "other."

And now it was happening again. I do not know if I could have stopped it but I knew I had not really tried, not with the vigor that it deserved.

I quietly left Liz's apartment and drove home in the middle of the night.

chapter thirty-three

I did not hear from Liz in the weeks after I skulked out of her apartment. Theo emailed me once, and then called, but I didn't respond and he did not try again. I assumed that Liz told him I had learned that there really was a Neanderthal growing in the chimpanzee, and what my reaction was. I suppose he may have been annoyed that I had stolen a sample from his lab, but I didn't lose sleep over that. I was feeling exhausted, all the time, emotionally and physically drained by the previous months.

I tried to resume my normal life and managed to get the results from the Panola birdstorm data published. It went quickly, in weeks rather than the usual months, because the journal's editor really wanted the article. The growing size of the outbreak was making people nervous.

I received an e-mail from Angus near the end of September. It said:

Dear Sara,

I read your paper in the American Genomicist Journal and I wanted to let you know that I thought it was superb. It is nice to see that some progress is finally being made on Panola. I imagine it could turn into a real ecological disaster if it keeps spreading.

In other news, I thought a lot about what you said about finding the right sort of woman. So I did a little research on the Internet and I spent a week of my summer holiday down in England at the place in the link below. It's sort of a camp for grownups.

I met a really nice girl there and we have been seeing each other for a couple of months now. Her name is Holly. She is the children's librarian in a town nearby, about a half hour south of here. She is English, but other than that she's really lovely and I hope you will get to meet her next January when you come for Julia's defense. It's going to be a good one. She's got some nice findings.

I hope things are not going too badly with the Neanderthal project. We have started getting more coverage of it on our news and frankly I haven't liked any of it. But I guess that's the press for you. That Barlas guy seems like a piece of work.

But I thought I should let you know that we received our Barlas Labs chromosomes and they look quite good so far.

Anyway, here is a link for the camp. That's Holly on the opening screen. =)

All the best,
Angus Gupta PhD, MD, MSc

I clicked on the link on the bottom of the page and was taken to the page for the Dark Adventures Caravan Park. It seemed to be where people went to get away from it all, to have a week in the great British outdoors, sloshing around in the mud, walking in the countryside, and getting tied buck naked to a tree by a leather-clad software engineer. The English, it seems, like to experience their hardcore S&M in the rain while wearing wellies and getting bitten by midges.

A photo of Holly filled the opening screen. The librarian was outside by a lake, naked with her arms bound at her wrists behind her back. She was face down and horizontal, dangling a few feet off the ground, suspended from the branches of a tree by four leather ropes that were wrapped around her shoulders and thighs. It reminded me of one of those racks that you hang pots on over a stove. She had thin rosy cheeks, mousey hair, and disproportionately pendulous breasts swinging in the breeze. There was a pink and yellow apple in her mouth. It looked like a Cox's pippin.

That's how you're supposed to do it, I thought. She's bound *to* something. A tree. She wasn't going anywhere.

The picture of Holly was displayed large on my 32 inch monitor when Mei came by my desk to see if I wanted to go to lunch.

"What you got there, Sara?" she asked.

"Ummmmm…Uhhhhhh…stupid computer viruses," I offered. "This junk is always coming up. You know what it's like."

"Really? I never get anything like that. Maybe you should take it over to the help desk."

"Yeah, that's a good idea," I said. "I'll take it down this afternoon."

After lunch I replied to Angus's e-mail:

Angus,

Thank you for your kind words about our paper.

I'm glad you met your soul mate at sex camp. I'm looking forward to meeting her – she seems sweet, from her picture. You might want to warn people in advance if you're sending them naked photos of your girlfriend, though. They might be at work.

As for the Neanderthal project, I am unfortunately coming around to your way of thinking. That is, I do think there might actually be a Neanderthal baby growing in that chimp's uterus. I don't know what to do about it. It seems the cat is out of the proverbial bag. I hope for a good outcome, but I don't know what a good outcome would be.

And, yeah, Theo Barlas. He sure is something.

Good luck with the viruses!

Hearts,
Sara

So Angus had found his soul mate. I wondered if your soul mate was just the person you wanted to have sex with the most. We try to make it into something deeper, but why?

That kind of attraction seems to come from a drive that is more essential than the part of us that worries about souls, the part of us that is ruled by higher thought, logic, and good sense. It seems to come from something more primal, the back of our brains not the front.

I do not think we can choose our soul mate. It just happens. So sometimes your soul mate is wonderful. And sometimes your soul mate is an asshole.

I didn't know what my soul mate was, even though I was beginning to confront the fact that I knew who it was. I had been afraid for so long that everything about Theo was fake, that he was a fraud. But everything he had ever told me was true. It was a horrible truth, though. Worse than a fraud. I felt connected to him, as if he was as much a part of me as my own arm, but I could not speak to him while there was a Neanderthal baby gestating inside the chimp.

chapter thirty-four

On a chilly evening at the end of September, I was sitting in my living room, sipping a ginger tea and wondering whether I would be able to keep down dinner. I had not made it to work that day and the kitchen seemed far away and nothing in it was appealing. I spent the day on the couch alternately watching the TV news coverage from Long Island and sleeping with the dog curled up at my feet, content to join him in his favorite activity, all-day napping.

"Will there be a Neanderthal? Or is this a scientific scam? With just weeks before the baby's due date, correspondent Erin Brooks reports from outside Barlas Labs."

The same woman who had ambushed Billy outside his gym stood in the middle of my TV holding a microphone saying a lot that added up to "Yes, we have no bananas." She was perfectly coiffed with a pressed suit and her makeup was so thick it looked as if it had been applied by a mortician. Behind her was the scene outside the lab: news trucks, protesters, food trucks. On one side people were carrying signs and bed sheets painted with slogans: "No New Species," "God hates Neanderthals. That's why their extinct," and "One True Human." The other side had the contrary view: "Welcome Home, Neanderthal!" "Freedom from Extinction Now," "Forward to the Past." One, "Legalise Pot," was both off-topic and poorly spelled. A line of policemen stood between the opposing sides. I wondered if Officer Barnes was among them.

Sitting on my couch, almost asleep, I was numb to all of it. Nothing was in my control. For weeks now waves of nausea had been washing over me. Some days were worse than others. I was missing work. I was so tired that I felt like I would melt through the couch's cushions. And still, in the midst of all this, or maybe because it was so tied to all of this, the Neanderthal project and Theo took precedence in my mind.

A Neanderthal baby was going to be born and there was nothing I could do to stop it. The rules of natural selection, the rules of nature, would be broken. The paparazzo outside had left for Long Island. The dog had ceased his incessant barking. In the quiet of my apartment I felt like I was in the eye of the storm, with nothing to do but wait for the winds to come and blow everything down. Then the phone rang.

"It's time," Hank said. "They're getting ready to take the baby out."

"Now?" I said.

"Now. They just wheeled the chimp in."

"Why so soon?"

"Katarina was worried. It happened all of a sudden."

"What's wrong?" I asked.

"Don't panic. She said everything's fine. The baby's heart rate was a little high, that's all."

"How's Liz?"

"A wreck."

"What's it like down there?" I asked.

"At the lab? Twelve news trucks. Protesters. Every crackpot from here to Michigan. Some lady's set up a fortune teller booth in the parking lot. She's selling tarot cards with Neanderthals on them."

It was a carnival and the little baby was the freak show.

"Who's there?" I asked.

"Just Liz and the Barlas Labs people. Billy stayed in NY. He says he's going to be a decoy. Keeps turning the lights on and off in Liz's apartment."

"Is he walking around in a wig?"

"It wasn't my idea," Hank said.

No one had listened to any of Hank's ideas. He was unquestionably qualified, but he had not been consulted about anything, not about what information would be released to the public, not about where the chimpanzee would be housed, not about where the birth would take place. Nothing. But he was stuck managing the security mess outside. He did it for Liz.

"You're supposed to pick up your mom on the way down," he told me. "She's packing a bag."

"What? I'm supposed to come now?"

"Yup. That's how it works, auntie."

Four hours in the car, probably five if I picked up my mother. There were pills. I had gone to the ER to get rehydrated a few days before and the doctor had given me some pills to keep me from vomiting to death. They gave me a headache. The drive would be torture, but I had no choice. And part of me did want to see the Neanderthal. I was, after all, a scientist, still curious if horrified by it all. She would be born, for better or for worse, by the time we got there. I took a dose of the pills and stuck the rest in my handbag. I told Achilles we were going for a ride.

chapter thirty-five

MY mother and I tried to sneak through the crowd outside the lab unnoticed, but that was a naïve plan. Even though we tried to use a back entrance, as Hank had instructed us, we were spotted and recognized. In moments a crowd stampeded towards us.

The reporters were screaming. I picked up Achilles as my mother was swallowed by the mob. "Mom!" I shouted, trying to push my way through. Everyone was shouting questions at her. A video camera struck me in the head. It was a cacophony. Where was my mother? Was she in that? I kept getting jostled. I gripped Achilles so hard he yelped.

Then suddenly I felt Hank's hand on my arm. "My mom!" I said.

"We've got her."

He guided me through the crowd, past the screaming hoard to the office building's door. The crowd regurgitated my mother, escorted by one of Hank's guards. We passed through the building doors and they shut, muffling the commotion behind us. We traveled the silent corridor to the Barlas Labs' door. Theo led us through the empty cubicles and back to the laboratory.

I had doubted her existence. I had doubted her reality. For months I had declared her to be an impossibility.

And then, in that moment, in a chair placed in the corner of the lab, we saw her.

She was cuddled in Liz's arms, her little face, her little body. Her mother introduced her. "This is Svea."

And there she was.

Not an abstraction but a child with a name. The little Neanderthal baby existed.

Svea was the first newborn baby I had ever seen. I had seen my co-worker's babies, of course, brought into work for their fifteen minutes of fame, and babies in the supermarket. But those were older babies: a few weeks, a few months. Svea was my first very little baby, not even a day old. Only grandparents and aunties and hospital staff get to see these babies. She was so tiny. Little hands, little feet. She looked so tender and so peaceful there in Liz's arms, wrapped in her pink blanket, her eyes shut, her skin still ruddy from her birth.

I didn't look for the differences. I didn't care. I was overwhelmed with feelings of love for this tiny child, to hold her, to protect her. I didn't notice the differences. I observed them. I remembered them: her high forehead, her broad nose, her thick hair, the peach fuzz on her face that was soft and light but still a little different from what most babies have. I can analyze them if I recall her picture in my mind's eye, but at that moment I didn't see them. I didn't think. I just experienced being in the presence of this infant. I was incapable of anything else.

"Let me hold her," my mother said.

"I just got her to sleep," Liz replied.

Her mother's voice woke the child. Svea opened her eyes, looked around a little, aimlessly. She opened her mouth as if to say something, and then changed her mind, nuzzled into Liz, and went back to sleep.

I was in love. We all were.

It seemed strange to have Svea sleep in the lab as if she were still an experiment, so we moved her, her bassinet, and her blankets into Theo's office.

"When can she come home?" Liz asked.

"A few days," Theo said. "Katarina wants to make sure everything is alright."

Katarina had been checking on her every hour or so, dividing her time between Svea and her other patient, Linda, who was recovering well from her cesarean.

"She's perfect!" Liz said.

"Her temperature's a little high."

"That's just how she is," Liz said.

"We're only talking about a few days," Theo said.

"I'll stay here," Liz said.

"Of course."

I stayed at Barlas Labs that night. We all did. Liz fed Svea from a bottle, forgoing the contraption that piped the milk up to her breasts in favor of the quiet simplicity of holding the baby in her arms. When it came right down to it there did not seem to be a way for a mother to feed her child that wasn't natural.

For a few minutes I got to babysit. It was the only moment that Liz left Svea's bedside, and that was only because she hadn't eaten for a full day. I watched Svea as she lay sleeping in her bassinet on Theo's oak desk. She was only five and a half pounds. "You're lighter than my smallest dumbbell," I whispered to her. "I could do thirty reps with you."

The room was dim. I had turned down the lights because I thought she would sleep better. Achilles was curled up under the desk. I wondered what it had been like the last time she was alive. Or not her, but the Neanderthal who her DNA sequence was taken from. I wondered if she had had an aunt when she started out the first time, who had watched her sleeping like this. She was sweetness itself. Of course she had. The whole village would have watched her sleep.

Theo came in and stood next to me. He put his arm around my waist. "Your niece."

"My niece. She's beautiful."

"She is."

"I'm still scared for her, what she'll be like. Mentally."

"That she won't be smart like you?"

"No. I'm scared that she will be. That she'll be smart enough to know she's different, to understand how different she is, to know she's alone."

He didn't reply because Svea began crying again. I picked her up and tried to settle her.

"Is she OK?" I asked. "She seems to be crying a lot."

Theo didn't know any more than I did, so he went to get Katarina.

She turned poor Svea over and stuck a thermometer in her baby Neanderthal butt.

"I think she has an infection," she said. "I'm going to start her on ampicillin."

"What kind of infection?" I asked.

"Probably just a mild strep infection. We took cultures."

"Cultures will take two days."

"We're starting her on antibiotics now, to be safe."

"I can sequence a blood sample," I suggested eagerly. "Then we can see what is infecting her. That will be quicker."

"If you like," Katarina responded condescendingly. "Her blood draws are in the lab."

"Shouldn't we call a pediatrician?" I asked.

"I am qualified to treat all species, not just one," Katarina said. "All ages, all species."

And with that she left the room to get the medical supplies she needed.

She was right, in one way. Svea's physiology might be a little different from other babies, and Katarina's veterinary training might make her better able to respond to those differences than a pediatrician.

But I wasn't satisfied. She was implementing the standard medical treatment, but I knew the antibiotic would only work if Svea's illness was caused by bacteria. It would not do anything against a virus. I wanted to sequence her blood so we could see what was causing her fever. Her blood would contain sequences from the pathogen, just as Linda's blood had contained Svea's sequences.

I ran two samples on the Barlas Labs sequencer: one of DNA, which would detect bacteria and DNA viruses, and one of RNA, which would catch any RNA viruses that the DNA sequencing missed. Sequencing was not done routinely for patients with infections. The cost was too high. But Svea was not a normal patient, and I was not a normal aunt. I had access to the lab's sequencer. And even though Katarina was probably right, that Svea probably had a common bacterial infection that would respond to antibiotics, I wanted to be sure.

I started the sequencing run, and when I got back to the ad hoc nursery Svea looked a little worse. She was fussing, and her face looked a little red. Liz was having trouble getting her to eat. In the hours it took the sequencing run to complete, her temperature climbed.

Katarina put an I.V. in Svea's arm. "Don't worry," she sang. "We just might need to give her some fluids."

When we were alone, Liz teared up.

"I'm scared, Sara," Liz said. "She doesn't seem right."

"No, she doesn't."

"Do you think they made a mistake? Did Xiao make her wrong?" she asked with a voice full of anguish as she leaned over Svea.

"It doesn't look like a genetic problem, Liz. It looks like an infection."

"But she's not responding to the antibiotics."

"Maybe it's viral. The sequencing run will be done in a couple hours. We'll know then."

When the run was finished and the computation had only a few seconds left, I sat down in the lab with my computer and looked at the data.

I checked the DNA first. Nothing unusual there: a couple sequences from *E. coli*, a common contaminant in the lab. The rest was Neanderthal or human, most likely from me or Katarina when she took Svea's blood. Svea didn't have a bacterial infection.

"It must be viral," I thought.

With trepidation I looked at the RNA. Most of the sequences, 89% of them, were Neanderthal. There were a few I couldn't match. But the rest, seven percent of all the RNA in Svea's blood, were from one source.

Panola.

"Oh, no!" I said it out loud because it was bad.

Seven percent may not seem like much but for a viral infection, it was a huge amount. I was used to seeing infections where maybe a couple thousand out of a million reads belonged to the virus, and these were samples from patients who were very sick. Even in birds that died from Panola, the viral sequences were never higher than one or two percent.

Poor Svea. The virus was ravaging her.

I thought about her little body in her little bed. Panola didn't infect humans. We were able to fight it. Svea was trying to. Her fever was high because she was trying to make her body too hot for Panola. Her white blood cells were elevated because they were trying to eat the Panola.

But I was worried this wouldn't be enough. Human genes have evolved to fight infections. New viruses appear and we evolve to fight them. I had been exposed to Panola during the birdstorm and nothing happened to me. Linda's species, too, had evolved modern defenses. She was exposed but didn't get sick.

Svea's genes, on the other hand, had sat out the last thirty thousand years of the infection wars. Her long-dead ancestors were never tested by more recent epidemics like leprosy, smallpox, bubonic plague, yellow fever, Spanish flu, cholera, and AIDS. Each plague was deadly but people with the strongest genes survived to pass on the weapons that worked against the infections. Viruses had evolved, too, each one changing to get a little stronger, a little better able to subvert our defenses, enter our cells, and wreak havoc. The Panola virus had modern weapons. Svea's weapons, her genes and her immune system, were thirty thousand years old. She was fighting a nuclear enemy with sling shots and spears.

When we were caught in the birdstorm and Panola rained down on us, Svea was there too, inside of Linda's belly. Linda may have become infected, asymptomatically passing the virus onto Svea through her placenta. Or the virus may have stayed on her fur or in her blood, infecting Svea during labor. However it happened, Panola was making Svea very sick.

I was the world's leading expert on Panola, the person who had studied it the most, who best understood its genome and its proteins. But I didn't know how to fight it. I could tell you what its genome looked like and I could design the next experiments. But I was not a clinician. I could not treat her. Svea needed the care of a virologist, a doctor. She needed the best person in the world not for studying viruses, but for treating them in real patients. That was not me.

But I knew who it was and I had his phone number.

chapter thirty-six

I let the phone ring and ring but no one answered. The call went to voice mail and I tried again. And again. And again.

Finally, a thick Scottish voice shouted into the phone, "It's 3:30 in the bloody morning, who the hell is this?"

"Angus, it's Sara. The baby's sick."

"Who? Sara?"

"Sara Nicoletta."

"What? What baby?"

"She has a Panola infection. Angus, she looks terrible."

"What baby? Babies don't get Panola infections."

"It affects Neanderthal babies."

"Hold on. You're talking rubbish. Give me a minute."

There was silence on the other end of the line for a minute and then the sound of a toilet flushing.

"Now what are you going on about?"

"She had the baby. The chimp had the baby. And now the baby's sick."

"You're fucking kidding me!" he said. "A Neanderthal? For real?"

"Yes, they delivered the Neanderthal. And now she's sick. She's very sick Angus. You have to help me."

"She's sick?"

"She's sick. She has an infection."

"What are her symptoms?" he asked.

I told him Svea's details: her temperature, her blood counts, her weight, when she ate and how much. I told him how fussy she was. And then I told him she had a Panola infection.

"Panola doesn't infect humans, Sara," he said.

"Angus, I sequenced her blood. There's nothing else there. It's Neanderthal and Panola. A lot of Panola. Seven percent of the RNA in her plasma is from Panola virus."

"Seven percent?" he said. "Shit."

His assessment was the same as mine. Seven percent was huge.

"What do we do?" My voice cracked with desperation.

"Well I don't have a treatment for Panola," he said. "Specifically. But its closest relative is flu, right? That was what you found?"

"It's not flu, Angus."

"But it's related. It has a neuraminidase gene, right?"

"Yes."

"What's it like? The neuraminidase?"

"It's similar to flu's, but not exactly the same. The gene sequence has a few substitutions. It's evolving faster than the rest of the genes in the Panola genome."

"If there's only a few substitutions it probably functions the same as in flu. We'll treat it like flu. Put her on oseltamivir—Tamiflu. It stops the flu virus from spreading so it's our best bet for stopping Panola. Give me a second to look up the dosage…"

The Panola virus particles were entering Svea's cells and using her own cells' machinery to make more copies of the virus. To exit her cells and move on to a new host, each freshly made virus had to be snipped by the neuraminidase protein. Angus wanted to use oseltamir to attack the neuraminidase and contain the virus.

He told me the dose to give her and I asked him if Svea would be able to tolerate the medicine.

"I have no idea," Angus said. "I've never treated a Neanderthal."

"Okay," I replied. We had no choice but to treat a Neanderthal with Panola like a human with the flu.

"Let me have a look at her," he said. "Call me back on Skype."

I went to the room that was now Svea's nursery.

"What's that?" Katarina asked, as I set up my laptop next to Svea's bedside.

"It's Angus Gupta. Svea has Panola virus. She needs seven milligrams of Tamiflu, now. Do you have it?"

Katarina looked at Liz, and then at Theo. "She is much more likely to have a bacterial infection…"

I turned on the computer and began connecting with Angus.

"No, she has Panola. I got the sequencing back. Do you have Tamiflu in your bag?"

Katarina looked around again. Everyone looked back.

"I have a few doses. We use it to treat parvovirus in dogs," Katarina said. "I'll go get it."

"I'll have Hank get some more from the pharmacy," Theo said. "Who is Angus Gupta?"

"He's a virologist in Scotland. One of the world's best virologists, and the only physician who has studied Panola. He's my friend."

"Will that fix her?" Liz asked, still sitting inches from Svea's little body.

Angus came on the video.

"Angus, this is my niece, Svea," I said.

He was silent for a moment, staring at her. And then, "Wow. She's a Neanderthal."

"She's my niece."

"Wow."

"She's not feeling very well."

"I can see."

Angus performed an exam, from Scotland. I moved Svea's hands and feet for him, as he needed, which she did not like, and I read off the vitals as he told me to measure them. Meanwhile, Katarina came in with the antiviral medication and dispensed it into Svea's mouth. Her little face wrinkled up at the taste, but all of it seemed to go into her mouth. Katarina handed her to Liz to see if she could get her to feed and wash it down.

"Will this fix her?" Liz asked again, taking the now screaming child into her arms.

She looked first at Katarina. Katarina looked at Angus, three thousand miles away with an anguished expression on his face.

"I hope so," he said. "Her viral load is very high."

They were words, I am sure, that he had said before, but I do not think that made it any easier. I do not think that is something a normal person can ever get used to.

My mother put her hand over her mouth and left the room to call Luka. She told him to come down right away. I called Billy and told him the same thing.

chapter thirty-seven

A cytokine storm occurs when a body throws everything it's got at an infection it cannot beat. Cytokines are signaling molecules that tell the immune system to go to a certain part of the body to fight an invader. If the invader is not conquered, they signal again. More fighters come and fail, so cytokines signal for more. And then you have a storm. The body ends up with too many fighters in one spot. This causes problems: high fever, low blood pressure, difficulty breathing, and hemorrhage. In the end a cytokine storm can be fatal, a death in which your own body fights its way to a Pyrrhic victory over the invader. These storms can be as deadly as the infection itself. They were at the heart of the catastrophic Spanish flu pandemic that swept across the globe in 1918 and killed seventy-five million people.

Svea was swirling in the eye of the storm.

She could not be consoled now. Her fever had crept even higher. At times she would shiver. Her skin looked flush. She must have been so scared. Liz was beside her, holding her, begging her to calm down, to please calm down, to try to eat something, but it was no use.

I put another sample of Svea's blood on the sequencer to monitor the effect of Tamiflu on her viral load.

On Angus's instructions, Katarina gave Svea medicine to calm the cytokine storm, but it seemed to be having little effect.

I shuffled in and out of her room. I was still suffering from nausea and realized I did not have enough pills with me to quell it completely, so I was rationing them, taking half a dose. This left me queasy and tired, running to the bathroom to vomit every couple hours.

On the way back to the lab after one of these incidents I saw Xiao and Theo in the hall having a heated discussion.

"The experiment worked, Theo!" Xiao said.

"Who is going to see it that way?" he responded.

"This technology is important. Think how much good it can do."

"I know it is. But we can't release it now, not like this."

"We gave birth to a Neanderthal. We can release our data. We have a Neanderthal."

"We have a very sick Neanderthal."

"How were we to know she would get an infection? The experiment worked."

I was irate. "You call this *working*?" I shouted. I was incredulous.

Xiao looked at me and then spun around and walked back to his lab.

"How is she?" Theo asked.

He looked distraught, like he needed comforting, or absolution. But absolution was something I could not give him. Xiao was right. He could not have foreseen that the chimpanzee would be kidnapped, that a freak occurrence would expose her to a new virus, that she would be born with an infection. Her DNA sequence, it seemed, was good. The gestation inside the chimpanzee, it seemed, was good. The experiment, within the parameters they had set, worked correctly. But still, I could not absolve him.

"It was a bad idea." That was all I could say to him, through tears. "It was a bad idea."

Several hours after she began the medicine, Svea's viral sequence content remained stuck at seven percent.

"Angus," I asked the computer screen, "is the Tamiflu working?"

"Maybe," he said. "The virus isn't spreading."

"Why isn't she getting better?" Liz said. Billy was with her. He had his arm around her.

There was no answer. Even in the best circumstances, even in the best hospitals, regular human babies catch viruses that saw have a lot of experience treating. Even in the best circumstances, babies sometimes die. Svea was fighting as hard as she could. Too hard. And she wasn't going to get any better.

"We should try to make her comfortable, now," Angus said.

Liz took her in her arms. "Oh, sweetie," she said, which calmed Svea a little. As new as she was, she already recognized her mother.

chapter thirty-eight

We hadn't chosen Svea's godmother. I was already her aunt so choosing me seemed redundant. Instead we gave her two godfathers, Billy and Hank. It was not strictly kosher. Neither of them was even Catholic, but a lot about Svea's life hadn't been strictly kosher and Luka was not about to start an argument with Liz over semantics. Not now.

My brother, on his knees next to Svea, took the water bottle from Liz's bag. "Father in Heaven," he began, "when the Spirit came down upon Jesus at His Baptism in the Jordan…."

Katarina and Xiao had gone back to the lab. Angus had closed his connection from Scotland. I was against the wall facing Theo as he watched us from the hallway. His eyes were on Svea. His face was expressionless. My family and I were watching a child die. We were watching my niece die. I thought about the conversation he had in the hallway with Xiao and I was not sure what he was watching.

"You revealed Him as Your own Beloved Son. Keep me, your child, born of water and the Spirit, faithful to my calling…."

Theo made eye contact with me, and then it ended. In an instant it was all over.

Svea was, finally, silent.

Liz started shaking. My mother began weeping loudly.

My brother continued his prayers for Svea as she entered God's kingdom, with tears streaming down his face. "May I, who share in Your life as Your child through Baptism, follow in Christ's path of service to people…"

Theo was staring at Svea. I didn't see tears in his eyes. At that moment I didn't know if he saw her, or if he saw her body, a specimen, a proof of concept. I felt queasy again. The emotions. The grief. I felt them but did not experience them fully, not in that room. I was an observer, watching and acting. I was Svea's aunt. I had the wherewithal to reach into my pocket, take out my car keys, and press them into the palm of my mother's hand. She looked at me, confused for a second and then, as Svea's grandmother, she understood.

I walked out of the room. Dashed, actually, with my hand over my mouth, towards the Barlas Labs bathroom.

I could hear my mom speaking in the hall. "Go with her," she ordered. Theo didn't say anything. "Go with her. That baby she's carrying, it's yours, isn't it?"

Theo obeyed. Maybe it was the shock, but he let himself be ordered around, maybe for the first time in his life. A moment later he was standing outside the bathroom door, the same bathroom I vomited in the first time I came to Barlas Labs. But this time I was vomiting and crying.

I don't know how long we were there. When I was done, Theo said how happy he was. There was a real, unmistakable joy in his face and in his voice that made me feel a little guilty, that I had let him find out he was going to be a father in this way, that I had intentionally distracted him to allow my family to take Svea, and because I felt the same joy over the baby growing inside me, even though little Svea, my niece, had just passed away.

When we went back to the room, the contents of Liz's enormous handbag were in a pile on the floor: her French lipstick, her Italian sunglasses, thousands of dollars' worth of feminine detritus all dumped out and left for trash. The room was empty. Svea was gone.

chapter thirty-nine

In the small hours of Thursday morning, Hank's army escorted my family and Billy through the mob scene outside: the reporters, the evangelicals, the hippies, and the science nerds. Svea was inches from them and no one knew. They looked at Liz and they saw a story, a demon, a savior, a trophy wife, a wealthy flake. No one noticed the agony on her face. No one noticed how she held her purse clasped in her arms. No one saw a distraught mother cradling her dead child, wrapped in a cashmere shroud, hidden inside a handbag.

Hank hustled them through the parking lot, trailed by the shouting mob and TV cameras, while his security guards grumbled that no one had called for my car to be brought around. Achilles followed at their feet, barking his way through the crowd and biting at the ankles of those who blocked his way or stood between him and his baby.

Hank piled them into my car, my brother still wearing his white collar and taking a few moments to remember how to drive a stick. Then Hank turned back to his duties as guard, making sure they could get out of the parking lot safely. Hank's crew stopped most of the reporters from leaving the parking lot. Only one news van got through.

I watched on television as they followed my car for a while. Luka did his best to lose the reporters without breaking the speed limit. Then Theo called a press conference and the reporters trailing my family retreated back to Barlas Labs in hopes of getting something more interesting than a slow-moving IROC.

Theo told the mob that the Neanderthal baby had passed away due to an infection unrelated to her genetic engineering and that her body would not be available for scientific examination, per the wishes of the Nicoletta-Corbit family. A reporter asked the obvious, "Without a body, how do you expect us to believe there was a Neanderthal baby?"

On the news footage you can see Theo pause, his face wrinkled into an expression of discomfort.

"I can't."

Then the crowd broke into an uproar, reporters shouting more questions but producing only noise.

Theo went back inside.

My mother told me later that, freed from the reporters, Luka drove north. Billy sat next to him. My mother sat in the back seat with her arm around Liz, who held Svea in her lap. At sunrise, they reached the Adirondacks. They found a hardware store along the way and bought a shovel, the same one we later used to plant a weeping cherry tree in the backyard.

They found a trailhead along the road and walked into the woods.

They say they went for miles. I don't know where. The exact spot must be lost to memory now. But somewhere in the forest, not far off an overgrown trail, they found a small hill with soft dirt at the top and autumn leaves surrounding it in a blaze of color and sunshine. And this old woman, this man, and this priest dug a hole, just big enough and just deep enough, and lined it with rocks. The child's mother said one last goodbye to her daughter, and she placed her little body, wrapped in cashmere, into the ground. Luka fashioned a cross from sticks and his shoe laces. Liz wouldn't let him leave it sticking up. She wanted Svea's grave hidden and protected. So he laid the cross down over her body and covered it with a thin layer of dirt and leaves. Then they all kneeled and used their hands to bury Svea with earth.

When they were done the small white dog, his curly hair sparkling in the sun, sat down next to Svea's grave, not possibly comprehending what had happened but still understanding all of it. He looked up to the sun and he howled the ancient call of the wolf.

How many hours are there in a life?

The Neanderthal had been resurrected. She lived for less than a hundred hours but in that time she was a daughter, a patient, a niece, and even a cousin. She was loved, christened, and mourned. She was not an experiment, or a hominid, or a prototype. She was a baby. She was our baby.

And the Neanderthal was once again extinct.

epilogue

It was May and Theo needed a ride home.

He had gotten off easy. His father's money and connections ensured that.

The media had demanded something that looked like justice. Members of the public had invested a tiny amount of energy into deciding whether to join the pro- or the anti-Neanderthal camp. Now they were convinced that it had all been a hoax and they felt silly. They wanted Theo's head on a stick.

The district attorney's office agreed but was stymied by logic. He committed fraud, they said, but Theo's lawyers argued that no money had ever changed hands and their so-called victim, Liz, wouldn't return their calls. Theo had traversed the bounds of ethical research, they claimed. His lawyers pointed out that the week before, the district attorney had claimed the baby never happened. They argued that Theo had created a public nuisance, but his lawyers pointed out that it is not illegal to irritate people.

The legal maneuverings could have gone on indefinitely, but after a few weeks Theo called the district attorney himself to arrange a plea bargain. He would serve five months for the possession of a chimpanzee without a proper permit, starting as soon as possible.

Theo was going to prison and he wanted to have it all behind him when the baby was born.

"But you'll be a week late," I protested.

"She'll wait for me," he said.

And she did. Barely.

I was waiting in the car outside the prison doors when the contractions started. I didn't really know what they were at first, but when Theo stepped out of the prison gates, late and with a smirk on his face, I told him he was going to have to drive.

"You got the IROC painted," he said.

"I wanted you to come out in style."

"It looks good."

"We should get going," I said. "It's a four hour drive."

"We have hospitals in New York. She doesn't have to be born in Boston."

"Of course she does," I said. "She waited for you. She'll wait for me."

"And if she doesn't?" he asked.

"I'm sure you can handle it."

He made a grunting noise that did not contain words but communicated both disagreement and acquiescence.

Then he put the car in gear, turned on the tape deck, and Triumph played "Magic Power" as we headed for the Interstate.

If you enjoyed *The Neanderthal's Aunt*,
you might like other titles published by
ScienceThrillers Media.

ScienceThrillers Media specializes in
page-turning stories, both fiction and popular
nonfiction, that have real science, technology,
engineering, mathematics, or medicine in the
plot.

Visit our website and join the STM mailing
list to learn about new releases.

ScienceThrillersMedia.com

Share your thoughts about *The Neanderthal's Aunt* by leaving a
review on your favorite social media, or the book sites:

GoodReads
Barnes & Noble
amazon
iBooks

Follow author Gina DeMarco on twitter @DrGinaDeMarco

Contact ScienceThrillers Media
publisher@ScienceThrillersMedia.com

Science notes from the author

The characters and situations in *The Neanderthal's Aunt* are completely fictional. However, much of the science in the story is an accurate depiction of science and biological techniques in use today. These notes clarify where the boundaries between science and fiction lie.

The Neanderthal Genome

The draft sequence of the Neanderthal genome was published by Green and coauthors in *Science* in 2010. The genome was sequenced by Svante Paabo's lab at the Max Planck Institute in Germany, from DNA that was obtained from the bone of a Neanderthal woman found in a cave in Croatia, as described in the text.

Sequencing the genome was a monumental feat. It's difficult to sequence very old DNA because the chemical bonds that join the molecules break down. It is currently believed, for example, that dinosaur DNA, which would be 165 million years old, will never be sequenced because so many bonds have by now been broken that the sequences are all fragmented into pieces that are too short to be informative. While Neanderthal DNA is much more recent (thirty thousand years old), the quality of the Neanderthal genome sequence is still not as high as, for example, the human genome.

In addition, the Neanderthal bones are also contaminated with a lot of other species, such as bacteria. Researchers could not, at the time, efficiently separate the Neanderthal and contaminant DNA before sequencing so they sequenced everything. When they were done they distinguished between the Neanderthal and squatters in the bone by seeing which sequences looked most similar to the human genome, the computational equivalent of throwing spaghetti against a wall and seeing what sticks. It is possible that if the Neanderthal had pieces of DNA that were very different from anything in the human or other primate genomes, it might not have been recognized as Neanderthal.

Subsequent publications have improved the Neanderthal genome's quality by sequencing additional samples. However, it is worth noting that even the human genome, which has been sequenced thousands of times from readily available, high quality samples, has regions which still are not fully sequenced. Completely finishing a genome is particularly difficult in repetitive regions, where the same series of bases is repeated many hundreds of times. If repetitive regions are longer than the longest read the machine can generate then it is a lot of work to figure out the correct sequence for that region. Many of these repetitive regions are probably not very interesting and new technology is being introduced all the time to lengthen the sequences of DNA that can be read. However, the ability to sequence longer fragments may not improve the quality of the Neanderthal sequence because the DNA itself has already been broken down into relatively short fragments.

While we don't know how much tolerance an organism can have for errors in its DNA, it's highly unlikely that the current sequence is accurate or complete enough to create a viable Neanderthal. Ignoring the fact that we cannot generate very long strands of DNA yet anyway, there are likely to be errors in genes that are necessary for viability. Those errors would prevent the embryo from developing. Of course, an even worse alternative would be to create a baby that is viable but has an error in her genome. An error could leave her with an illness that causes suffering which would of course be inhumane.

Despite these extreme technical limitations, the publication of the genome inspired several people to advocate for creating a Neanderthal. Among these was *New York Times* science blogger John Tierney. Many of people's reservations about the project, both in the blog and in the readers' comments, were about the prospect that the

Neanderthal might be lonely or not fit in at his apartment's co-op board meetings. This blog and many of the comments on the blog were an initial inspiration for this novel.

A draft sequence of the Neandertal genome *Science.* 2010 May 7;328(5979):710-22 http://www.sci-encemag.org/con-tent/328/5979/710.long

Ancient DNA comes of age *PLoS Biol.* 2005 Feb;3(2) http://www.plosbiol-ogy.org/article/info:-doi/10.1371/journal.pbio.0030056

The Tierney Lab blog about the Neanderthal project http://tierneylab.blogs.nytimes.com/2009/02/13/why-not-bring-a-nean-derthal-to-life/

Chapter 3: Human and Neanderthal Divergence

Scientists will argue in bars about the actual time of the human-Neanderthal split (to the hilarity of bartenders, no doubt). Different publications give different values. Half a million years roughly rounds current estimates.

Chapter 10: Birdstorms

The Panola virus is completely fictional.

The timing of the novel required the birdstorms begin in the south east so they could move up the east coast with the spring migrations. I selected the name Panola from a list of places in Alabama because it rolls off the tongue. Alabama actually has two Panolas. I have never been to either but am sure they are very nice places unlikely to be a hotbed of viral activity.

Massive bird deaths do occasionally happen, though they are generally observed as dead birds on the ground rather than birds raining down on one's head. In 2011 there were reports of massive bird deaths with hundreds of dead birds found on the ground in separate incidents in Kentucky and Arkansas. The cause of these deaths is, to my knowledge, unknown and has not been traced to any specific cause, viral, environmental, or otherwise.

Dead Birds Mysteriously Appear in Kentucky, WDRB News. 2011 Jan 4.

http://www.wdrb.com/story/13779745/
dead-birds-appearing-in-kentucky

Chapter 20: The List of Reasons to Make a Neanderthal

Most of the ideas in the fictional blog post were inspired either by John Tierney's 2009 blog post on the reasons for resurrecting a Neanderthal or from the *New York Times* readers commenting below. The charity walk is based on one reader's suggestion for a "Walk for Harry". I think it was suggested tongue-in-cheek.

The idea that Neanderthals made cave paintings is taken from anthropologists' speculation based on dating of the oldest known cave painting in the El Castillo Cave in Spain to more than 40,800 years ago. Neanderthals were firmly established in Europe at that time but modern humans were only just making inroads into Europe.

Jha A. Neanderthals may have been first human species to create cave paintings. *The Guardian*. 2012 June 14

http://www.theguardian.com/science/2012/jun/14/
neanderthals-first-create-cave-paintings

Pike AW, Hoffmann DL, García-Diez M, Pettitt PB, Alcolea J, De Balbín R, González-Sainz C, de las Heras C, Lasheras JA, Montes R, Zilhão J. U-series dating of Paleolithic art in 11 caves in Spain. *Science*. 2012 Jun 15;336(6087):1409-13.

http://www.sciencemag.org/content/336/6087/1409

Walk for Harry http://walkforharry.blogspot.com/

Chapter 22: The Genetic Basis of Lactose Intolerance

Lactose, a sugar found in milk, is composed chemically of two smaller sugars: a molecule of glucose bound to a molecule of galactose. Glucose can be used directly by the body to produce energy. Galactose can be easily converted into glucose. Thus, to be used as a fuel, the lactose must be split into these two smaller sugars.

The hydrolysis reaction that breaks the bond between the glucose and galactose is catalyzed by the enzyme lactase. Lactase is produced in high amounts when babies are first born because human milk is high in lactose, and the baby needs the lactase to use the sugar. Lactose intolerance results when a person is weaned and loses the ability to produce enough lactase to break down all of the lactose in the milk a person drinks.

People from populations who farm dairy cows have a higher likelihood of being able to digest milk without getting cramps than people who do not farm dairy. In Northern Europeans it was demonstrated by Bersaglieri and colleagues that this tolerance is due to evolutionary selection acting on the gene LCT, which produces the protein lactase (enzymes are types of proteins). They established this by looking at the DNA around the gene. The stretch of DNA showed little variability between people, as if it had entered the genome in a big chunk. Seeing big chunks of DNA which do not vary much between people is evidence that the stretch of DNA entered the genome fairly recently, because over time chunks of DNA get broken up by mutations and swapping of the DNA between the two pairs of the same chromosome (e.g. between the chromosome 2 inherited from your mother and the chromosome 2 inherited from your father.)

It is possible to estimate when a particular mutation in DNA entered the genome by looking at how similar the DNA is in different people. In this case, the authors estimate that the mutations that make LCT produce lactase into adulthood arose 5,000-10,000 years ago, consistent with the advent of dairy farming in Europe. In evolutionary time, this is a very recent event. For this version of the gene to be so prevalent, the authors infer that it must give a huge advantage to the people who have it, meaning that those able to persistently produce lactase were far better able to survive into adulthood and pass their genes on to offspring than people who did not have the nutritional advantage of being able to drink milk.

While Scandanavian populations have the lowest incidence of lactose intolerance (5%) other populations are also fairly good at digesting milk. The majority of people in northern India can digest milk just fine, for example, but not people in southern India.

However, the lactose tolerance observed in different populations did not necessarily arise from the same mutation as that is seen in Europe. In fact, Ingram and colleagues suggest that several different combinations of DNA changes conveying lactose tolerance have arisen in different human populations.

Bersaglieri T, Sabeti PC, Patterson N, Vanderploeg T, Schaffner SF, Drake JA, Rhodes M, Reich DE, Hirschhorn JN. Genetic signatures of strong recent positive selection at the lactase gene. *Am J Hum Genet.* 2004 Jun;74(6):1111-20.
http://www.ncbi.nlm.nih.gov/pmc/articles/PMC1182075/

Ingram CJ, Mulcare CA, Itan Y, Thomas MG, Swallow DM. Lactose digestion and the evolutionary genetics of lactase persistence. *Hum Genet* 2009 Jan;124(6) 579-91.
http://link.springer.com/article/10.1007%2Fs00439-008-0593-6

Chapter 25: DNA sequencers

The Runcorn Sequencers are a fictional brand of sequencers, but are loosely based on a new generation of DNA sequencers that use nanopore technology, such as those produced by Oxford Nanopore. While the real sequencers are small and handheld and do stretch the DNA or RNA though a small hole made of proteins, protocols for preparing samples for sequencing, particularly from tissue, require some sort of extraction step which would take longer and use more equipment than what is described in the text. Protocols, however, are always improving.

Chapter 37: Spanish Flu

If you look at charts of human death rates across the 20th century, you'll notice a big spike up during the years 1918-19. The Spanish flu was a particularly deadly strain of influenza that swept across the globe that year, infecting half a billion people and killing an estimated 50 to 100 million. Data shown on a chart is inherently cold, but the spike represents horrendous devastation and loss of life. It was a particularly cruel virus in the way it selected its victims.

It killed many by inducing a cytokine storm where the patient's own overzealous immune system reacted to the virus, leading to their death. Hardy young people with robust immune systems were actually more prone to cytokine storms than the elderly and frail. Unlike other flu viruses, the Spanish flu struck down people in the prime of their lives.

Newborn babies may also be more prone to cytokine storms. Because their immune systems are not fully developed, they do not yet have many of the sophisticated tools that adults use to accurately target invading pathogens. Therefore, they are more reliant on the crude inflammatory responses that act as a first, general response against infection. Overzealous inflammatory responses are the type of reactions that can lead to cytokine storms.

Jie Zhao, Kwang Dong Kim , Xuanming Yang, Sogyong Auh, Yang-Xin Fu , and Hong Tang Hyper innate responses in neonates lead to increased morbidity and mortality after infection. *Proc Natl Acad Sci U S A.* 2008 May 27;105(21):7528-33.
http://www.pnas.org/content/105/21/7528.full

Taubenberger, Jeffery K.; Morens, David M. 1918 Influenza: the Mother of All Pandemics. Centers for Disease Control and Prevention. January 2006
http://wwwnc.cdc.gov/eid/article/12/1/05-0979_article.htm

About the Author

Gina DeMarco is a biologist working in the field of DNA sequencing. She has a doctorate degree in biology and a small dog.

Gina DeMarco is a pen name.